TAKE YOUR TURN, TEDDY

TAKE YOUR TURN, TEDDY

BY HALEY NEWLIN

NEW DEGREE PRESS

COPYRIGHT © 2020 HALEY NEWLIN

All rights reserved.

TAKE YOUR TURN, TEDDY

ISBN	978-1-63676-555-6	*Paperback*
	978-1-63676-662-1	*Hardcover*
	978-1-63676-132-9	*Kindle Ebook*
	978-1-63676-133-6	*Ebook*

"*Take Your Turn, Teddy* is a powerfully disturbing tale that delves into the twisted horrors that can spur from childhood trauma. This heart-racing narrative will grab hold of you, ensnare your every sense, and keep you on edge through every blood-filled twist and turn."

—Sophie Queen, Author of Riley's *Excellent and not-at-all Fake Exorcism Service*

"Newlin had me turning the pages as if the characters' lives depended on it."

—Richelle, Host of Queens of Horror Book Club

"*Take Your Turn, Teddy* is a wonderfully dark story with a vividly gripping tension. Newlin's prose and storytelling takes you on a truly wild ride through a twisted narrative full of blood and everyday terrors that linger long after you've finished the last page."

—Claire L. Smith, Author of *Helena*

"It's something you haven't experienced before that perfectly blends the psychological thriller and horror genre. A visceral novel full of terror and death"

—Frank Reynolds, Host of *Is It Worth It*

For Jeremy,

You were my Samwise Gamgee of this journey, protecting both the story and me as the carrier of it. You reminded me that the shadow, the darkness, is only a passing thing. "And when the sun shines, it will shine the clearer."

Thank you for always being my light.

For Nanners (Hanna),

Who collected me piece by piece in the moments when doubt shattered my connection to this story. You reminded me I was stronger than I felt. And no matter how much the shadow told me I was alone, I could turn to you, my oasis in a vast desert and my island in a stormy sea.

For my reader before the readers,

You've been with me from the start. I take great comfort in knowing no matter where I am in the world—whether I deliver chapters to you myself or send them in an email from Timbuktu—you'll always be ready to read and waiting for more.

Lastly, for my editor, Clayton, who helped me do the crime and the time. I owe the spookiest parts of my being to you, the first person who helped me see that my stories wanted to be darker and I was meant to write horror.

"Alone. Yes, that's the key word, the most awful word in the English tongue. Murder doesn't hold a candle to it and hell is only a poor synonym."

—STEPHEN KING

CONTENTS

——

NOTE FROM THE AUTHOR   13

PART 1.   **THE ACT YOU'VE KNOWN FOR ALL THESE YEARS**   **19**

PART 2.   **A VILE, MERCILESS KILLER**   **157**

PART 3.   **THE MAPLE STREET MASSACRE**   **275**

PART 4.   **COUNTING CASUALTIES**   **301**

PART 5.   **CONFESSIONS OF A MAN GONE MAD**   **341**

EPILOGUE   381

ACKNOWLEDGMENTS   389

NOTE FROM
THE AUTHOR

───

"Villainy wears many masks, and none so dangerous as the mask of virtue."

Dear Readers,

I have grown since we last spoke. I have learned even more about the offerings of the quaint genre of horror—for readers and creators. But more than anything, I have learned a lot about myself.

It has been a difficult year for me, one where the inner demons I had let come to the surface when writing *Not Another Sarah Halls* couldn't be silenced. And the more I tried to press a pillow over their faces, the more powerful they grew. With every attempt to beat them, I sank lower, feeling six feet under despite the hammered beating of my anxious heart.

In writing *Not Another Sarah Halls*, I tried with everything I had to make myself vulnerable to you, readers, in honor of what I was asking you to do—allow horror to prompt self-reflection. Allow the genre to take you deep into your inner consciousness, open the locked boxes you have created for the stowaway demons of your mind, and ask, "Why do you make me vulnerable? How do I beat you?"

With that, I uncovered a wave of darkness I didn't know how to face. The anxious tics, the panic attacks, the feeling of being physically present but emotionally absent—within and without as my favorite author, F. Scott Fitzgerald, would say—became a part of my everyday life. And this wasn't the first time.

I've struggled with anxiety and depression my entire life, but especially the past year. I overthought everything. I misread body language or misdirected anger and plugged it into my worsening mental health condition. I was giving up control to the sinister orchestrator within my mind. And I let that shadow run amok, even allowing it to tell me that the shortness of breath, the sleepless nights, the bursts of anger, and the darkness were normalcy in my life.

As I've studied the craft of storytelling, I've heard professors, established authors, and publishing professionals say time and again, "Write what you know."

So, it was no surprise that when I began building my protagonist in *Not Another Sarah Halls,* who I named Autumn as a reminder of the change that's always waiting around the corner, she also struggled with depression and anxiety.

When readers thank me for the inclusion of sensitive topics in *Not Another Sarah Halls*, one scene comes up nearly every time—Autumn's near suicide attempt. For readers who are here for the first time, this isn't a major spoiler, but it is a critical element of Autumn's character arc.

Autumn has scars across each of her arms, reminiscent of a release when she needed to feel something aside from the internal pain that plagued her peace of mind.

But one scar stands out more than the others. It was the only pink singe of a blade that lay vertically on Autumn's wrist. And that scar, by far, stretched the farthest. It ate the most skin.

Autumn says the scar "sits permanently puffed above my pale skin, a bulging reminder of how close I had come that day to ending it all."

The day Autumn made that nearly fatal cut, she had a moment when the sight of the physical wound made her realize she was choosing death. She realized she didn't want to die, only to find an end to her pain. Though it felt nearly impossible as someone who has sunk that low before, I knew I had to pull Autumn out of that scene. She was the only one who cared about the string of cold cases in Oakhaven. She was the only chance of breaking the curse in the town. Autumn had to be there for the rest of the story.

Writing that scene, and pulling Autumn from it, served as an out-of-body experience for me. To make an impact, to offer hope to others who struggle with mental health, I had to pull myself out of my own preconceived idea that the demons of my mind would cloud my life with their darkness and discouraging taunts forever. I had to believe something within me could outshine the shadow.

So, like Autumn, after the scene with the deepest bite of the blade, I got help, and I white-knuckled that sense of control I thought was long gone.

For the first time in my life, I confided in a doctor and was diagnosed with chronic depression, generalized anxiety disorder, and bipolar disorder. After speaking with me, my doctor also speculated that I had traces of an eating disorder in high school, a torment that still visits from time to time.

The more I talked about it, the better I felt. It was like in *Not Another Sarah Halls,* I had uncovered a new formula of life: triggers + unresolved trauma + the belief of having no control = monstrous manifestations. These mind-made conjurings were far worse than anything I had ever written or read within a horror story.

Autumn's story was about regaining control of both her life and her town. You got to see what it was like for her to put herself before the shadows within. *Not Another Sarah Halls* was meant to show the impact of confronting our inner demons in order to battle manifestations in the outside world. When Autumn let the voices of the lady with the broken bones consume her, she was distancing herself from uncovering the truth of the disappearances in Oakhaven.

While *Not Another Sarah Halls* was meant to be a story of guidance, *Take Your Turn, Teddy* is more of a cautionary tale.

Psychologist Carl Jung theorized that four core archetypes make up the human consciousness. These are realized through a unique experience, such as a traumatic incident like that of the night Teddy and his mother pack everything they can fit into her station wagon and drive fifteen hours away from his father and the life he had always known.

One of the four archetypes, the shadow, exists in the darker side of the psyche, representing wildness, chaos, and the unknown, each of which takes their turn with Teddy through the physical manifestation of the shadow. In his book *Archetypes and the Collective Unconscious,* Jung said of his archetype, "The shadow is a living part of the personality and therefore wants to live with it in some form. It cannot be argued out of existence or rationalized into harmlessness."

While we can't completely shut the shadow out, sometimes allowing it to spill over in bursts of anger or jealousy, we do have control over how much of the shadow comes to light. Repressed ideas of hate and aggression bring the shadow archetype to the forefront.

The cunning shadow manifestation in this story tells Teddy that some people ignore their shadows and let them starve.

To keep what he believes to be his only friend in the Indiana township, Teddy gives his control to the latent dispositions of the shadow until its chaos consumes all of what makes him who he is. As his relationship progresses with the shadow, so do Teddy's acts of greed, envy, hate, and aggression. The violence and betrayals allow the shadow to gain more control over Teddy until it dominates his mind and demolishes the retaining wall, releasing a wave of blood in the name of loyalty (truly a mask of desperation).

As I did in my first novel, I urge you, readers, to bask in what I believe to be horror's highest quality: the way it asks you to consider what the situation of the story would look like for you. How would you be vulnerable to the manifestation presented?

In *Take Your Turn, Teddy*, my intentions are not to give a negative perception of those who struggle with mental health. Instead, I seek to personify depression and the darkness of our minds. I want to show that each mental trial is an exercise in control—either giving it up or fighting to reclaim it.

People who suffer from depression, anxiety, PTSD, or any other mental health illnesses, believe that when you're in a dark place, the darkness has won. But that's not true. The ultimate control comes from us, a lesson Teddy will have to learn in hopes of regaining his true inner self.

The hungry shadows in our minds want us to believe our control is long lost. But it's not. As Shirley Jackson says of fear, "We yield to it, or we fight it, but we cannot meet it halfway."

I learned so much from Autumn's character. I lived through her decision to get help for her suicidal thoughts and anxious tendencies. And that changed my life. But my battle is long from over. In fact, the better I get, the more I come to understand that my depression, anxiety, and bipolar disorder will always be with me. The shadow lives in all of us. But I am far more equipped to fight it than I have ever been, and now, thanks to all my readers who have shared their stories with me, I know I'm not alone in the continuous fight for control in my life.

I leave you with comforting words from the master of horror himself, Stephen King, "Things can get better, and if you give them a chance, they usually do."

Thanks for going on this journey with me, my spooky friends.

I believe in you all more than you'll ever know. Thank you for believing in me.

Yours (Horrifically),
Haley Newlin

PART 1

THE ACT YOU'VE KNOWN FOR ALL THESE YEARS

1

Excited chatter filled the bus coming from Oakhaven Elementary. The kids had gotten an early release because of an electrical difficulty at the school. With just a few days left before summer vacation, administrators were feeling lenient.

Teddy sat on the bus with Pete Marsh, who had lived next door to him his whole life.

Pete glanced over at the unopened package in Teddy's hands. "I've got a busted set. Who did you get today?"

Teddy peeled back the wrapping on the pack of baseball cards his mother had just given him that morning. As they did every time they got new cards, Teddy and Pete waited to open the packs together on the bus ride home.

Teddy shuffled through the set of ten. No one too exciting in the first few, though he did get a Ted Williams. But Teddy had so many of Williams already. Teddy's dad had collected cards when he was younger and passed them all on to him.

But the last card was *everything*—one Teddy would add to his framed collection. One that would impress someone with an array of Hall of Famers and Cy Young Award Winners—someone like his dad, Arthur Blackwood.

Before Teddy could say a word or mention how excited his dad would be, Pete protested with envy, "What? How do you always get the good ones?"

Teddy held the card before them, marveling at its divineness, and whispered, "I got Hammerin' Hank."

"Not just Hammerin' Hank," Pete said as he waved his black curls from his face. "That's a limited-edition World Series card."

The bus's breaks screeched to a halt as Mrs. Womack looked up in her rearview mirror and yelled, "Alright, Blackwood, Marsh. We're at your stop."

Teddy and Pete looked at the rows of empty seats before them and then out the window. Teddy was surprised to see his red oak-colored house already. The excitement of the Hammerin' Hank had made the ride home fly by.

With barely so much as a wave, Teddy ran from the bus to the garage door. He turned his key in the lock at the center of the door and threw the weight of it just above his head so he could climb under. Teddy was excited to see his father's navy blue 1970 Ford Ranch Wagon parked inside.

Dad must've gotten an early release too.

Teddy maneuvered around the bikes and baseball bats, careful not to let his bookbag hit the car. The alarm on that thing was so delicate, and Teddy wanted to surprise his dad.

Teddy stepped into the house, bursting with excitement. "Hammerin' Hank. Wait till Dad sees this."

He went through the yellow floral wallpapered kitchen and set the less exciting cards on the counter. His dad's office light was on, so Teddy continued slowly to be sure he wasn't interrupting a phone call. He pressed his back against the paneled wall, out of sight, and waited for a "This is Arthur Blackwood." But the room sat quietly.

Teddy peeked around the corner. It was empty. *Odd.*

He heard movement down the hall—a gentle but consistent thumping.

"Dad?"

No answer. But the thumping continued on the far side of the wall. Teddy pressed his ear to the door to his parents' bedroom and heard heavy exhales, like when his mom used the stationary bike in the basement. The thumping picked up, as did the exhales.

Teddy could tell then that it was a woman's breathing he heard. Soft moans came with each sound of breath. He hadn't seen his mother's car parked in front of the house.

"Oh, Arthur. Arthur," a voice said.

The door in front of him rattled like an energy shot across his parents' room.

"Faster, Arthur. Faster."

The voice didn't sound like Teddy's mom. But, if his dad had a friend over and they were playing a game, Teddy wanted to play too.

Sometimes his dad would let Teddy sit with the guys and watch on Poker Night.

He thought on the "faster, faster." What game could they be playing? Teddy wondered if his dad had moved the Magnavox console into his parents' bedroom like he had when he was stuck home for two weeks after his knee surgery.

Dad is slow at Table Tennis. Teddy tried to teach his father to play, but at best he became a little less reminiscent of a zombie spaz. That's what Pete always called Teddy when they played catch and Teddy got distracted by something in the street or on the radio they kept outside.

Teddy still had the Hammerin' Hank card in his hand. No matter what his dad was doing, he would want to see this.

His father might even want to show his friend something as rare as this limited-edition find.

The other side of the door was quieter now. *So, maybe I'm not interrupting now.* It was like when Teddy waited outside his father's office before going in. Talking meant his dad was with a customer or his boss. Quiet meant, at worst, Teddy would get a finger signaling one more minute. Then his dad would take his glasses off and say, "What's up, Ted, my man, my grand slam?"

Teddy reached for the gold door handle and pushed it open, saying, "Dad, you won't belie—"

Teddy bit into his lip and brought his eyebrows together in confusion, causing vertical furrows between them.

Dad and his friend weren't sitting on the floor playing the Magnavox. The woman was atop his parents' bed on her hands and knees, the way Pete and Teddy crawled under his mother's window when they wanted to sneak out and watch the thunderstorms at night.

The woman's dark hair flew from the front of her face to her arched back when she heard Teddy. Her pale, petite breasts hung from her chest. Her rose-colored lipstick was smeared not only on her face but on his father's too. It took him a minute because her hair was lighter than it used to be, but Teddy knew her. It was Amber Dae. Amber used to babysit Teddy before she went to Plymouth for college.

"Amber? What are you doing here?"

With a slick sound, Teddy's father shouted and pulled away from the woman as he grabbed his work shirt to cover himself.

The shout startled Teddy and he stepped back toward the hall. Amber scrambled for her dark green Plymouth sweatshirt wadded up on the floor, holding the satin sheet over her chest.

Amber didn't say anything, but the heaviness of her breath and quickness in her movements showed how frazzled she was.

When Amber failed to grab the sweatshirt while maintaining the sheet, Teddy reached for it and tossed it to Amber. Then, he immediately wished he hadn't. The sweatshirt hit the bed in front of her. Amber's eyes avoided Teddy, and her attempt to avoid him made him feel sick to his stomach.

Amber readjusted one of her arms for coverage as she slipped the forest-colored crewneck over her head.

Teddy looked to his dad for some kind of explanation, but all he said was, "Wait in the hall, Teddy. Now."

Was he in trouble? Was he not supposed to go in? He obeyed his father and closed the door behind him. Teddy stood against the smooth paneled wall in the darkness of the hall.

Teddy wasn't sure what he had seen. He didn't know what it meant or why he would be in trouble for it. He really was glad to see Amber. Maybe she did something wrong. But that didn't make Teddy feel much better. He didn't want her to be in trouble either. Before he started talking to Pete on the bus rides home, Amber had been Teddy's first ever friend.

Teddy heard faint voices coming from his parents' room. "You said no one would be home before three."

"Jesus Christ, Amber. Do you think I thought my ten-year-old would walk in?"

"You don't get it. He *knows* me, Arthur. This is bad. Bad for us, bad for him. This is so bad."

"Stop. It's okay. They must've let him out early. Teddy doesn't know what we were doing. I'll go talk to him. Wait here and get dressed."

Teddy could hear the nervousness in Amber's voice as she said, "No. I think you should take me home first. What if Lila comes home?"

The last part confused Teddy. Was his mom supposed to be surprised by Amber coming home? Maybe his dad was planning something special for his mom, and Amber was there to watch him. But then why would she want to leave?

Teddy brought his hands to his face and slid to the floor. He was so confused, and his dad seemed upset with him. Now Amber was upset too. He wanted to cry.

His dad sighed. "Uhh. Fine. Wait here. I'll be right back."

Arthur opened the bedroom door, and the light conjured Teddy's shadow on the wall. He almost spoke to it, as if it was a friend—someone as young as he was but maybe less confused. Someone who could explain to him what he had seen. But Teddy's father's shadow appeared on the wall and merged with Teddy's, creating a dark mass of grey.

His father crouched down in front of Teddy. "Hey, Teddy, my little Bambino. I'm going to take Amber home. I thought you could tag along, and we could get some baseball cards. What do you think?"

Teddy could hear sniffling coming from his parents' room. Something wasn't right. He could feel it in his stomach, and the lump in his throat told him he wanted to cry.

All Teddy wanted now was his mother. Teddy shook his head. "I'm going to wait here for Mom."

His father's eyebrows raised, and his eyes looked panicked. "No. No. No, Teddy."

Teddy's father pushed his palm forward as if pumping the brakes on his intensity and took a deep breath. Teddy noticed his father wasn't wearing his wedding ring. There was a small, pale line in place of the usual bright, gold band.

That, too, turned Teddy's stomach. His father had done this in the past, and it resulted in an evening of shouting from his parents' bedroom. Teddy hated nights like those.

As Amber had struggled to do with him, Teddy couldn't meet his father's eyes.

His father spoke softly, "Teddy, let me explain something to you. Are you listening to me?"

Teddy brought his knees to his chest and rested his head on them. He nodded.

"Okay. Sometimes adults get overwhelmed. You know what I mean? They get stressed about money or their job, or something as simple as figuring out what to cook for dinner. Everyone deals with that stress in different ways. Amber helps me, so I don't come home and yell anymore. Do you remember what that was like?"

Teddy remembered hearing dishes hit the floor as he tossed and turned in his room. He remembered the muffled yet loud voices from the kitchen. It usually ended with his mother crying. Sometimes, after his father came home yelling like this, Teddy's mother wouldn't talk for a few days. She would just sit in front of the record player in the living room, drinking wine and working on her next article for work.

But sometimes, if he'd sit with her as she flipped through the records to pick a new one, she'd hum the tune and then add some kind of commentary. Teddy tried hard to remember the ones she talked about, so when she got upset, he could put those songs on for her.

Last time, it was "The Wind" by Cat Stevens. She'd hummed to the opening lyrics and said, "I've always found this one incredibly comforting."

Teddy enjoyed those moments with his mother, but the yelling that came before was awful.

"Teddy, are you with me? Don't you remember how bad things were when I came home stressed and yelling like that?"

Teddy nodded.

"Now, with Amber, I can blow off all that steam. Your mom and I have never been better."

Teddy nodded, sort of understanding. At least as best as he could.

"I need you to keep this between us, okay, my little Bambino? Just for a while."

Teddy nodded.

His father rubbed his beard and took a deep inhale. His father put his hands up, maybe with a little frustration, and said, "Okay. You can stay here. I'll see you when I get back. We can play catch until Mom gets home."

His father grabbed Teddy's shoulder and gave it a consoling squeeze. Teddy wasn't sure why, but in his confusion, he didn't want it. He lifted his shoulders in discomfort, as if his dad was a creepy stranger.

"Hey, Teddy. Everything will be alright. I'll be right back."

His dad opened the door, and Amber nearly shoved past him. She pulled her sweatshirt down and began straightening her hair, walking through the hall with raised elbows as she tied it back.

Teddy didn't try to talk to her, and once again, she didn't even look at him. He tucked his chin back into his folded arms on his knees.

His dad looked back at Teddy and gave him a reassuring wave. The garage door rattled opened, and soon after, the Ranch Wagon hummed.

Teddy pulled the Hammerin' Hank card from his pocket and was left alone with the shadow on the wall.

2

To Teddy's surprise and disappointment, his father didn't come right back. And after witnessing his father with Amber, Teddy wasn't even sure he would know how to act when he did. It didn't make sense to him. He stumbled to his room and lay flat across his Jetsons bedding. He traced the cartoon images on the comforter and sang the show's tune aloud, finding Elroy, daughter Judy, and Jane his wife. Teddy circled back, singing the names of the three characters. First, Elroy. Teddy found his blond hair, wave, and smile on the bedding. Then Judy with her futuristic white-moon-colored ponytail. And Jane. Jane had orange hair just like Teddy's mom; only his mom's hair wasn't chopped above her shoulders. Instead, her hair draped down her back like a shiny cape. Sometimes, while she was cooking, his mom would pull all of that length into a puffy hair tie, and as she danced around the kitchen singing The Beatles or Led Zeppelin, her orange hair would bounce and swing in peaceful, subtle waves. Teddy rubbed his hand across Jane. He thought Jane was pretty, as he was sure Elroy and Judy did too. But to Teddy, his mom was the prettiest person in the world.

Right next to Jane was George Jetson. Teddy couldn't help but wonder if after Jane dropped from the spaceship and to the shopping mall, if Mr. Jetson sat behind his desk all day, or if he came home to an empty house with a friend he needed to feel better—like his father said Amber had done for him. He wasn't sure why, but the uncertainty made him angry with Mr. Jetson. Was it anger? He didn't know how to feel about any of it. What he wanted to know most was how his mother would feel.

Teddy rose from the bed and turned the comforter over to its light blue underside. He didn't want to look at Mr. Jetson anymore.

He sat in his room and waited for his father to return. Teddy didn't think he would show him the Hammerin' Hank card. It didn't seem to matter anymore.

Instead, Teddy took the card and dragged himself into his father's office. Along the back wall was an array of wide dark oak shelves. Against the orange shag rugs, the bookcase always reminded him of the colors of autumn. He and his parents would walk to Benji's for ice cream. Then they'd walk the town with their ice cream cones and admire the color of the leaves in the months where summer and winter were beginning to merge. All before the cryptic cold snuck in and turned everything to ice.

The thought sent a chill through Teddy as he shook his shoulders and said, "Brrr."

He flipped the light next to the case that illuminated his father's rare collection of the best baseball players known to man. Next to The Great Bambino himself, Teddy laid his World Series edition Hank Aaron card. He thought it belonged with the greats, even if he and his father didn't put it up there together.

Teddy heard a car door slam shut out front. He ran from the office, fearing his father would come in and want him to stay and talk about the card. Teddy waited for the rattling sound as the rusty garage door opened. But, the golden doorknob in the living room jiggled with movement from the key on the other side. The car was parked in front of the house and not the garage, which meant his mother was home.

Her hands opened and closed around crinkling paper bags. Teddy could see the yellow packaging of Nestle Toll House cookie dough peeking out the top of one. She and Teddy, on select nights, made cookies together while cleaning up dinner.

"Hey, my Teddy Bear. Wild rice soup tonight?"

It was Teddy's favorite dinner. His mother was in a good mood, which meant her boss at the Oakhaven Chronicle was happy with her latest column. Teddy nodded with a forced smile and took a few of the bags from his mother. She set hers on the counter and, with a single pull of a pin, let down her long red hair. It fell onto her shoulders in long waves.

She stepped into the laundry room and shut the door. With a slam of the dryer door, Teddy waited for her to change out of her bright, corduroy bell-bottoms.

His mom came back wearing a British Invasion t-shirt and black athletic shorts. Her hair was back on top of her head but in a more relaxed ponytail.

"Okay, Teddy Bear. Let's get dinner going. I bet Dad's had a long day at the office."

Teddy was sure he hadn't. He tried to smile, though, to cover any expression on his face that would suggest otherwise.

"You can pick the tunes tonight. Go on. Whatever you'd like."

She waved Teddy to the living room to the cream Crosley record player. He opened the dark wood entertainment center and flipped through the extensive vinyl records collection, trying to pick something that would pick up his spirits and hold his mother's high.

Teddy took out one he had seen a hundred times—one his mother had sung him all his life. It had too many people to count on it, some he recognized like Marilyn Monroe and Edgar Allan Poe. Four men were standing behind a drum with lettering as colorful as their yellow, pink, blue, and orange suits. At the bottom, the band's name was spelled in bright red flowers, The Beatles.

"Come on, Teddy. Hurry up," his mother called from the kitchen.

Teddy pulled the record from its sleeve, careful to hold it between his fingers and not let any smudges get on it, just as his mother had taught him. He dropped the needle and turned the volume knob to the right, letting the rock-infused hit dance its way across the room to his mother. And as if teasing him of his efforts to make her happy, Paul McCartney sang of a band that was guaranteed to raise a smile. And his mother did.

Teddy was happy to see his mother in such a good mood. Things were getting better as his father had said. His mother was standing at the yellow Formica countertop, swaying her hips off-beat, as if McCartney was singing a slower tune. Maybe she was dancing to the rhythm of her own, peaceful energy. The orange color of her hair, along with the yellow counter and pastels of the floral wallpaper, reminded him of the poppy field Dorothy and her loyal band of misfits skipped through on their way to Oz. Teddy's smile faded. That field was poisonous. Teddy started to wonder if, like the field, his home was beautiful but truly carried a plan of deceit.

The kitchen knife made thick thuds as it split the carrots and sank to the cutting board. His mother continued to sway as she cut the vegetables at a steady pace. Teddy could see the natural smile on her face. His dad was right. Without all the yelling, things were better. His mother was happier, which meant his father had to be too. And if they were happy, so was he. Maybe there was such a thing as a simply beautiful poppy field. All treats and no tricks.

"Shit!"

A carrot hopped from the cutting board and onto the far side of the counter.

Teddy saw a steady spot of blood growing on his mother's finger. She ran it under cold water and yelled behind her and over Teddy, "Honey? Honey, are you working? I need you to finish cutting these carrots for me!"

Teddy froze in uncertainty.

She grabbed a kitchen towel and wrapped it around her finger. "Sorry for cursing, sweetie. But man, that hurt like he—" She bit her bottom rose-colored lip and giggled aloud. "It just really hurt. I don't want to touch all this food with a bloody finger. Your dad can help. It'll be kind of nice to all cook dinner together. You can DJ for us. How 'bout that?"

Teddy was nervous with uncertainty. He knew his dad wasn't there, but he'd promised to keep what he had seen that afternoon between them. He didn't know what to do, so he just stood there watching his mom scramble around the sunset-colored kitchen. Only when she removed the cloth from her hand again did he snap out of his anxious trance. The reminder of blood seemed to wake him from it, saying, *This is urgent. Do something, man. Move.*

"Uh. That's okay, Mom. I can finish cutting them."

"No, no, Teddy Bear. Those carrots are thick. You'll just turn around and do what I did. Maybe if I yell loudly enough, I can get your father in here."

She gave Teddy a playful wink and grinned.

"Oh, Arthur? Can you come help me, please?"

Teddy could hardly stand the tension. Why wasn't his father home yet? Teddy tried to be as sly as possible when he studied his mother's face for any sign of suspicion. But she just held the cloth tightly around her finger, wincing from the pain. Teddy couldn't help but notice her wedding ring on the hand she was using to apply pressure to the wound. It was a dark midnight-colored sapphire with a cluster of diamonds surrounding the center stone. Teddy remembered just a few months ago when his mother hadn't worn the ring, but instead it lay on the corner of the bathroom counter— seemingly hissing at him to look at it, like the ring of Sauron in his Tolkien book.

His mother began calling for his father again.

"Sweetheart? Arthur? Come on, sweetie. You've worked all day. Come see us."

But the house sat empty as they waited for a response with nothing but the increasing sound of his mother's impatient breathing.

Her breath was getting heavier by the minute. The record player was still spinning and filled what little space the building tension would allow with "Lucy in the Sky with Diamonds."

"Arthur?"

She exhaled hard and stomped her feet down the hall to the office. "Arthur, did you not hear me calling for you? I need your help w—"

She must've seen no one was in the office.

"Teddy, honey? Is Dad not home? I told him I wanted him home earlier tonight so we could all have dinner together."

She was still stomping back to the kitchen, coming for an answer. Teddy wondered how someone as small as she could create so much noise with their steps.

Teddy backed away until his back hit the counter-top. There was nowhere else to go. He wasn't ready for the yelling. He took in a deep breath and suspended it inside him. He felt as though any sudden movements would undo everything—catastrophe.

She shot her green eyes at him. Teddy thought they almost seemed to have an outer ridge of orange that matched her hair, or the fury of fire.

Teddy's face must've spelled out some form of anxious-ness because his mother studied him for a moment, saying nothing but shooting a suspicious glare.

"Right. Well, can you get in the cabinet in the laundry room and grab me a Band-Aid? I'll get the rest of these car-rots cut."

She turned from Teddy and spread her arms out as she white-knuckled the edge of the counter. Her breath had yet to let up.

Teddy obeyed his mother and rifled through the cabinet in the laundry room, finding their last Band-Aid. He grabbed the Neosporin for good measure too. He hoped that maybe if he could start the album over, perhaps they could restart their night together.

But just as he closed the cabinet door beside the washing machine, he heard his mother say, "You've got to be fucking kidding me."

Maybe she thought she said it low enough, but Teddy crept around the paneled wall to find her squatting at the bottom of the fridge.

"There was a whole bottle of wine in here this morning. How is it all gone?"

She hurried to the wine cabinet and flung its doors open. Teddy immediately knew what his mother wanted wouldn't be there. The glasses clanged together as she investigated those too.

She mumbled frustrations under her breath and slammed the dark oak doors. "I just wanted to come home and make dinner and drink my wine. I just wanted some time to relax."

Lila's face fell to her shaking hands, and she began to cry. Teddy's socks created soft shuffling sounds on the tiled floor as he went to his mother. "Mom?" He tried to use the softest voice he could. "Are you okay?"

She looked up at Teddy with smeared mascara and swollen eyes. Teddy looked back with wide eyes, fearful of what she would read in them.

"I'm sorry, Teddy. I've just been a little stressed. I am trying to find ways around it, but things just keep getting ruined."

Teddy slowly went to the floor and sat beside his mother. He grabbed her hands and ran his thumb and back forth across the top of them, a soothing method she had done for him his whole life.

"Maybe you should find a friend to help you relax. Someone like Daddy's friend."

She brought her head up so fast she startled Teddy. Another tear slid down her freckled cheek.

"Daddy's friend?"

"Yeah. She comes here and helps him relax, so he doesn't yell anymore. It's been so nice. Hasn't it? Not having him yell and be so mad when he gets home?"

Her eyes shot to the wine cabinet and then fell to the floor, avoiding Teddy.

"Yes, Teddy. That has been nice." Her voice was off. Shaky, almost hollow sounding. "Yes, it has."

She grabbed Teddy's hands and brought him to his feet with her. She turned off the stove and, in a quick swipe, slid all the carrots and vegetables of the wild rice soup, yet to be cut, into the trash.

"How about you and I go out for pizza. Maybe Benji's after? We can stop by the Marshes' and see if Pete wants to tag along too."

Teddy hesitated. Was he supposed to be excited? Normally he would be. But that afternoon left a weight in his gut—one that seemed moments away from rupturing and making an even further mess of things.

"Just let me change out of these shorts."

She pulled her hair down from the ponytail and released a more controlled exhale with it. Teddy watched as his mother's shadow followed her down the hall and paused at the doorway of his parents' bedroom. She hesitated for a moment before going inside and closing the door. The sound of glass hitting the floor followed.

3

___

After the outburst from his mother and the strange encounter with his father he was still trying to process, Teddy lay in bed with a belly full of pepperoni pizza and Benji's vanilla soft serve, smiling. Even though he had to lie to Pete about what his father said about the Hammerin' Hank card, he had fun with his friend. For the time being, Teddy was able to push the unfortunate events of the afternoon to the back of his mind.

Still, his mother seemed off throughout the evening. It was like she was lost in thought as her green eyes looked beyond the pizza place, past Benji's, and into another dimension. And as the night went on, Teddy swore the orange rim in her eyes ignited to a fuller brightness. When Pete asked Teddy if his mother was okay, Teddy shrugged his shoulders and said, "Probably just tired from work."

Pete didn't push Teddy for more, and Teddy was thankful for that.

On his nightstand, next to his Jetsons bedding, was a baseball-shaped alarm clock. His grandparents had sent it to him from Indiana as a gift for his birthday last year. The clock illuminated a red brightness that read 10:30. How had it gotten so late? Teddy wondered what time his dad would come home. When they got back from the pizza place, Lila didn't call Arthur's name. She opened the front door, walked through the kitchen, and peeked into the garage. She nodded to herself and headed for her room.

"I'm going to do some cleaning, Teddy Bear."

Teddy began to groan, but his mother interrupted, smiled, and said, "You go read or something."

He didn't have to help clean, and he got pizza and ice cream—what a night. Teddy couldn't believe his dad had missed it. The only thing missing was going to dinner together and coming home to play catch while his mother sat on the back porch with a glass of wine, smiling as she watched.

The thought of wine stung as he thought of his mother getting so upset that afternoon. When his father did come home, he wondered if the booming of an argument between his parents would suffocate the giddy feeling he had after such a great night.

He heard movement across the hall in his parents' bedroom. It sounded like the shriek of duct tape being stretched out. Teddy got up and crept to the door of his bedroom. He opened it slightly, allowing just a line of vision. Then, the door flew open, and a box slid out, marked with thick lettering that said, "WORK CLOTHES."

Teddy's mother stomped into the hall and grabbed the box. A moment later, he heard the front door open. It was only a few minutes before the door opened again. This happened several times in a matter of minutes. What was his mother doing going in and out of the house like that? Was she taking boxes to Goodwill this late?

The thought made Teddy anxious, though he wasn't entirely sure why. He tiptoed back across his room, pulled open the drawer on his nightstand, and flipped through the stack of books inside. At the bottom was one his parents read to him when he was younger, *The Little Prince.*

The first page had a drawing of a boa constrictor tightening around a fearful little creature. The author described his experience reading a book called *True Stories from Nature,* where he learned about the primeval forest. He went on to share that boa constrictors swallow their prey whole, without chewing, and then are unable to move. Then, they sleep for nearly six months to allow digestion.

Teddy carried the book to his bed and climbed back under the Jetsons cover. He couldn't play catch with his dad, but maybe reading a story that his parents used to read to him would give him that same feeling.

He sank beneath the comforter and allowed its warmth to wrap around him. Just as he began to read on to the part about the man drawing what the boa constrictor with a full belly may look like, only for grown-ups to say it was a hat, Teddy's door swung open.

Teddy's mother was still wearing her jeans and British Invasion shirt. She hadn't changed into her pajamas yet. She held a purple plastic tub that used to have all of his father's old baseball jerseys inside.

"Teddy Bear, I need you to get your things and put them in here. Get as many clothes as you can. I'll fold your bedding up. You can use it in the car on the drive. Leave whatever you can't get into the tub."

Teddy was confused. "Leave my stuff? Mom, what's going on?"

His mother shook her head. "I can't explain now, Teddy. We have to go. Please, get up and get your things?"

"What about Dad?"

He wasn't quite sure why, but Teddy began to cry. Not sobbing, but just a simple, mysterious tear rolled down his freckled cheek. It was as if the tear carried some undisclosed sadness that Teddy hadn't yet fully felt himself.

His mother took a deep breath and softened her voice, allowing panic to slither away momentarily.

"We are going to see Grandma and Grandpa. We're going to stay for a little bit, so I just want to make sure you have everything. I want to get on the road, so we need to be quick."

They had never decided to see Grandma and Grandpa this late. They always left early on Saturday mornings.

He listened to his mother, feeling as though he were in a trance, and went to his closet and began taking clothes off hangers. He grabbed a sweatshirt from the bin and threw it back on the bed.

"No, Teddy. You'll need long-sleeves too."

"It's hot in Florida, Mom."

His mother shook her head. "We're going to their old house in Indiana."

Teddy had only seen his grandparents in Florida, where they moved after retirement. If Teddy had ever been to the Indiana house, it was a dream of a dream now.

He wasn't sure what to call the way he felt. It was a sinking feeling. One that fell to the pit of his stomach and sat heavily—as if he swallowed the pizza from dinner whole without chewing it. And like the boa constrictor in the story, Teddy felt like he couldn't move. Part of him wondered if he wasn't the boa constrictor at all, but instead the unfortunate prey who was being squeezed tighter and tighter by this big thing circling him, ready to be swallowed whole and digested over the next long, six months.

Teddy's mother, trying to stay calm, was frustrated with his pace. "Here, you take the bedding to the car, and I'll grab your clothes. Deal?"

Teddy nodded. He stripped his bedding, tucking *The Little Prince* in the wadded sheets for safe-keeping, and shuffled down the hall and out the front door. The interior lights of the Beige Chrysler wagon lit up the leather seats inside. Boxes were stacked to the ceiling of the car. He opened the passenger door, the only seat other than the driver's that wasn't hidden by mounds of plastic tubs and cardboard boxes. He threw the bedding inside. He tucked his head in and examined the boxes.

Just then, rocks on the asphalt churned underneath a car coming down the street. The car's headlights spotlighted Teddy, and he jumped. Then, the car picked up speed and zoomed down the street. It braked hard at the station wagon, its trunk door still hanging freely above the car.

It was his father. Teddy could see his shoulder jerk as he cranked the window down.

"Teddy? What the hell are you doing? Where's Mom?"

Teddy didn't answer, and his father didn't wait for him. He took one look at the contents of the station wagon and pulled into the drive, not wasting the couple of seconds it would've taken to pull into his usual spot in the garage.

Teddy's father went straight to the front door and threw the door open. He stood there, paralyzed by confusion and fear. He looked at the darkness of the pewter house next to his own, the Marshes'. Teddy couldn't help but think of Pete waiting for him at the bus stop tomorrow morning, waiting to show Teddy his new cards. Part of him wanted to go to Pete's window and knock until he let him in. Teddy could spend the rest of the school year hiding out there.

Teddy's thought was interrupted by the sight of his parents through the glass screen door. The front door was still ajar. His mother was pointing in his father's face. She stepped closer each time his father took a step back.

Then, when they stepped behind the blinds' invisibility, Teddy could hear the roar of his father's booming shouts. He didn't want to go in, but Teddy hoped they would stop fighting if he did.

Teddy trudged through the damp grass and to the screen door. It was his mom's turn again, and she had plenty of ammo to light his father up.

"Get the fuck out, Arthur. You don't get to come home and fuck her in our bed, stay out with her all night, and then come back to our son and me. Get the fuck out!"

His father took a deep breath. Defusing a bomb took patience, tact. Teddy was surprised. With his father's anger, thinking clearly in moments like this wasn't something he typically did well.

His father's voice was low and calm. "I just needed to blow off steam. You were working so much. You were stressed."

Teddy looked to his mother and could instantly tell his father had cut the wrong wire. His mother exploded. "It wasn't just her, Arthur! You fucking know that. You can say I'm uptight. You can say I spend too much time at work. But it's always been the same problem."

His mother stepped closer to his father, their noses nearly touching.

"You've never been able to stick with me when things get hard. Instead, you go shopping for someone else to fuck and then parade her through our house."

She looked at Teddy. His stomach somersaulted. *Don't say it, Mom. Please don't say it. Don't tell him I told.*

"And in front of our son, for fuck's sake."

The tension beat into his head and sent splitting aches throughout. He couldn't help it. The dense knot in his throat grew and poked harder and harder at him until he began to sob.

But his cries were drowned out. As if proving a point that he was his father's son, he and his dad seemed to snap simultaneously.

"If you don't want me here, that's all you have to fucking say!"

Teddy's mother began to sob as she fired back. "It's not about not wanting you! It's never been about that. It's about needing to know you love me. You've chosen someone else so many goddamn times, Arthur. Everything we should go through together, I do alone, and then when I've pulled myself out of that mess, I'm stuck cleaning up whatever the hell you've done in the meantime."

His mother's energy surge seemed to have melted from the burning red in her freckled cheeks, down her chest, and to the floor. Her tears were soft and slow. And the anger in her eyes seemed to have left too. She looked at his father and whispered, "I won't share you, Arthur. I can't."

Thinking this was his cue to give them a moment, Teddy took a step toward the hall, putting one foot out of the war zone.

His parents didn't seem to notice, so he took another step. Teddy's father raised his hands to the top of his head and then slammed them to his thighs. The sound made Teddy stop.

"What are you asking me to do then, Lila?"

Teddy waited. If she could give him the roadmap for how to fix things, maybe he really could. But instead, his mother wiped her tears and, with an unyielding tone of confidence, said, "Leave. Leave so we don't have to."

She said it with unbreakable determination, spoken from a place of pain and exhaustion, one without faith and too tired to carry on. A place that his father himself had set fire to. Teddy looked to his mother to piece the foundation together from the ashes, as she always had.

When his father didn't answer, his mother pushed past him.

"Teddy, go get the rest of your things. I just need to grab something else."

Looking for an escape route all along, Teddy ran down the hall. Tears beat down his face as he bypassed the tub of clothes and dove onto his bare mattress. Teddy threw his fists at it without a clear understanding of where all this anger came from. There was so much he still didn't understand. He threw his fists in uncontrollable energy that misguided his aim. His fist beat from the mattress into his own face.

Teddy cried as he held his face. Then he sat up and smacked both sides of his head. "It's your fault, you... you... stupid fuck!"

Teddy threw his legs off his bed and yelled it again, "You stupid fuck!"

He waited for his parents to come storming down the hall, pulled from their own argument, because of Teddy's cursing.

But the yelling from the living room went on. It became white noise in the background while Teddy floated above it.

His eyes and throat ached from his outburst. As Teddy tried to slow his breathing, he looked to his moonlight-created shadow and whispered aloud, "I didn't mean to mess it up. I didn't mean to tell."

The volume from the living room was moving closer, as his parents stormed down the hall. Teddy's mother came into his room and picked up the purple tub of his clothes.

"Teddy, get the rest of your things. Now."

She never got stern with him like this. She never had to. And before this afternoon, she had never cussed like that in front of Teddy. Or even really raised her voice. It was never her style. She wasn't submissive but rather showed her anger in silence. The kind that made the person on the other side yell louder to compensate for the absence of volume from their counterpart. Is that why his dad yelled the way he did? It couldn't be. It wasn't her fault. He knew what his mother did to try to help keep his father's yelling at bay.

Even though Teddy didn't understand, with the certainty she carried, he knew she was beyond talking to his father. She said they were leaving, and she meant it.

"Lila, you're being irrational."

The anger was building in his father's voice. Teddy wished he had an escape pod—one he could tuck in and fly away to the moon, where maybe parents didn't yell and fathers didn't need friends to make them feel better because they were just happy when they came home.

Maybe on the moon, he wouldn't have any secrets to keep from his mother or from anyone. It would be the end of trying to understand why adults did the things they did. Maybe there wouldn't be any adults at all—just Teddy, the stars, and his shadow.

The roaring around him continued as his father yelled at his mother. Her determination infuriated him. He jumped around her, bursting with a fury that was ready to tip and spill.

Teddy's father grabbed his mother's wrist and pulled her toward him, making the tub spill on the floor.

"You listen to me," his father spat in his mother's face. "You're not taking our son. No one is going anywhere!"

Teddy trembled, not knowing what to do or how to move. Part of him wanted to take his chances of zipping past them and running for the trees where he'd climb until he reached the moon, away from it all.

His mother jerked her wrist free. "Teddy, grab the last box here and get in the car. My keys are on the counter."

Teddy didn't move.

"Now, Teddy."

Teddy grabbed the tub, scooped his clothes inside, and did as his mother said. His father grabbed his shoulder with a tight grip that made Teddy's knees bend underneath him. His father's hand was strong and made Teddy let out a mumble of pain.

His mother shoved his father away from Teddy. "Don't touch him! Don't you ever touch him like that! Do you think yelling over everyone and grabbing your son like that makes you a man? It doesn't, Arthur!"

The words sank in like acid into the skin—burning as it seared through the layers.

"You don't have the strength of a man, of a husband, or a father. You're a fragile little bitch."

His father charged his mother and smacked her across the face repeatedly. She fell into the hallway and against the wall. She brought her fists to the outside of her face. She was trying to lessen the whipping pain of the strong hands flying at her. Teddy's father didn't let up on the intensity of his strikes.

"Stop! Stop! Please, you're hurting her!"

Teddy sobbed through his pleas. But his father went on and on, ignoring the cries of pain from both his son and wife. His father's anger caught fire and was burning them alive. Teddy knew he had to put out the flames before his father killed his mother. He had to save her even though he was more afraid than he had ever been in his entire life.

He shot to his closet and grabbed the baseball bat his father had gotten him for his ninth birthday. He got up on his tippy toes and raised the bat above his head, the way a knight would wield a sword, rather than a ballplayer in the batter's box. Through tears, Teddy brought it down against his father, hitting him square in the back of the head. When he fell to the floor, Teddy hit him once more. His father convulsed in pain and fell unconscious.

Teddy threw the bat down and crawled to his mother in the hall. Her freckled face was swollen and blaring red. It was like her face alone had suffocated the fire and was holding it in so it couldn't spread to Teddy. He couldn't help but think of the women in his comic books, how brave they were.

"Mom? Mom, are you alright? We have to go now. I'm sorry. I'm so sorry. I didn't understand."

His mother slowly moved her hand to Teddy's. She held it and ran her thumb back and forth across the top. Even then, as her face pulsated from the hits, she tried to comfort Teddy.

Teddy barely heard her when she spoke with her swollen mouth. "You're right. We have to go." Her eyes ran over his father in the hall.

Blood spattered over his lips where they parted to release the slightest hint of breath.

"Go and never come back."

The finality of her words scared Teddy, but what frightened him most was what might happen if his father woke up and looked at his son, who had struck him down.

Teddy helped his mother rise to her feet. She leaned on Teddy, and he tried to balance the weight of the tub of clothes in one hand against his hip while stabilizing his mother on the other side.

"We have to go now. We can't take anything else."

Teddy set the tub on the porch and helped his mother to the car. He dug under the passenger seat and pulled out four canvas bags with "Greg's Grocery" written in cursive.

She put her seatbelt on and looked up at Teddy. "We have to go."

"I just need one more thing."

Before she could argue, Teddy turned and ran for the screen door. In the corner of the living room was the Crosley record player. He folded it in its suitcase shape and emptied as much of the shelves as he could, stuffing the records into his mother's reusable grocery bags.

He heard a shuffle in the hall, followed by a small groan. Teddy peeked into the hall to see his father's hand raising to the back of his head.

Teddy grabbed one final handful of records. On the top was Frank Sinatra. Teddy thought of all the nights his father came home singing "The Way You Look Tonight" outside his parents locked bedroom door. He grabbed the Sinatra record, flipped the jacket upside down, and watched the disk fall to the floor. Teddy raised his foot in the air and stomped on the vinyl, and did it again and again, splitting it into little bits.

Teddy nodded with approval, grabbed the canvas bags, and ran for the car.

His mother was more coherent now. She reached over the center console and threw the passenger door open. She hardly waited for Teddy to get inside before she pressed the gas.

With the records crammed against his chest, Teddy put his hand to the window as his street sped by. To Pete, to his father, to all he had left behind in Oakhaven, Teddy mumbled a heavy "goodbye."

4

On that long car ride from New Hampshire to Indiana, Teddy dreamt of a bull with a septum piercing and strong shoulders, kicking in the dirt. He stood at the center of an empty arena with no audience members but Teddy, floating somewhere above him.

But he heard a soothing voice, soft and sweet, asking the bull to calm down, asking it to work through the issue calmly. The voice was comforting to Teddy. It wasn't until it said, "Please, come back to me. Don't let your anger carry you away," that Teddy realized the voice belonged to his mother.

The bull flared his nostrils, and before him appeared a woman. Her long, red hair curled only at the ends and stopped just above the waistline of her athletic shorts. The back of her black t-shirt listed venues in Paris, Seattle, New York City, and at least thirty other cities. Teddy had seen t-shirts like that all his life. They were concert shirts, like the ones his mother collected.

Teddy turned to the crowd to find there wasn't one. No one to see the terror of the beast. No one to know its fury. No one but Teddy and the woman before him. The woman he was sure was his mother.

Like a criminal to a police officer, the woman held her hands above her head, showing she meant no harm. She moved closer to the bull, her steps soft and careful, almost fearful. The bull showed no sign of backing down. Despite the increasing urgency of the danger before her, Teddy's mother didn't raise her voice. She worked with ease and grace to avoid the fatal pierce of the horns.

With each step she took, the bull seemed to grow in size. His horns not only grew larger but the ends became sharper.

Teddy felt his heart pulsating in his chest, into his cheeks and his ears as if his blood carried its own panicked rhythm as it beat through him.

Teddy wanted her to get back, to stop trying to ease the raging anger of the bull. It was a lost cause. He knew that, but she only inched closer. How could she not see the threat of the beast?

"Shhh. You're alright, darling—deep breaths."

The bull shook his head, shucking the comfort of her words. He lowered his head, exposing the mountainous strength of his expanding shoulders, and kicked his hooves in the dirt. A dirty cloud of dust sank into Teddy's nose and down his throat. He coughed through it but felt as though the dirt had trapped him in a chokehold.

The arena shook, as though an earthquake were only miles out. Bits of concrete fell at the edges of the arena, decreasing the air quality even further.

Teddy watched his mother through the haze. Though he couldn't see his feet, they wouldn't respond. Teddy felt stuck in something like he was sinking into the jaws of the arena itself.

"Mom! Stop! Get out of here!"

Then, Teddy couldn't even speak. He sank lower into the dirt, and the air claimed his last bit of lung space. He couldn't move. He was helpless—held victim by the bull and the after-effects of his anger.

But his mother took another step forward. She hummed a love song by The Beatles. The sound of the melody pulled a memory from Teddy's brain that he had forgotten. At one time his parents would dance around the record player. But in recent months, his father used songs like "And I Love Her" as an apologetic ploy—one he knew would tug at his mother and make her open the locked bedroom door.

Teddy coughed and was able to clear out some of the fog trapped within him. He hummed to the familiar song's chorus, hoping the effort from him and his mother would be enough. All he could do was follow her lead and hope.

The bull snapped its neck away from his mother and looked right at Teddy. Its eyes were a deep, dark brown that looked as though the iris and pupil were merging.

Teddy panicked and reached his hands out before him, trying to hoist himself from the earth. Then, he saw the gentle movements of his mother, and Teddy tried to slow his own. He didn't want to be the thing that set off the beast. *Proceed with caution*, he thought.

But he was too late. The bull turned back to his mother and, without a moment's hesitation, rammed into her. His horns dug two deep gashes into her chest and pinned her to the arena's wall. Blood pooled from her mouth, and her arms spread widely with the bull's force. Teddy was horrified to see his mother suspended like a sacrificial Jesus Christ.

Then the bull ripped her from the wall and thrashed around the arena, shaking and splitting the earth. A jagged crack stopped just before Teddy, and he could taste his own salty sweat that dripped from his upper lip.

The beast kicked his back legs and threw his horns toward the sky, sending his mother's helpless body flying. When she came down, searching for the ground, the bull caught her atop his nose. He threw her against the arena wall. His horns, coated with crimson gore, pierced her back as she stumbled to her feet.

The bull shook his mother free from the grip of his horns, threw her limp body just before Teddy, and trotted to the other side of the arena. His cavalier response to brutalizing his mother was sickening.

Teddy struggled to lift himself from the sinking pit of dirt. He could feel its hands tighten around his ankles as he tried to free himself.

Blood poured from his mother's mouth as well as the two deep gashes in her chest and two on her back. The seams of the wounds stretched as she tried to inhale.

"Hang on, Mom! I'm coming. Please, just hang on."

Teddy kicked with all his might and lifted himself from the dirt. Minding the fragile crack in the ground before him, Teddy hurried to his mother's side.

"Mom, I'll get you out of here. We can get you some help. I'm so sorry, Mom. It's all my fault. I shouldn't have told you. This is all my fault."

Teddy whimpered, and his mother raised a hand to his face. Her thumb was turned backward, nearly touching her wrist. Teddy quivered as she rubbed it across his face. Even in death, even with blood spewing from her chest, mouth, and back, she tried to comfort Teddy.

His mother tried to speak but was cut off by the blood in her throat. She coughed and sprayed his face with blood. Teddy's stomach turned.

Through his peripherals, Teddy saw the bull kicking again. He hadn't had enough.

Teddy turned to him. "Stop! It's not her fault. I told. I told!"

The bull centered its focus on Teddy. And while holding its gaze, he ran through him, like he wasn't physically there at all. Like he was invisible—a ghost in that world. Or an unworthy target.

Teddy turned back to his mother. The bleeding was too heavy. There was nothing he could do. She let out a final whimper of pain, and then, her quivering and her breath ceased.

* * *

Teddy jolted forward in his seat. His mom had an arm stretched out in front of him, ready to catch him.

"Sorry, hun. The light turned on me."

Teddy turned to both sides, eyeing his whereabouts. He was still in the car. He felt the cold sweat sticking his shirt to his chest and the dryness in his throat from breathing so heavily.

His mother eyed him up and down. "Teddy, sweetie. Are you alright?"

Teddy turned from his mother, glad to see her alive but still not ready to accept the night they just had. The bruises and swelling of her face were bulging reminders that he couldn't take right now.

Still, Teddy wondered, if he could protect his mother at the house, why couldn't he in the arena?

5

The beige Chrysler wagon rolled down a gravel road, and as the bits of rock chewed into the cracks of the wheels, Teddy felt the car slow down. He stared out the window for hours, dozing in and out of the arena with the bull, and avoided his mother's developing bruises and bloodied scabs across her face. More than anything, Teddy tried not to meet her hurt yet hopeful eyes at all costs.

With his eyes locked on the rows of rusty train cars and split, decaying trees, Teddy asked, "Are we there yet?"

"Oh, well, hi there, Teddy Bear. We're here."

Teddy could hear her sniffling. The same way she did when his grandma's perfume tickled her nose and put her into a sneezing fit. But that smell was nowhere to be found out in the woods of that Indiana township.

Teddy sat up against the warm leather seat and rubbed his stiff neck.

The train tracks went on and on, stretching farther than Teddy could see.

Nothing was out there except the train cars, which were so neglected that not even the town's teens had bothered to vandalize them. There were abandoned train cars in New

Hampshire too, but the color of the spray paint on those was much livelier than this acidic rust.

In front of the ongoing row of train cars was a big steel building with "Abraham's Abattoir" stamped across the front. A potent smell of pennies permeated the air. It smelled like the jar his mom had kept in the kitchen when he was really little. If she had change from the grocery store or at the bottom of her purse when she'd switch to another one, she'd dump it into the jar and say, "Someday we'll take a nice vacation."

On nights when things were particularly quiet at dinner, he would hear the jar slam on the counter as his father dug through to find enough bills and coins to quench his thirst. Or after his parents had a knock-down-drag-out fight, before the garage door zipped open late at night, Teddy would hear his father's anxious hands digging through mounds of change. The mounds quickly became ant hills, which led to more fights. They never got to go on that vacation, and part of Teddy always knew they never would. Now, he knew it for sure. The thought filled his eyes with tears.

Careful not to let his mother see, Teddy turned toward the window and searched for a chance to clear his head. He pointed to Abraham's Abattoir and asked, "Mom, what's that?"

She glanced at the sign and her tired eyes widened. She locked her eyes on the road ahead, "Oh, that's just..." There was a pause. "Just a, uh, it's where food is processed. Yeah, you know, where it is processed before it goes to the grocery store."

"What kind of food?"

The sound of a blaring steam trumpet made Teddy jump.

"It's just the train, sweetie. It runs through a few times a day and then once or twice at night, if I remember right."

"You mean we'll hear that every day, more than once?"

Teddy's mother smiled. "Things will be different, but I think different is what we need."

Teddy's mother continued down the gravel path and turned at an opening in a wooded area. No houses, no schools, just trees, miles and miles of trees. And, unlike the ones in New Hampshire that were always full and bright with color, there were patches of entirely bare trees with their skeletal limbs exposed. So many branches interweaved, and they reminded Teddy of a spider web that trapped dwarves and hobbits in a Tolkien book he had read. He shivered at the thought of snapping spider fangs in Bilbo's face.

Through a small break in the miles of trees, Teddy could see the front of a house. It was a pretty brick color, and a yellow swing was attached to a far livelier tree in the front yard. He had a feeling it was planted more recently and was well-tended, unlike sectors of the forgotten forest before it.

Okay. Just had to get through some of the rough patches.

A girl ran from the front porch and hopped on the swing. Her blonde braid flew over her shoulder as she pumped her legs, and the seat carried her higher. She waved at Teddy and his mother as they drove past.

"I wonder if she'll go to your school. She looked about your age."

Teddy shrugged. "So, where is our house then?"

Just past another patch of woods where that same cluster of trees with dead limbs and strange twists separated them from the appealing house with the girl and the swing sat a large two-story farmhouse.

Only blotches of grass were left where the front yard should've been, and even that had little life in its yellow straw-like strands.

The front of the house may have been white siding at one point but was now a grey color with sporadic lines of peeling paint, as if some towering monster had clawed at it with hopes of scratching out its prey.

The ripped curtain in the front window only offered partial coverage to the stacked cluster of a table and chairs.

Teddy's mother shifted the car to park and unhooked her seat belt. But Teddy sat in his seat, eyeing the house. He felt like a rock had settled in his stomach.

His mother climbed out of the car and crouched down to Teddy's eye level. "Come on, Teddy Bear. Let's start unloading the car."

She popped the trunk and began unloading boxes. His mother grunted when she came across the boxes that didn't quite allow the flaps to close in, the ones that were ready to compromise their contents at any moment.

Teddy sat frozen in the overheating leather seat, just a few feet from his dreadful new home. The curtain slowly pulled away from the window, exposing greyish-colored boney fingers. Someone was there, holding the curtain back to look out to the front-drive. The sun gave the figure a spotlight. Teddy could see the shadow of a head and shoulders. Someone was in the house.

"Mom?" His fear made him impatient when she didn't answer immediately. "Mom!"

"What, Teddy?" she called from the trunk.

"Someone is inside the house! I saw them. Look, look! In the window."

Teddy's mother, as she had when she was angry with his father, stomped her feet to the front of the car.

But the curtain returned to its position of partial coverage. She looked at Teddy with stern eyes as if to say, *See? Nothing.*

"Okay, Teddy dear. Come get your things. We need to get you some sleep."

She opened the door to the backseat behind the driver's side. Her face looked harsher than it usually did. She was worn, frustrated, maybe even a little annoyed.

"But, Mom. I'm telling you..."

Her shoulders raised with tension. "Teddy."

Teddy knew better than to say anything else. But as he unclicked his seat belt and got out of the car, he kept a careful eye on the window with the torn curtain.

The breeze through the trees carried the smell of pennies from down the road to their front yard. Once they had settled in a bit, Teddy wanted to ask his mother about the smell that came from that building they had passed.

He put one box on the ground and then checked on the window again. The curtain was still. But his nerves were wired.

"When did grandpa say the last people moved out? I mean, are we sure they're gone?"

"Yes, dear." Her voice was dry and short.

With another deep breath, she was able to lighten her voice.

"They're gone. Come on, sweetie. We're both just tired from the drive. We'll get these boxes inside, and I'll help you get your bed set up."

Teddy was hesitant to go into the house alone. He held his box and stepped behind his mother, hoping she'd go in first.

"Go on. I have some things to go through out here. Go pick your room. You'll be upstairs. There are at least two rooms up there, and then I think a home office, but pick whichever."

"But Mom, I—"

She handed him the key. Gravel crunched under a car coming down the road. Teddy and his mother turned to look. Teddy could see alarm in his mother's face. *What is she expecting?* Teddy wondered.

A bright red car came down the road. A younger guy had his window cranked down, and The Beatles blared from the radio loudly enough to hear before he got to the end of the woods in front of the house. Teddy and his mother watched the man, waiting, but he hardly slowed his vehicle and only offered a lazy wave as he passed.

Teddy's mother sighed and returned her attention to unloading the car. "Go on, Teddy. Go start unpacking. I'm right behind you."

He glared at the window, waiting for even the slightest movement so he could make his mother see it too. But it was still.

"I'll be right behind you, Teddy. I just mislabeled some of my boxes so I'm trying to figure out what to take in and what can be stored in the shed in the back."

With her hands on her hips and a little laugh, she said one more time, "Go on, Teddy. I'll be right behind you."

Teddy nearly dragged his feet across the dry, dead grass. The dust from the yard clung to the white trims of his Adidas Shelltoes. He was beginning to think that nothing bright, not even his white tennis shoes, would last long in this house. If anything ever wasn't so dark and dreary, it had gobbled it up the way the Kraken ensnared ships and sailors in its deadly whirlpool.

The steps creaked as Teddy climbed to the front door of his new home. The front porch had splintered wood and gapes in the floorboards, showing the darkness underneath. He imagined a tentacle of the Kraken rising from one of the holes, wrapping around his pantleg, and carrying him away to the icy depths below. Instead, he heard soft squeaks of what he assumed were either mice or rats. Either way, something was down there. Teddy hurried through the door, kicked his boxes inside, and closed the door behind him.

Teddy closed his eyes and leaned against the dry wood of the front door as he took a deep breath.

Hello.

Teddy's eyes peeled open and his neck snapped to the curtain he had seen move. Nothing was there. He could've sworn he heard someone.

"Hello? Is someone here?"

The house sat silently.

With careful steps, Teddy inched toward the front window. Between his thumb and index finger, Teddy lifted the torn fabric. He jumped back, scaring himself.

Nothing was behind that curtain. Nothing looked out at his mother in the drive other than him.

Teddy wasn't sure that made him feel much safer as he stood alone in the house.

The living room was dark and cold. It had sheet-covered furniture and light fixtures with pull strings rather than switches. The walls, marked with bands of yellow, peeled like the paint outside.

Teddy grabbed a piece of the wallpaper and pulled it down, peeling it with greater force than time and wetness had. There was damp paneling behind it, like his home in New Hampshire. He closed his eyes and envisioned the paneled hallway of his childhood home. For a moment, he felt a sense of comfort. But then, Teddy saw his mother's blaring red face as her body slid down the wall. His father, chest raging with anger, fumed above her.

Teddy shook his head and pushed the wallpaper back into the wetness of the wall. It stuck.

He heard a creak in the floor behind him. Teddy jumped and spun around. Nothing was there but sheet-covered furniture, his bright plastic moving tubs, and the damp, peeling wallpaper. Teddy swallowed hard and went back to the window he thought he had seen movement in when they pulled up. He lifted the curtain once more. Still nothing. His body shivered involuntarily.

At the far side of the living room was a long staircase that, like the rest of the house, had traces of water stains.

As expected, the stairs felt thin and weak, making each step audible. The handrail was dusty, and the corners of the walls had cobwebs.

Teddy couldn't help but wonder how long ago the previous family left. Because when he and his parents went to visit his grandparents in Florida for a week's vacation, the house didn't collect this much dust, and he never saw so many cobwebs—not even in his father's office, which he only cleaned the first day of the year. It was like the house carried its own sickness. The dust was a visual symptom, like hives, and it was set on dying.

The rooms upstairs were small. Teddy didn't think his baseball diamond rug would spread neatly in any of them. The first room had a vent that let the copper smell from outside blast through. He thought it would only get stronger when his mother turned on the heat. A large desk sat in the middle of the room with papers scattered across it. Teddy took one step closer and a chill breathed down his neck. He stepped back into the hall and closed the door.

The next bedroom was terribly small. He took one glance, hoped the final room would be better, and closed the door. Its hinges squealed.

Past the bathroom with the same pull string light fixture like the one at the center of the living room was the biggest bedroom. It had a decent size window on the far side of the room. Teddy set his boxes on the floor. The creaks in the floor made him feel like wherever he walked, someone was just a few steps behind.

He raised from his boxes on the floor and looked for any other company, like the owner of the hand he thought he saw downstairs. But he was alone. Teddy returned to the window to see if maybe the backyard was less desert-like than the front. It wasn't. The grass was dry and the massive tree looked like a corpse—a rotten, decaying remembrance of something that once lived tall and full. Like the trees in the woods they passed on the drive, this tree was bare and its branches looked like arched skeletal hands, ready to nab the first thing that ran below it.

The same chill he felt in the office teased the back of his neck and then slithered down his shoulder and onto his arm. Teddy watched his skin break out in goosebumps that felt normal back home in the New Hampshire fall wind. Here, it wasn't a breeze. It was an icy, abnormal cold that sank into his skin and froze him in fear. He had never been unable to escape the cold. In Oakhaven, the icy wind would beat into his cheeks, but when he came home and stood inside the house, the cold stayed outside. Here, the cold lingered.

Teddy stared at the yard below. He told his arms to move and then his legs, but he was still. He heard footsteps, softer than the pounding of his mother right before a big blow-up with his father. Somehow, he now thought, quiet was worse.

Move. Right leg, turn. But he was still.

The chill intensified and forced a shiver throughout Teddy's otherwise frozen body.

Right, leg, move. Move. Move. Move.

He thought it with such force, he began to say it aloud, louder, and louder. "Move. Move. Mooove!"

Nearly tripping over himself and the box he set below, Teddy ran from his room. He stumbled into the hallway and his door slammed shut behind him. All the closed doors flew open and snapped back shut, piercing the quiet with their shrieks of age and wear.

Teddy watched the lights from the window burst into the hall and then be ripped away by darkness when the doors slammed.

He ran down the stairs and to the backyard. He put his hands above his head as he ran, taking cover from the tree he was sure would nab him otherwise. His heart pounded in his chest, like it was trying to escape Teddy's body and the horror from the house all on its own.

"Mom! Mom!"

She turned to Teddy. "What! What? Are you okay?"

Teddy was trying to catch his breath.

"What happened, sweetie?"

"The doors. All of them. I couldn't move. I tried, I could hear myself telling my body to move and I couldn't."

"Shh. Shh. Hey, Teddy Bear."

Teddy's mother pulled him into her chest.

She wrapped her hands around his head, holding him close.

"It's okay, Teddy. This is an old house in an old town. It makes me jumpy too."

He pulled away from her, sniffling his runny nose and wiping his wet eyes.

"But they were… they were slamming shut."

"Oh, sweetie. That's probably my fault. I opened some of the windows downstairs to air the place out. The wind probably pulled them all shut."

Teddy shook his head. "No. No. I shut them when I went upstairs. They were shut. They opened and slammed shut again. Again and again."

His mother crouched down and brought herself to Teddy's level. "Teddy, honey. We're both very tired. We're both on edge. We need food and sleep. Take a deep breath and come inside."

When Teddy hesitated, his mother smiled and said, "Unless you prefer to spend the night out here."

She stuck her tongue out at Teddy and laughed to herself.

Teddy looked up at the tree, its claws ready for him the minute he walked through. *I wouldn't make it out here all night.*

Teddy's mother ran her fingers through his hair, and they went back inside. She grabbed her knitted purse covered with buttons that said things like "Give Peace a Chance," "Make Love Not War," and a few with the four Led Zeppelin symbols.

Before Teddy could ask where she was going, she pulled a yellow slip from the fridge.

"I saw this before I went out back. There's a pizza place not too far from here. I think I still remember where it is. Want to do that for dinner? We can do the grocery shopping tomorrow?"

"I want to come," Teddy said with more force and haste than he meant to let on.

"I want you to stay and unpack. Besides, I need to make a stop."

"I don't mind waiting in the car. Please, Mom. Let me go."

She shook her head. "No, Teddy. I need to drive by myself for a few. I just need to clear my head a bit. You'll be fine. I'll be one hour, tops. That gives you plenty of time to unpack your room before dinner."

Teddy tried to quiet the heaviness of his breath. He was trying to hear the house move—the doors, the curtains, whatever subtle or obnoxious thing it did next. He wanted his mother to see it too.

"I can unpack when we get back. Please."

Teddy was whining. He could hear it in his voice, but the fear made him desperate.

His mother walked from the kitchen to the front door saying, "Your room, Teddy. Get the boxes unpacked so we can a get a mattress in there tomorrow."

She grabbed her keys and pointed up the steps, signaling Teddy to get going.

She closed the door behind her. Teddy's eyes wandered the living room, waiting for the house to seize its moment, but it was still.

Teddy went to the window, and as someone had when they arrived, he pulled the torn curtain back to look down the drive. He felt a chill inch down his neck and over his spine. He waved to his mother as she blew him a kiss. When she pulled past the mailbox and out of sight, the orchestrator of the symphony of terror waved his hands and cued the slamming doors upstairs.

6

_____

The next few nights in the new Indiana house for Teddy were full of taunting images of his battered mother, the heaving breath of the bull, and the roaring train as it ripped across the tracks.

The train sent vibrations into Teddy's room each morning. The walls shook, and the floors hummed. Teddy wondered if he'd ever get used to that awful noise.

Teddy sat up in bed and rubbed his tired eyes. He had never felt sleep deprivation like this in his life—not even during summer baseball camp when they'd play a game until nearly 10 p.m. and be up and on the bus by 8 a.m.

Last night, the bull had circled his mother in the dusty arena. She ran, helplessly stumbling on her own feet. She would occasionally stop with her hands stretched before her. She would plead with the bull, "Please, not in front of him. Don't do this."

Teddy had heard variations of this plea his whole life. "Please, Teddy can hear you." Or, "Stop it. Teddy is asleep."

Only now did he realize that those nights she pleaded with his father were more than harsh words and screams. For all he knew, they were all variations of what he had seen the night they left, how his father's hands flew with such power into his mother's delicate face.

It had never occurred to Teddy to hit his father before then. But he did with the bat his father had given him. And, for some reason he couldn't quite make sense of, that really stung.

When he awoke from the nightmares in the arena, Teddy knew his mother's face would begin healing eventually, and she was downstairs safe from the bull. But Teddy wondered, when the arena faded, and his new room replaced it, where was the beast?

In the new house, the taunts of Teddy's nightmares didn't end when he got out of bed. His ears caught every creak in the hall or on the stairs. Every noise invited torment to his peace of mind—one that left Teddy in suspense, waiting for the doors to simultaneously open and close.

Last night, when the nightmare from the bull and the stench of Abraham's Abattoir woke him, he heard the same *Hello* he'd heard when they arrived. The voice was hollow-sounding. Almost as if someone were shouting it down a well, and he happened to be sitting at the bottom of it. It was soft and gentle. Its delicate nature made Teddy jump, the same way a person might when something tickled them lightly.

Teddy climbed down from his bed and followed the smell of breakfast to the kitchen. His mother was not only cooking breakfast but painting a trim around the kitchen. The fridge was pulled from the wall, and a mound of lemons were stuffed in the sink. His mother always hated the smell of fresh paint.

Teddy's mother brushed perspiration from her brow and smiled at Teddy. She wiped her hands on her smock and said, "Hey, Teddy Bear. Do you think you could take care of those dishes for me this morning?"

Teddy froze, staring at his mother's right eye. It was so swollen she could only squint. He wondered how much longer it would take for the swelling to go down.

"Mom, have you iced your eye today?" Teddy asked.

His mother looked surprised. She placed a hand on her eye and winced. "No. You're right, sweetie. I'll take more Tylenol and ice it after I finish the trim."

She motioned to the dishes. "Don't worry about me, sweetie."

Teddy turned his back to her, wondering how he was supposed to not worry with a constant reminder of the night on her face and the arena tormenting him when he closed his eyes to sleep. The night wanted him to remember it. At least it seemed that way to Teddy, and it only made it all the more painful for him.

Hello, Teddy.

The echo-sounding voice returned. It wormed into Teddy's mind, taking center stage and pushing aside his thoughts about the night they left.

Teddy dropped the plastic cup in the dishwater. The rusty well water splashed onto his white baseball camp jersey. He turned behind him as calmly as he could. Teddy's mother, with a paintbrush in her hand, smiled back.

"Did you say something, Mom?"

She shook her head. "Nope. I was just singing to myself. I wish we had some music while we worked this morning."

Teddy smiled. A hint of their past life, their traditions, that wouldn't make his mother cry. He skipped to the living room to find their cream Crosley record player. Teddy was pleased with himself for going back for it.

Teddy spotted the bag of records and stopped. It was under the window where he thought he saw someone when they pulled into the drive of their new home. He was hesitant, despite the curtain's position that didn't seem to point to some kind of being on the other side of it. Part of him wondered if ghosts really took on a full form that he would be able to see. What if all he could see was its hand, the way he did when they pulled in. Teddy put a hand over the nape of his neck, trying to ease the rising hairs.

Teddy reached for the bag with caution. He planted his feet where he stood, squatted, and reached out as far as his arm could go. He figured if there was something there, it couldn't gobble him up. He would only need to free his hand.

Hello, Teddy.

Teddy fell back on his feet and to the wooden floor. Like a crab on the beach, he used all fours to scoot away from the window. His eyes widened as he waited for a sinister smile to emerge from behind that curtain, following the same dead, ghostly hand he saw a few days ago.

Teddy's mind was racing, telling him to move, but the fear pinned him to the floor. Was it curiosity? It couldn't be. Not with the dry knot swelling in his throat.

It's me, Teddy.

Teddy lowered his chin to his chest and cocked his head, but he couldn't see behind the curtain.

"Hello? I—I don't understand."

I'm warmer now than I've been in a very long time, Teddy.

Teddy felt a disturbance behind him, an unsettling chill he couldn't put his finger on. And just like he had been with the curtain, he was both afraid and curious.

"Please, leave me alone. I don't know who you are."

The chill wrapped its arms around Teddy and encapsulated him. It isolated the fear and made him abandon curiosity. Teddy, nearly tripping over his own feet, stood and ran to the steps. His feet pounded up the stairs and carried him to his room. Teddy slammed the door shut and pressed his back to it. His breath was hard and shallow. Teddy grabbed his throat to console the burn of each inhale.

When Teddy's breath settled, he stomped his feet to his bed and tucked himself under the covers. "I hate it here. I hate it. I hate it."

He ripped the comforter above his head and cried in the blanketed darkness.

His mind raced, from getting pizza with Pete, what he might've said had he known it was the last time, his father with Amber, the way Amber couldn't look at him as she followed his father into the garage, the way his father turned on his mother so quickly, and the way his mother's face looked as she sat against the paneled wall in the hall. And now, hearing voices in the house.

Together, the chain of events spelled one feeling for Teddy—helplessness. He said it aloud through his weak, trembling voice, "I feel helpless."

The voice pushed the thoughts aside.

But you've helped me, Teddy. Don't you see?

Teddy only cried harder. He wanted the voice to leave him alone. If he was going to be alone, he wanted to do so in peace and without the torment of his memories or whatever wandered the halls of that house. They could both exist, but he wanted them to wander alone.

Talk to me, Teddy.

Teddy pressed his hands to his ears.

"Leave me alone! Leave me alone!"

Teddy screamed, each word clawing its way up to his dry throat.

"Please, just leave me alone!"

Then, a splintering sound burst through Teddy's room and shot his bed a few inches from the wall. The wall coughed a cloud of drywall and dust. His small bookcase on the other side of the room fell on its face and spilled the binders of baseball cards.

Teddy's eyes widened as he looked at the wall in disbelief. The straggly cracks that began at the trim traveled to the center. The lines tried to curve but were cut off by a harsh hand. In what looked like carvings from sharp claws, the center of the back wall of Teddy's room read, "Hello."

7

Teddy put his feet on his cold bedroom floor. It creaked in response. With a gentleness, as if not to wake the monster sitting beneath the wood floorboards, Teddy crept to the window. Day or night, the sinister claw-like limbs of the tree outside his window didn't offer any comfort. Instead, to him, it felt as though they confirmed the living nightmare he was in.

Teddy missed his room in New Hampshire. At that moment, he missed his baseball curtains the most. He remembered feeling disappointed when his grandmother sent those to him for his birthday instead of another pack of cards like he asked for. It was like getting clothes for Christmas. But now, as the branches seemed fixed on growing outward at an expeditious rate and into his room, to *get* him, he wished they were in one of the boxes that needed unpacking, marked TEDDY'S STUFF.

Teddy hated that tree. It reminded him of a scary story Pete's father told them one Halloween. It was too cold to go trick-or-treating that year, so Pete and Teddy built a fort, and Mr. Marsh added the scare-factor. He turned out the lights and put a flashlight below his chin.

The story was about four boys, Pete and Teddy's age, who were playing in the woods and found the skeletal remains of a woman shoved into a cavity of a large elm tree. One of the boys ran back to his house and took an ax from his father's tool shed. They took turns chopping away at that old tree until they found an entire skeleton, some hair, and a lady's bloodied blouse.

The kids argued over telling their parents or keeping it a secret. Two of the boys wanted to bring other kids from their class to see the skeleton. The others were afraid.

A week later, the boys began seeing notes everywhere—written in the bathroom mirror or the dirt beside their bikes—that said, "Who put Bella in the Wych Elm?"

Pete's dad lowered his voice and said, "Some say her spirit still wanders, looking for whoever put her in the tree."

Teddy looked at the tree outside his window and shivered. He thought if his mother wasn't crying when he went downstairs, he would ask her about getting curtains.

Teddy felt himself continually trying to reestablish reality versus imaginary in that house.

He scanned his room that was beginning to look slightly reminiscent of the one back home. Teddy's mother bought a cheap and beat-up dresser with cubbies for him to store his baseball cards. His baseball rug tried to cover the dullness of the old, stained wood floors. His walls were still bare. Cracks in the drywall ran from the ceiling to the center of the wall. They looked like straggly fingers chasing something that sank into the floor before they could catch it.

Teddy pulled apart his accordion closet doors and stacked a pile of baseball jerseys on his bed. He figured he could use them to cover the cracks in the wall. Maybe it would make

his mother happy to see him putting them up—a hint of normalcy and familiarity.

Things felt off between Teddy and his mother in a way he couldn't explain. When he told her about the nightmares and the slamming doors, she seemed worn and on edge. Teddy was still getting the hang of trying to think of her in the things he did. His fear told him to run to her, but she was afraid too. Maybe not in the same sense as he was, but of the newness. She said it herself, "Everything is different. And different is scary. But we have each other, Teddy. Just try to make the most of it."

Maybe the jerseys on the wall would show his mother he was trying. As his mother's son, Teddy had to try to answer her efforts with the same forced smile and positivity she had given him all these years.

Teddy threw his night t-shirt into the potato basket his mother had given him to use as a laundry hamper. He pulled on his nylon shorts that he heard the high school kids back home call "hot pants."

Teddy opened his door and winced as it creaked. He poked his head out as if expecting a stampeding bull or a walking corpse, asking, "Who put Bella in the Wych Elm?"

He tiptoed through the hall, trying to minimize the floor's teases of something or someone walking behind him.

Why do the creaks always echo?

He couldn't help but peek over his shoulder and mumble, "I don't know who put Bella in the Wych Elm."

At the bottom of the stairs, the same torn curtain that Teddy thought he saw move when they first arrived was pulled far to the side. The screenless window was cracked just enough to let in some of the outside air. It, of course, had that same penny smell. Teddy brought his hands to his temples and shook his head from side to side.

Teddy tried to tell himself not to get worked up. He was supposed to be making the best of things.

Teddy stepped from the bottom of the stairs, and a green tub in the living room caught his attention. Teddy remembered seeing his mother with it in the garage the night they had pizza with Pete. The night they left.

Teddy sat beside it and popped the lid off. It was his baseball stuff. On top was a signed baseball he got from a Manchester Yankees game. He couldn't even remember the name of the non-legible scribble, but Teddy remembered that day with his dad. He and Teddy sat upper deck with their mitts, ready to catch any foul balls. Teddy's dad told him on the drive there how he and his friends would sit far in the outfield with their mitts ready, hoping to leave with a souvenir. Teddy wanted to catch one to make his dad proud. But the wind carried all the foul balls to the third baseline. Around the same time, Teddy's dad told him all about a right fielder who was nearing forty home runs that season, a player named Hank Aaron.

Teddy kept digging in the tub and found two baseball mitts. One was newer, a small, oiled caramel-colored Rawlings mitt. But there was another one. What once was a bright cream color was now dingy and dull. The black stitching was fraying in some places, but overall, the glove was intact. He had seen it a thousand times when he played catch with his dad while his mother sat on the back porch sipping her wine. On a good night, she would throw a few with them too.

Teddy turned the mitt over and rubbed his thumb over the faded, printed name ARTHUR BLACKWOOD.

Teddy didn't know if his mom meant to grab his father's mitt, but he was glad she did. He threw his glove back into the tub and slid his hand into the larger cream-colored one. Teddy positioned his pointer finger on the outside, just as his father had worn it.

Teddy threw the signed ball into the mitt again and again as he peeked into the kitchen. Empty.

"Mom? Are you down here?"

Teddy went to her bedroom door and knocked. Nothing. He pushed the door open slowly but heard a whining creak behind him. It was the same awful sound the doors made upstairs when they all opened together.

Teddy threw the ball into the mitt harder and faster. "Mom, where are you?"

Teddy was alone. The chill, the same one he felt days before standing at the living room window, enveloped him. His shoulders raised. The cold was coming from all over the place as if he was surrounded.

He started to head for the kitchen and the back door, but with the first step, the air was colder.

Without turning around, Teddy stepped back into the living room. His eyes swept through the damp wallpaper in the living room. He looked for any kind of movement. But the house was still.

He felt like the cold demanded something—an explanation or a reason of sorts. All Teddy could think to say was, "I don't know who put Bella in the Wych Elm."

Teddy felt his palms sweating in his father's baseball mitt. He started to take it off and go back upstairs, but then the doors began once again. Altogether, they creaked open and slammed shut.

The ball he held in the other hand toppled down the basement stairs. It made a continuous thud until it reached the bottom.

"Crap."

Teddy almost hoped his mom would call up the stairs saying, "Teddy, don't say crap."

But the darkness below stayed silent.

"Mom? Mom?"

Teddy shouted for his mother, but she didn't answer.

"Mom, are you down here?"

The doors slammed shut again and again. Teddy ran for the front door and was met by the same icy blast. A mental image of Bella's talking corpse on the other side turned him around.

Teddy ran through the hall between the living room and the kitchen with the back door in sight, but right as his feet hit the tile, the frozen chill became even more apparent.

Teddy stood suspended between the two rooms, just above the top of the basement stairs, with his hands over his ears.

"I don't know who put Bella in Wych Elm! I don't know! I don't know!"

Inch by inch, Teddy felt the cold tiptoe from the living room and the kitchen to meet Teddy in the middle.

He only had one more place to run. Teddy closed his eyes and beat the wall on the side of the stairs, looking for a light switch.

There wasn't a switch. Teddy slammed the basement door shut and ran down the stairs as fast as he could.

He could feel his heart clobbering in his chest like it was trying to beat its way out of that hell house too.

The basement was almost entirely dark. A small window that was covered by junk allowed just a slither of light that only allowed Teddy to see a few shapes here and there.

The smell of the trash replaced the penny smell that dominated upstairs. It also had an undertone of the bathroom when his dad would leave wet towels wadded up in the corner for days.

Teddy waved his hands before him, unsure what he was looking for in the abyss of darkness that was the basement. He swatted his face as something ran across it. Teddy envisioned creepy spider legs running across his face.

He moved his face back, but whatever was there only left for a moment before it hit the other cheek.

Teddy smacked at it harder. "Die. Die."

But when he brought his hand to smack at the spider again, he caught something between his fingers and palm—a string. Teddy gave it a good tug, and a static yellow emanated from a dusty bulb.

So many oddities were piled up in the basement: wooden rocking chairs, mounds of water-stained books, and an old sunburst clock that froze at 3:33.

A young, sweet voice said, "Please take me with you."

Teddy stumbled back and yelled, "Geez!"

A doll with red hair and pigtails wearing playtime shorts sat in a rocking chair just inside the light's reach.

Its grinning face was locked on Teddy. He bit into his lower lip and tasted blood as he tore away the skin.

He looked closer to see what might've set the doll off. He could see its last owner marked the bottom of her foot, JACKIE.

It was a little girl's toy. That made it seem less scary to Teddy. He realized the doll was to Jackie what the ball was for him.

Then he remembered his ball.

Teddy crouched down to the dark corner his ball rolled to and said, "Get the ball and get out of this creepy place."

He moved stacked boxes of old stationery to the floor and pulled a dusty chair out. Mounds of dust rose from it.

Behind the chair was a pair of yellow-gold eyes.

Teddy jumped back.

"Is someone back there?"

Teddy stepped back and lowered his chin to his chest as he looked down at the eyes.

They weren't nearly as fearsome as he first thought they were. They didn't have circular pupils but vertical slits, and their brightness held Teddy's attention.

"Hello?"

The eyes reminded Teddy of a cat. He went closer and crouched down, still a little afraid himself. But the eyes had a certain softness to them. Maybe even a vulnerability. They made Teddy think it had to be just as scared as he was. Too afraid to move, the feeling had become too familiar to Teddy in the last few days.

"I'm not going to hurt you. Here, kitty, kitty." Teddy never had a cat before, but that's how Pete would call his cat, Roosevelt.

The eyes seemed warmer and friendlier the more Teddy looked into them.

"Are you stuck down here all by yourself, buddy?"

Teddy already thought he could convince his mother to let him keep the cat. It would be great. When he would wake up from his nightmares, he could roll over to the cat beside him for comfort. Maybe then Teddy wouldn't feel so alone. And every noise he heard he would start to think was just the cat.

With a smile on his face, Teddy said, "I won't hurt you, honest. We can be friends. Come on out."

The eyes closed gently and opened.

"Come on. Come on out. I'm a friend."

Teddy dug into his pockets, hoping he had something that might help draw it out. But his pockets were empty other than a few bubble gum wrappers.

The eyes closed gently and opened again.

Teddy, on his hands and knees, leaned down to the eyes. "You need a friend. So do I. It's okay. Come on out."

A whisper, so faint, echoed, *You're right. I could use a friend.*

The voice didn't seem to come from the corner but just above Teddy. It was as if the words showered over him and sank into his head.

With his hands that were reaching for what he thought was a cat, Teddy drew back.

Teddy opened his mouth but found he didn't have the words.

The voice continued, *We could be friends.*

Again, the voice didn't come from in front of him, but over him. They stepped in front of Teddy's thoughts and momentarily took their place.

The eyes nodded in assurance as if to show its satisfaction with the idea.

"Wh-Who are you?"

Teddy turned from the corner and looked to the ceiling. It was full of dust and water stains, but nothing else.

The whisper seemed to circle Teddy and slither up his back into his ears. *As you said, a friend.*

"How are you doing that? Your voice. It's not normal."

The whisper tickled Teddy's ears and wormed into his head. *Oh, it's a trick. A trick I haven't done in quite some time. I can only do it with my friends.*

Teddy bit into his lip and looked back up to the closed basement door.

The figure was still hidden in the dark corner of the basement. But its yellow-gold eyes locked on Teddy's every move. Without giving it too much thought, Teddy was creeping closer to the stairs.

Right before he turned to climb them, the voice came again. *You must be a very special friend if I can speak to you this way.*

Teddy stood frozen in confusion and fear. "Are you taking my thoughts?"

The figure closed its eyes and shook its head.

More like interrupting.

"How did you get down here?"

Just as Teddy began envisioning a dark figure falling through the damp and dull floorboards above, his thoughts were interrupted.

My last friend, I needed him, and he left me. I got so weak and scared. I thought I'd hide down here. I wasn't sure another friend would ever come along. But here you are.

Teddy looked to the steps again, wondering if he should run for it. Instead, he asked, "What are you?"

The eyes looked soft and friendly, which seemed to be the only thing that stopped Teddy from running.

A shadow, Teddy. Shadows only talk to their friends. We could be friends. Just like you said.

Teddy felt guilty. He did say that. How could he tell this thing because it wasn't a cute little kitten, he didn't want to be friends?

Friends.

The word made him realize how badly he missed Pete. He had known Pete his whole life. It could be a while before he met anyone like that here.

Teddy felt a chill as the eyes moved closer but still remained in the dark.

Before Teddy could ask the shadow where that cold air was coming from, the thought took a side-step and was replaced with: *You know, Teddy. I can only talk because you want me to.*

Teddy bit into his lip again. "What does that mean?"

You said you were a friend. You noticed me.

Teddy's eyes went from side to side as if something in that dim, wet basement could give him a clue.

"I thought you were a cat. When I saw your eyes, I was just—"

Teddy's thought was finished for him.

Just looking for a friend.

Teddy didn't know what to say. The shadow was right. Even if it was in some mangy barn cat, Teddy was looking for a friend. But he was still afraid.

Friends play games together, Teddy. Would you want to play a game?

Teddy looked up the stairs, eyeing his exit.

"I—uh. I don't know. My mom wants me to unpack."

The shadow rolled the ball to Teddy.

It's your turn, Teddy. Roll it back.

Teddy lowered himself to the ball on the floor, careful not to sit in the wetness. He grabbed the ball and gave it a speedy shove into the dark corner where he saw nothing but the golden color of the shadow's eyes.

And the shadow rolled it back.

8

———

A warmth rose from the floor under Teddy's feet, up to his legs, and to his chest. To him, it felt like the warmth had entered his heart. He felt the tears coming again, and he felt fragile and sensitive like he hadn't given himself the time he needed to cry it out, given what happened.

You made me feel warmer than I have in a very long time.

That made Teddy both happy and sad. Everywhere he went in the house, he felt a chill. Teddy felt sorry for the shadow. It occurred to him that the shadow might feel that cold even more than he did.

"Is it cold down there?"

It is. But when I have a friend, I don't feel it so much.

Teddy nodded and wiped his dripping nose. "I'm sorry I ignored you. I was scared. I get a chill sometimes in the house and..."

If you keep talking to me, if we can be friends, I can keep you warm, Teddy.

That was comforting to Teddy. It was strange to feel that way as he stood in his new room with the cracks in the wall and the spooky tree just outside the window. Teddy went to the toppled bookshelf and turned it right side up. He began to pack up the baseball cards in the binders, but the voice in his head came again.

You can show me if you want to.

Teddy raised the cards in his hand, motioning them to the other side of the room as if the shadow was standing there. Teddy realized he was alone.

"Bring them downstairs, you mean?"

We can do it here.

"But I can't see you."

You don't need to. Tell me it's okay.

"What do you mean?"

Tell me it's okay to talk to you, to listen. Then you can tell me about them as you pack them away.

Teddy was confused, but he hadn't talked to anyone about baseball since that day on the bus with Pete. He missed it.

"Okay. It's okay for you to talk to me."

And is it okay for me to listen?

Teddy arched his eyebrows in confusion, but went ahead anyway and said, "And it's okay for you to listen."

Go ahead, Teddy. Tell me about each one.

The tears on Teddy's cheeks dried. He collected a stack of cards in his hand and spent the afternoon telling the shadow about the best pitchers of all time in the major league.

"This one is Bob Gibson. We don't like the Cardinals, but this guy is incredible. He's already pitched in two world series. And a few years ago, he pitched so well they had to change the pitching rules so the other guys could score!"

Teddy laughed and paused. He was sure it had only been a few days since he laughed. Still, it felt like a childhood friend who grew to become a stranger.

He laughed again, this time forcing it a little, but happy to hear the sound.

Teddy rolled onto his back and looked at the water-stained ceiling. "You know, I had one of the best hitters too. I have a lot of them, but one was really special to me."

Can I see that one too?

"It's back home, back in New Hampshire."

Why didn't you bring it with you?

"We left so fast. When I opened the pack that had it and went to show my dad, he was—well, he was busy. Besides, Dad taught me everything I know about baseball. I thought even if we weren't going to be together anymore, the cards should be, all the best ones anyway."

Well, it's still an impressive collection without it.

Teddy shrugged his shoulders and grabbed the marker from his binder. He used it to mark any repeat cards he had, so he knew he had more than one if they got separated. It helped Teddy keep track of which of the good ones he could trade to Pete.

Teddy didn't want to talk about baseball anymore. He wanted to laugh and forget about his father, who was fifteen hours away. He didn't know how he felt about everything that happened or what it all meant, but he knew he was tired of feeling helpless.

Teddy walked to the cracks in the wall and sat on the cold floor. He took the marker to the eggshell-colored surface, drew three vertical lines, and then three intersecting horizontal lines.

"Do you know this one?"

Teddy watched as an invisible hand carved an X into the top right corner.

Teddy smiled and answered the X with an O below it.

After a few rounds, Teddy realized the shadow never spotted the diagonal wins. Pete had always caught those and usually beat Teddy. But that day, with the shadow, Teddy went five to nothing.

It was just a game; he knew that. But he felt a satisfying sense of control, spotting where he would be in trouble as the shadow engraved X's across the grid but stopping them before they could tip his winning streak.

Winning was new to Teddy. It existed beyond the cards he collected. It was here, in the new house, with the shadow. And winning made Teddy smile.

9

———

I have a gift for you, Teddy.

Teddy stopped at the center of the staircase. He couldn't help but look over his shoulder, as if the shadow was just a step above him, whispering in his ears. Teddy was still getting used to a lot of things, the shadow included.

He took another step, and the loose wood creaked beneath him. Feeling better than he had in a long time, he stomped on the step and said, "Quiet, you."

When the floor didn't reply, Teddy nodded in approval. "I win."

You always win, Teddy.

Teddy smiled, embarrassed. "Not always."

But it was true. Whatever game he played with the shadow, if there could be a winner, he won. He liked that feeling. Teddy's mother noticed his smile as he rounded the staircase corner and stopped just short of the kitchen at the basement door.

She smiled back and said, "Pancakes or waffles, Teddy Bear?"

Excitement lit his eyes. "Pancakes, please."

Then, Teddy waited for her to turn to the cabinet and grab the mixing bowl above her. When she did, he gently opened the basement door and tiptoed down the steps.

When he went down to see the shadow, he didn't let his mother see. Teddy was worried she would come down after him and say he'd get sick from the moisture or get an idea to take away all the toys. Teddy didn't need them, but he didn't like the idea of the shadow down there all by itself.

The thought of the last girl and the toys made Teddy wonder if the shadow's last friend was the little girl whose name was scribbled on the foot of the creepy, talking doll. Was she the friend who left it? Maybe he would ask.

Teddy barely set foot on the damp cement before the shadow said, *My friend, it's so good to see you.*

Teddy crossed his arms and rubbed his hands up and down the sleeves of his denim jacket.

"How do you stay down here, Shadow? It's so cold."

The shadow reached out a hand as its yellow eyes beamed through the darkness. The hand arched, raising all the two-dimensional fingers except the pointer. Then, as if it were bulging from a pop-up book, a long nail rose above the shadow and grazed Teddy's hand. A comforting warmth, gentle and smooth, spread through Teddy. It was just like sipping hot cocoa with big marshmallows—his father insisted—after they decorated their lawn with a friendly gentleman of snow, stick limbs and all.

Better?

Teddy nodded, and his eyes doubled in size. "How did you do that?"

I can do lots of tricks, Teddy. I'll be able to do even more once I feel better.

"Am I still helping?"

As it always did, the shadow closed its eyes softly and opened them again—a gentle way of saying yes.

That's why I wanted to give you this gift. As a thank you.

Teddy felt this really did make him and the shadow friends. Whenever he stumbled across something he thought Pete would like, like a pack of special edition baseball cards, he would ask his mother if he could rake the leaves or do the dishes to pay for an extra pack.

The anticipation made Teddy smile.

The skeletal hand tucked back into the darkness and then shoved forward a black and silver box with a window at the top that mimicked a beehive. It had lettering at the bottom and a red button that Teddy was eager to push. The back of it looked like a steep slide Teddy could send his army men down.

It was a Polaroid camera. Teddy had seen commercials for them. He and Pete really wanted one. They planned to mow yards and raise the money to buy one together that summer.

Try it out, Teddy.

Teddy adjusted the camera so he could see the clear spot to look through. He spun around and pointed the camera at the pile of forgotten things left by the last family. The flash illuminated the corner of the room, but the basement was quick to swallow the light. A small, thick sheet rolled out the bottom of the camera. Teddy grabbed it and waved the photo as he had seen on television. But, when the image developed, Teddy was horrified. It captured Jackie's doll. Its eager face and frozen, beady eyes flickered in the flash of the camera. Teddy threw the photo to the ground.

Teddy fell to the floor, brought his knees to his chest, and buried his head. "I hate it here. The house always scares me. That stupid doll scares me. I want to go home."

Teddy heaved and sobbed.

"My dreams scare me. The tree scares me. The steps scare me. It *all* scares me. I want to go home."

The shadow sat quietly in its dark corner and watched Teddy cry until he wore himself out. After a few minutes of sobs, Teddy pressed his palm to his dripping nose and sniffled.

Teddy looked to the watchful yellow eyes. He didn't want to hurt the shadow's feelings, but he didn't like the camera. There wasn't anything in that house he'd want to capture. His mind remembered and created enough images as it was.

"I'm sorry, Shadow."

Teddy put the camera in front of the shadow's corner. The yellow eyes followed each of his movements. Discouraged, Teddy buried his hands in his pockets, bowed his head, and backed up the steps.

"We can play tic-tac-toe later. I'm sorry, Shadow."

Teddy could smell the pancakes and the sweet vanilla his mother always added an extra spoonful of. He focused on that. If he could just think about the warm, gooey syrup, maybe the tears would subside quicker, and he wouldn't have to explain to his mother.

What do you want to see?

Teddy turned back. The dark basement sat still below.

"What do you mean?"

The picture. If you could take a picture of anything, anywhere, what would you hope the little box would print out for you?

To Teddy, the answer was obvious and immediate.

"Home. I would want to see my home. Pete in his baseball cleats in the dead of winter because it was his way of holding out for spring."

Can you see it in your head?

"Well, sure if I tried. I'm sure I could imag—"

Pick up the camera, Teddy.

Teddy froze.

Pick it up. Trust me.

With a little reluctance, Teddy moseyed down the steps and picked up the camera again. He half expected the doll not to wait for the flash this time and jump out as soon as he covered his face.

"Shadow. I don't know. My mom has breakfast waiting. She'll be calling for me soon."

This is a new game, Teddy. You picked the last game. Now it's my turn. Isn't that how friends play?

Teddy's fingers fidgeted over the buttons on the front of the Polaroid. He wanted to play fair. He and Pete always played fair.

"Er—I mean, yes."

The shadow closed its eyes and opened them. The gentleness to this was becoming increasingly comforting for Teddy.

Determined, Teddy said, "Okay, Shadow. It's your turn. How do I play?"

Imagine your house.

Teddy cleared his mind, closed his eyes, and his mind's busy workers created an image of the red oak-colored house he grew up in.

Imagine it's winter.

And just like that, snow blanketed the roof of the house, and the snowman Teddy and his father built last winter sat at the front of the yard.

Imagine your friend is there. He is wearing baseball cleats.

Pete came from the back of his house, mulled over the side yard, and sank into the snow. He puffed and grunted as he pulled his wet pant legs from the snow. He was wearing a baseball mitt over his knitted gloves, which made Teddy laugh aloud.

Now, Teddy. Press the button now.

The Polaroid shuttered and then hummed as it printed the photo.

As if it were a parcel on fire, Teddy waved the photo in excitement. And at the center of the white borders of the photograph was his home back in Oakhaven. A snowman sat at the front of the yard, wearing his dad's plaid-patterned scarf. And coming around the house was Teddy's childhood friend. Pete was in cleats with a baseball mitt over his knitted gloves.

"It's Pete!"

The fog of the image faded, and Teddy could see Pete had one foot raised mid-air, the other buried in the thick snow.

Teddy laughed. He laughed until his sides hurt, and for the first time, when his eyes were wet, it was because he was happy.

The shadow cackled a laugh too. The two laughed together, just like Teddy and Pete had all those years on the bus rides home. Teddy's smile, even in the dark, scary basement, was beaming.

"Teddy Bear! Breakfast is ready."

Teddy dropped the photo and fumbled for it. "Oh, shoot. Mom is calling me." He felt around for the photo and stuffed it in his pocket before hurrying up the stairs.

When he reached the top of the stairs, Teddy stopped and whispered to the shadow through a smile, "Thanks, Shadow. Goodbye."

The yellow eyes inched from the corner, and Teddy looked at them with a new sense of feeling less alone as he waved goodbye.

Teddy closed the door and rounded the entryway to the kitchen. As he lowered into the old wicker chair that he was certain belonged on the lawn, Teddy's thoughts of drenching his pancakes in his mother's homemade syrup were interrupted.

Goodbye, Teddy.

10

"Can you do a baseball field?" Teddy asked the shadow.

Teddy felt a little low that day. As the summer heat beat in through the window and warmed his back, he sat slumped over in his Roger Maris jersey.

Of course, my friend. You know how it goes.

Teddy nodded. The process was fun and rewarding, showing Teddy memories: places he'd loved but never seen in person, or hadn't seen since the move, like his house back in Oakhaven.

Teddy focused on the back wall of his room, where his bed was. After more games with the shadow, Teddy felt less attached to some things from his old room. One of those things was the Jetsons bedding. Teddy cut holes into the fabric and tore at them, leaving the edges worn and frayed looking. He balled up the comforter on laundry day and handed it to his mother. She tossed it in the wash, and when she pulled it out, Teddy stood behind her and said, "Oh... man."

The trick worked. Money was tight, but his mom drove up to the sewing shop down the road and bought him a handmade quilt.

A fresh start, the shadow had said. And it was right. Teddy did feel better, like he was no longer sleeping under the crushing weight of a seemingly perfect family. Teddy was surer each day that George Jetson wasn't one hundred percent the husband and father he was on screen. He wondered if any of the adults on TV were. Or did all adults have a mean streak like his father? Or carry a ton of hurt like his mother?

Teddy was learning adults were more mysterious than any childhood ghost story Pete's father could tell or some being lurking in the new home's basement. He was figuring out the shadow. However, his mother, his father, so much of them, still felt like question marks to Teddy.

Do you have a favorite field, Teddy?

Teddy thought about it. His first thought was Yankee Stadium, though he had never been. But after some thinking, he said, "Wrigley Field." It was Pete's favorite; he loved Ron Santo and Ernie Banks. Pete was excited for summer, to watch Cubs games in the Santo jersey he got for Christmas.

"Yes. It's Wrigley Field. I've never been, but maybe one day I'll get there. I know it. Here, I have a picture of it in one of my card binders."

Teddy shuffled across the floor.

It's okay, Teddy. We don't need to see it. You imagine it, just like before.

Teddy closed his eyes. He could see the ivy that covered the outfield wall. To his right, he could see Pete's curly hair blow in the Chicago wind. A batter stood in the box, and the catcher crouched behind him. The pitcher threw a knuckle-ball, and Pete and Teddy's eyes lit up as it soared across the infield. Teddy, with his eyes closed, held the Polaroid in his hand.

Now, Teddy. Press it now.

Teddy arched his eyebrows, ignoring the shadow. The wind began to blow harder as the clouds rushed toward one another, darkening the sky. Teddy felt his hand move to the top of his head to hold his hat down. Pete yelled, "We better get out of here! There's a storm coming."

Pete began to collect his things and rose from the seat. The wind became heavier. It was angry. "Teddy! Let's get under the awning."

Teddy nodded in agreement, but then he heard it. The ball, zooming to the catcher's mitt, had vanished. The players vanished. On the field stood a beast, flaring its nostrils and kicking in the grass until it was dirt.

Teddy tried to get up, but his body and brain were in different universes. The disconnect pinned him to his seat.

He was walking up the stairs from their seats. The wind carried the popcorn from the bag in his hand, and Pete let go of it.

"Teddy! Come on!"

Teddy tried to shove his body forward to throw himself out of his seat with all his might but a crushing force held him back.

The bull's eyes zeroed in on Pete, and it began to charge.

It was happening all over again. Teddy didn't think he could take seeing the bull batter anyone else he loved. His eyes swelled with tears. He mustered up as much of a shout as he could with the tears and said, "Stop! Please, no!"

Teddy tried to swing his limbs and rise from his seat, but it was no use. He whimpered in fear and frustration.

Teddy. Teddy. You're okay.

The bull pushed past home plate and dove into the vacant stands. The rest of the crowd had already fled. Or did he forget to put them there in the first place?

The bull zoomed up the steps, past Teddy, and to Pete. "Stop! Stop!"

The bull forced Pete to the steps and stomped across his back. It turned at the top of the steps and huffed a heavy breath as Pete struggled to regain any muscle strength. A hunger for power, power through pain, sparked in the bull's eyes.

Put me there, Teddy. In front of Pete. Do it!

Tears rolled down Teddy's cheeks. "Don't hurt him!"

Teddy, you have to do it now.

Teddy squeezed his eyes tighter and imagined the shadow figure. At that moment, Teddy realized he had never seen the shadow aside from its hand and glowing eyes. So, Teddy imagined a hooded being that looked like Death with glowing eyes. The shadow stood before Pete, who was coughing, spewing the steps with blood and bile.

The bull charged the shadow. "Shadow! Look out! Look out!"

The shadow raised its skeletal hand at the beast. Just before it nearly passed through the shadow and into Teddy's friend, the bull detonated. Chunks of its hide, limbs, and blood soaked the cement. Teddy wiped the blood from his eyes and held his jersey in front of him, drenched with thick crimson wetness and that smelt of copper. It fell from his forehead, down the bridge of his nose, and into his mouth. Teddy's mouth opened as he gagged.

Feet pounded up the steps outside of Teddy's vision. His bedroom door swung open. "Teddy! What's the matter?"

Teddy opened his eyes and saw his mother in the doorway, holding a dripping paint roller. Oddly enough, Teddy's mother was painting the kitchen brick red. The paint spotted Teddy's floor like drops of blood. He felt his face and was alarmed at the moisture. But when he held his hand out, the liquid was clear. They were tears.

Teddy turned in a full circle. He was in his dull room in the new house. There were no animal organs or pools of blood nearby. *Blood. The smell.*

Before Teddy could finish his thought, Teddy's mother said, "Teddy? Did you do this to the walls? What happened up here? And why were you shouting? You scared the hell out of me."

He hadn't realized how many games of tic-tac-toe he played with the shadow. The walls were covered. Even the posts that held the mattress on his bed were marked with lines of tic-tac-toe and homemade scoreboards, showing Teddy as the reigning champ, undefeated.

But that wasn't what she meant. She traced her red paint-covered hands over the cracks in the wall. At the center read the first message from the shadow—well, the first to catch Teddy's attention. The one that said, *Hello.*

"I—uh."

It was there when you moved in. You were shouting because you were playing, the shadow whispered in Teddy's mind.

Without thinking, Teddy repeated, "It was there when we moved in. I was shouting because I was playing."

Teddy's mother looked at him, her eyes weighed by concern. They danced around each corner of the room, noticing all the marks. The scorecards said, "T & S."

Teddy's mother didn't ask about those, but she brought her hands to her face and sighed. His mother's face was still discolored from his father's hands. "I haven't asked. I'm sorry. We should've talked more about this. How are you doing, Teddy Bear?"

If his mother was hiding her pain, was he supposed to too?

Teddy shrugged his shoulders. "Fine. I miss Pete and Dad."

Teddy felt as though he had just used a curse word. The thought just popped up and rolled off his tongue. He bit his lip and looked at his mother, waiting for a big upset, maybe tears, but she only nodded.

"I'm sure, Teddy. It was a big change fast."

Her hands were shaking, and the paint roller she held to her side teased her pant leg, brushing against it just a bit at a time. She wasn't ready to talk about it. Teddy knew if he pressed her further about his dad, if he asked questions, she would comfort him. But maybe he needed to do more to comfort her, so he let it go.

Teddy lifted the camera and said, "Look what I found in—"

He hesitated. Teddy didn't want his mother to find the shadow. He thought she would be afraid of it and maybe get rid of it, or lock the basement door and throw away the key. After all, the yellow eyes scared him at first too.

His mother's face lit up with excitement. "Oh, wow! And it's in great condition. It looks almost brand new!"

That made Teddy feel a little guilty. "Oh, you're right. Do you think the last family left it by accident? Can Grandpa get ahold of them and ask? We can mail it back."

Teddy's mother set the roller on the ground, neglecting to notice the mess she left on the hardwood floor. She sat beside Teddy, ran her fingers through his hair, around his cheek, and down to his chin. Her usually soft hands were dry with days of labor, but the gesture still made Teddy's mind feel at ease.

"You keep it. Finders keepers."

"Are you sure?"

"Things will start to feel more like normal, Teddy. I promise. Now, let me see your pictures."

Before Teddy could say anything, his mother flipped through them, and the worry lines on her forehead became prominent, followed by a deep frown.

"The lines, Teddy. There's more and more in each picture." She lowered the pictures to her lap. "Are you playing up here by yourself?"

Teddy didn't answer.

His mother rose from the floor with the prints in hand and flipped through the rest of them.

"Look through them, Mom. I've got some good ones of the stars, baseball fields, a snowman."

She shuffled the pictures and then flipped faster and faster as panic took over her face.

Teddy's mother went to the bookcase and spread the photos on top of it. Teddy stood beside her.

Teddy saw the old house and wondered if that was bothering his mother. But she leaned on the shelf and looked back at him and said, "Honey, these are just pictures of the walls."

The two of them stood together in silence. Teddy's mother looked at him, waiting for an explanation. Her eyes were wide with worry.

The front door creaked open, and Teddy's mother nodded as if to say, "Well, then."

She ran her fingers through Teddy's hair and handed him back the pictures.

"Hello? Mrs. Blackwood?" a voice called from downstairs.

His mother's shoulders rose. "Ope. That will be Mr. Abraham. Your grandfather sent him to help fix the locks and the washing machine."

She smiled at Teddy and said, "Why don't you come paint with me?"

"That's okay." He picked up the camera. "I want to explore outside a bit more."

His mother went down the stairs, and Teddy turned to the wall in his room. He cleared his head and thought of Benji's Ice Cream Parlor back home with the bright green summer leaves hanging above.

Teddy raised the Polaroid to the wall, and out popped a photograph of the old ice cream shop in Oakhaven. He could taste the vanilla bean on his tongue.

11

"I just think he misses it back home," Teddy's mother said.

Teddy sat at the top of the steps, prepared to make a run for his room if his mother came up. Mr. Abraham had set the kitchen up with a phone, and Teddy's mother spoke to his grandparents daily.

Teddy, looking dead on, said, "She's worried about me."

The hissing whisper interrupted Teddy's train of thought and answered back, *She doesn't understand. She doesn't have to.*

Teddy shrugged. Part of him wanted his mother to know he wasn't as alone as she thought he was. The shadow kept him company. If she knew, she wouldn't worry.

"We could try to tell her? Maybe together?"

No! We can't.

The quickness of the shadow's words startled Teddy. It seemed as though it spat them, causing his shoulders to rise in tension.

I'm sorry. The last friend I had, Teddy, he told. He told them about me, and then we couldn't be friends anymore.

The shadow said "he." Teddy thought maybe the shadow's old friend wasn't the little girl who owned the scary doll after all.

"What was your old friend like?"

It doesn't matter, Teddy. You're my friend now.

Teddy smiled and nodded. "I am."

Teddy heard his mother drag her wicker sandals across the kitchen floor as she spoke into the phone.

"No. No. We can't. We just settled here. I can't uproot Teddy again and take him another fifteen hours." Teddy's mother sighed and said, "Dad, I know. Okay, I know, and I appreciate that, but this is what's best for us."

She was quiet, and then with grit in her voice, Teddy's mother said, "I haven't heard from Arthur. Now I have to go."

That did it. It reeled Teddy in. Usually, he would listen and think over what his mother had said on the phone to try and make sense of it on his own. But this time, she mentioned Teddy's father.

Teddy rose from the steps, and they answered with a creak. Teddy dropped one foot to the step below him. As if it built an invisible wall, the shadow tiptoed into Teddy's head, and he stopped.

Teddy, let it go. It won't help you.

"She hasn't talked about my dad since we left."

Teddy was about halfway down the steps when the horn of Mr. Abraham's Chevy truck sounded. Dust lifted from the house as the eleven o'clock train began to rumble by too.

It was enough to shake some sense into Teddy. He was aware of her tone. She didn't want to talk about his father—not with Teddy's grandparents and not with Teddy. Teddy decided against going downstairs and turned back to his room.

When the front door opened, he picked up the pace. Mr. Abraham seemed nice, but it was still too much for Teddy. He couldn't put his finger on it, but something about Mr.

Abraham popping in and out set Teddy on edge, like being hit with a pitch at a baseball game. Intentional or not, the pain made him angry.

When he opened his door, the skeletal limbs of the trees outside annoyed him too. They should be full of green. It was summer.

Teddy grabbed a baseball and rolled it across the floor, hard enough that it came right back. He did it again, harder, and the ball shot back as the wall's trim separated and fell to the floor. A cluster of frazzled bugs scrambled out.

"Ugh!"

Stomp on them, Teddy.

Teddy scrambled away from the multi-legged pests, frightened.

They scared you. Now, you kill them. Do it, Teddy.

Teddy crawled to his closet and grabbed his white Converse, slid his hand inside, and pounded on the bugs below.

A wave of anger came over him as he pounded again and again into the floor, whether there were still bugs under his might didn't matter.

You got them, Teddy.

Teddy swallowed hard as he tossed the shoe to the side and backed away from the bugs.

Feel better?

"Yes. Better."

You're angry, Teddy. Not just about the bugs. Tell me why.

Teddy's eyes fell to the floor, and he pulled his knees to his chest.

It's alright, Teddy. I'm your friend.

"I miss him, but I'm mad at him."

He hurt you, Teddy.

"And my mom. He hurt her bad."

Come see me, Teddy. We can take more pictures. I can make it better.

Teddy wiped a tear sliding down his cheekbone. "Okay. I was going to show you the pizza place me and Pete used to go to."

There was a creak in the hall. Teddy turned and yelled, and a higher pitch squeal answered.

It was the blonde girl he had seen on the swing at the house they passed on the other side of the woods.

Mr. Abraham's voice came from the living room below, "Ali? Are you alright?"

With her pale blue eyes locked on Teddy, the girl yelled back, "Yes, Daddy!"

As if they had met hundreds of times, Ali shook off the shock and sat on the floor beside Teddy. With a sweet smile, she said, "Who were you talking to?"

Teddy waited for the shadow's instructions, but they didn't come. His mind was full only of his own confusion and the scare this girl had given him.

Before Teddy could answer, Ali had already moved on. She pointed to the fracture in the wall. "Whoa! How did that happen?"

Again, Teddy's head was silent. Ali stared at Teddy, waiting for his response.

"Oh, uhm—I don't know. It was like that when we got here."

Twice. Teddy had lied about the wall twice now.

Ali cocked her head to the side like a confused terrier. "It wasn't like this last time I was in here."

That ignited a flame of curiosity in Teddy. Maybe she knew the shadow's last friend.

"You mean you've been in my room before?"

Ali paused, lowered her voice, and said, "Well, not your room. It used to belong to one of the Warren girls."

Girls. Teddy wondered if it was possible that one of the Warren girls knew the shadow, even if they weren't the friend he spoke of. Still, Teddy heard the shadow say, "My last friend, *he told*."

A group of footsteps beat into the creaking steps. Under Mr. Abraham's work boots, they sounded hollow.

With an aging version of his daughter's hair color and a fair amount of scruff on his chin, Mr. Abraham poked his head around the door.

"Hiya, Teddy. I see you've met Ali."

Ali went and stood in front of her father. He wrapped his arms around her as she faced Teddy. Mr. Abraham looked at the marks at the wall and then back to Teddy as if he were looking at a circus freak.

With a concerned tone, Mr. Abraham tried to move forward for the time being. "I was telling your mom, Teddy, I believe this fall, you and Ali will be in the same class."

Teddy hadn't thought too much about school in Indiana. It made him nervous. He'd be sure to bring it up with the shadow later. Maybe Teddy would even ask the shadow to create a picture of his old lunch table where he and Pete sat. He could carry it in his backpack on his first day.

"The swings are pretty good too," Ali said, rocking back and forth on her heels. "I can get higher at school than I can at home."

Teddy only gave a shy smile. He was relieved when his mother stepped into the room. She turned to Mr. Abraham.

"Checked the office too. AC is running in every room. Thank you again. I found that old book you were looking for too. Doesn't look to be in very good shape."

Mr. Abraham grabbed the worn, leatherbound book from Teddy's mother. Teddy couldn't help noticing that Ali's eyes flared with… what was it? Excitement? Alarm? Teddy couldn't quite tell.

Mr. Abraham nodded, cleared his throat, and said, "Thank you very much. Mr. Warren was a friend."

Mr. Abraham shook his head and motioned to the kids, "Lila, I was just telling Teddy about his new school."

Teddy's mother looked at him on the floor and smiled. "It will be so nice for you to have a friend when school starts. Won't it, Teddy?"

Teddy was quiet.

"Mr. Abraham says school here is on a different schedule than back home. They get out two weeks earlier and go back two weeks earlier. I think that will be nice," his mother said.

Teddy wasn't sure which part he was supposed to find appealing, but he faked a reassuring smile. He wondered where the school or even other people from the town were. All he could see was woods and corn.

As if Ali could comb her way into Teddy's thoughts like the shadow could, she groaned, "We're so far out from everyone else." Then, her icy blue eyes zipped to Teddy, who was just realizing he was still on the floor, "At least now I'll have someone to play with."

Teddy could hear the shadow's whisper. *Friends play games.* It slithered from his ear, over his shoulder, and down his spine. Teddy felt himself shiver.

Ali noticed. "Since Daddy fixed the air, it probably does feel chilly to you now. Come on. Let's go outside and play. It's hot out there."

Teddy looked at his mom, who nodded her head forward, as if to say, "Go on."

Ali grabbed Teddy's hand and ran for the stairs before stopping and nearly tripping Teddy. "Mrs. Blackwood, is it okay if we play in the creek?"

Mr. Abraham chimed in. "It's not too far into the woods there. Just back a little. If we're outside, we can hear them. I can always hear Miss Ali giggling as she splashes around in there.

Teddy's mother folded her lips in as she considered it. "Teddy's not a very strong swimmer."

Teddy felt himself blush. "I'm not that bad."

He was.

"Ali, you know where the drop-off is. Don't go out any farther. Not even on your tippy-toes. Feet have to be flat on the bottom, and no water over your shoulders. Got it?"

Ali nodded and giggled.

Teddy's mother made her way through the group and went down the steps; they followed. "We have some old t-shirts in one of these boxes."

Teddy's mother crouched onto the floor and the knee that her distressed jeans left bare swiped across the dusty floor. She opened one and kicked it away. Then she found the one she was looking for, peeked inside the flaps to be sure, and slid the box to Ali and Teddy. "Grab one. Both of you. You can wear these to the creek."

When Teddy opened the box, he shuffled through and pulled out a navy cotton one. He held it up for his mother to see.

"Even this one?"

Teddy couldn't ask her about his father, but he could make nods to him naturally in moments like this.

The navy shirt had big, orange Hawaiian flowers on the front. The yellow-pink sunset design in the background was fading. Teddy knew his father put that t-shirt in the dryer time and time again, even though his mother told him it would make the graphic crack.

Teddy's mother looked at him. She lowered her head as she tried to determine her own feelings about the shirt, about a relic of Teddy's father.

Before she could say anything, Mr. Abraham snapped them both out of it.

"Ali can run home and get her bathing suit. A t-shirt might get heavy anyway. Teddy, maybe some old shorts would do better."

Teddy's mother folded the shirt and put it back in the box. "Good idea. Go ahead and go change, Teddy."

Teddy headed up the stairs, but before he made it to his room, he heard his mother say through sniffles, "Things are still pretty raw with us. I mean, there are reminders of Arthur everywhere. And it's not like I can dump it all out or set it on fire like a teen girl getting revenge. Those things mean something to Teddy too."

"Just not the same thing," Mr. Abraham answered. "I can't imagine. When we lost Lynn, figuring out what stayed and what went was hard. I could finally let something go, and then Ali would lose it."

Teddy hung in the inside of his doorframe and continued to listen.

"Your father called me, Lila. He asked that I check in on you from time to time. Do you think Arthur knows you're here?"

Teddy's mother exhaled, "I don't know. I mean, I try not to think of that. I just want things to be better. I don't want to be afraid. You know?"

Mr. Abraham said, "I do, Lila. Promise me you'll put some more ice on your face. There's still some swelling."

Teddy waited for his mother to go into detail about the way his father hit her, pinned her to the paneled wall, and struck her while her only son screamed for him to stop.

But his mother moved right past it.

"Can I ask you something, Mr. Abraham?"

"John."

"Okay, John. With Ali's mother, Lynn, when did Ali seem to get better? When did she begin to move on? I know it hasn't been long, but... I... just have to know."

Teddy wondered when things would begin to feel normal as well.

Mr. Abraham's tone got heavier, as though he were in pain. He hesitated, and then he said, "I'm not sure she ever really did."

Teddy hung his head, feeling defeated, before stepping into his room, closing the door, and leaving the muffled voices on the other side.

12

When Teddy came down the stairs in an old t-shirt from summer baseball camp and basketball shorts, he saw Ali standing in the living room with her back turned to him. She had cut-off denim shorts pulled over a one-piece neon green bathing suit. Her blonde hair nearly reached the waistband of her shorts.

Mr. Abraham, or John to his mother, was gone.

Ali turned when she heard Teddy coming down the stairs.

"Geez, slowpoke. I thought I was going to have to go by myself."

Teddy couldn't help but smile at how fast Ali was getting comfortable with him. She talked to him in a way that felt like they had known each other for years rather than a few hours.

Ali grabbed Teddy's hand and said, "Well, come on."

They ran through the hall, past the basement door, and out the back door. As Ali pulled Teddy along through his backyard, Teddy ran past the scary tree without even noticing it. For the first time since the move, Teddy was outside without staring up at its claw-like limbs.

Ali yanked his arm toward her as they went down a mostly covered path by leaves and overgrown trees. It scared Teddy how easy it might be to get lost in there.

But he was with Ali, and she knew the way.

Ali's neon green bathing suit was like a traffic cone amidst the dirt brown and forest green colors. When they came up to the creek, Teddy had difficulty hiding his disgust. The water wasn't like that of the pool he and Pete used to go to. It was so muddied, and Teddy didn't like how it left everything underneath hidden.

The ground slanted steeply just before the creek. It was as if the pond tilted the earth as part of a cruel trick to make kids, like him and Ali, slide right into the jaws of whatever lurked in the murky water.

Ali shimmied off her shorts. Teddy wasn't sure why, but he felt himself blush. He stood back and watched her throw her pants aside and run into the pond. As the dirt shifted below, pockets of foggy dust rose to the surface.

Ali was already giggling and tossing the water around, just like her father said she would.

Ali turned to find Teddy still not in the water and gave him a look of impatience. "What? Do you think it's going to bite? Get in!"

He did think it would bite. What scared Teddy most was he didn't know what *it* was.

"You be Richard, and I'll be Nixon. I won't let you step over the drop-off," Ali shouted to Teddy.

The drop-off. Teddy already feared the pond before even remembering the drop-off. The part where Ali stood now was only the parlor of the house of terror. Other levels of scare were still waiting for him.

"Nixon! Nixon!"

Despite being afraid of the pond, he caught himself laughing at the absurdity of Ali. Was he supposed to know what she meant? She sure thought so.

Teddy smiled and said, "I don't know how to play this game."

Ali swam closer to Teddy. "Sure you do. You get in, close your eyes. And I'll swim around calling Nixon after you say Richard. Then, with your eyes closed, you have to come find me."

Laughing, the fear of the pond subsided, at least for the moment. Teddy stepped in toward Ali. The legs of his old summer camp shorts ballooned around him, and Mr. Abraham was right. His t-shirt was heavy as the weight of the water clung to the cotton. He stripped it off, wadded it into a ball, and threw it to the pond's side.

"My friend Pete and I always called that game Marco Polo."

Ali nodded. "Everyone does. But this way, the game is just ours."

Teddy thought of the shadow. They played and made up games together too. The shadow was his friend, and he was supposed to visit him. Teddy decided he would go to the basement right when he got home and apologize. But for now, he wanted to play with Ali. Then Teddy realized he had more than one friend here now. That realization expunged any of the fear he felt at the pond.

Teddy stepped further into the pond. The water was cool, but with the sun on his back, it felt a lot more balanced than the chills he got at the house.

Without any further thinking, Teddy closed his eyes and said, "Richard!"

He heard a small splash in the water before Ali answered, "Nixon!"

Teddy turned and stepped forward. Small, sharp rocks lay at the bottom of the pond. But he kept moving forward.

"Richard!"

Ali giggled, and Teddy could hear she was closer. "Nixon!"

He stepped just a few feet closer with his hands out and grazed Ali's shoulder before she could swim away.

Teddy opened his eyes. "What? I got you already?"

"It's not polite to make the guests lose."

Is that why he always beat the shadow at games? Was Teddy the guest in its home, so it let him win? Teddy felt a pang of guilt and maybe a hint of anger.

We're friends, Teddy.

Teddy turned and looked in the trees. He saw nothing but green leaves and a few scraggly trees, but most were tall and well.

Ali giggled and splashed Teddy.

Teddy returned his attention to his new friend and splashed her back as they swam further into the creek. As Teddy tried to keep up with Ali, he understood his mother's questioning of his strength as a swimmer. He resolved he would spend the summer getting better at it.

The water moved quicker around them, but they could still touch the bottom with their feet flat.

Teddy felt something nick the bottom of his feet. He called to Ali, "Ouch. The rocks are kinda sharp at the bottom."

"Don't worry. You get used to it."

Teddy half-expected Ali to close her eyes and move into the next round of the game, but instead, she lay back. Her blonde hair floated just beneath the water's surface. It broke up the impurities as it spread around her head, and she closed her eyes.

Teddy thought Ali looked like a princess from a book his mother had read him growing up. It was *Sleeping Beauty.*

Ali peeked open one of her eyes, and Teddy jumped, feeling embarrassed.

"Well, what are you staring at me for? Lay back."

Teddy did as she said, and his bright, white tummy shot up at the sun. He could see why Ali liked doing this. He felt weightless.

"Daddy said you and your mom aren't from around here. I mean, there's no way you could be. I would've met you by now. I know everybody."

She said it in a way that sounded proud.

"Daddy always tells me to hush when I talk to everybody everywhere we go, but I just like being friendly. Daddy says it's a small-town thing. I don't know what that means, but I think I like seeing how different everybody is."

"You talk a lot more than my friend Pete back home."

Teddy bit his lip, hearing how rude that may have sounded, but Ali just laughed. He laughed too.

"My mouth runs a mile a minute, or that's what my daddy says."

Teddy smiled. "I don't mind. It's pretty quiet at the house."

It's quiet in the basement.

Teddy shook his head. Was that his thought? He didn't think the shadow could reach him out here. Teddy figured he was having thoughts or hearing things out of guilt for leaving the shadow at home, waiting on him. He made a mental note to stop by the basement before he went to his room when he got home.

Ali raised one hand to her forehead to block the sun from her eyes and turned slightly toward Teddy.

"What do you think of the house? Daddy has been helping the Starlings with it since I was born. Daddy says Mr. Starling is your grandpa."

Teddy nodded. "Yeah. I've only been here once or twice, but I was really little. I don't remember it much. My grandma and grandpa moved to Florida a long time ago. I always liked going to their house in the summer. We got to go to the beach. But we haven't been in a few years. They mostly just mail me birthday cards and gifts."

"I've never been to the beach, but this is nice too. Isn't it?" Ali asked. Though she wasn't looking at Teddy anymore. With her eyes wide open, she looked straight above her, and Teddy did too. The treetops seemed to weave together, only allowing sunlight in focused spots.

"Have you ever seen anything like it?"

Teddy had, and his thoughts just spilled out. "I used to have this babysitter, Amber. When she came over, she would bring all kinds of cool things for me. One time, she brought this yellow tube. It had a lens on the end of it. She told me to look through it like I was a pirate eyeing an island ahead. Only, on the other side were all these colors and patterns. When I turned the end, it would move into different patterns. This kind of looks like that."

"Amber sounds nice."

The weight returned to Teddy, but only his throat as he said, "Yeah, she was, until—"

Teddy waited for Ali to ask questions, but she didn't push him. Teddy was thankful for that. She lay in the water and shared the silence with him.

Teddy shook away the thought of Amber and his dad and asked Ali, "Did you know the family before us? The ones my grandpa kicked out?"

Ali kicked her feet to the bottom of the creek and stood. "They weren't kicked out. But we're not supposed to talk about the Warrens."

The smile Ali had worn all day seemed to drop and sink to the bottom of the creek. "Daddy made me promise."

Teddy kept wondering if one of the Warrens was the shadow's past friend, the one who made it want to keep its relationship with Teddy a secret.

"I've been to the basement a few times."

But not today.

"Right, I'll come today. I promise."

Ali turned her head. "What?"

Teddy straightened himself up too. He had to get his guilt under control.

"Nothing. Nothing. What I was saying was, when I went to the basement, there was a bunch of stuff, some of it almost brand new."

Teddy decided not to tell Ali about the Polaroid. He didn't want to give it up if Ali wanted it, especially if it belonged to one of the Warrens she knew.

"Like what?"

"Well, there was a doll. A freaky looking, and talking, doll. Its foot said, 'Jackie.'"

"Jackie's doll is still there?"

Ali's hands flew over her mouth as if the words were pouring out uncontrollably.

"No more, Teddy. You'll get us into trouble."

She's keeping secrets.

Teddy nodded in agreement, assuming his guilt became talking suspicion.

Ali tried to change the subject. "What else was down there?"

It was Teddy's turn to keep a secret.

"Nothing."

13

———

Teddy had spent the day with Ali. He was sure to check on the shadow before their next activity, playing in the cornfield. But, when Teddy went to see the shadow late that afternoon, it was quiet and firm, and it made a request that he had always thought was against the rules.

Bring her.

"To you? No, Shadow. You said we had to keep our friendship a secret. I don't want you to have to go away."

Bring her to me.

The shadow's gold eyes felt like a burning spotlight to Teddy. He wondered if this was what his mom's friends from the Oakhaven newspaper meant when they said, "the hot seat."

She knows.

Teddy was confused. He lowered himself to the cold basement floor. When he shivered, the shadow reached out and placed its hand on him.

Teddy ground his teeth and shot back.

"Ow!"

The shadow had never burnt him before. Teddy examined the top of his wrist. The skin was a little red, but the burn wasn't too severe.

He looked at the shadow with his eyes wide in surprise. "You hurt me."

Sorry. I saw you were cold.

Teddy unbunched the sleeves of his t-shirt and pulled them down on both sides.

"You think Ali knows about you?"

The shadow's whisper hissed back at Teddy.

She's heard you speak to me. She knew the last family.

"The Warrens?"

Teddy thought if he said the family's name, maybe the shadow would tell him about his last friend.

Don't you want me to be warm, Teddy? Don't you want to be my friend?

Teddy was finally adjusting to the house in Indiana, and he wouldn't have done that without the shadow. Even with Ali, Teddy still spent time alone. And without the shadow, that alone time would make him feel bad and make him feel more afraid of the house. He needed the shadow.

"Of course."

Then we have to be sure she won't tell.

Teddy didn't like it. He was afraid of scaring Ali off once she heard the shadow's voice or saw its golden eyes. He was used to the shadow's features now, but they used to scare him too.

Still, with a sense of a need to please his friend, Teddy agreed.

"We're going to play in the cornfield behind the house. Can I bring her after that?"

The shadow's hand fell to the concrete floor and flattened back to a two-dimensional figure. Its eyes gently closed.

"Okay. I can do that."

Teddy went up the stairs, and the shadow tiptoed into his thoughts.

Be careful, Teddy.

Teddy nodded and went out the basement door, shutting the darkness behind him.

14

"Are you sure we won't get lost?"

Ali laughed. "You worry too much. I've gone in a hundred times. It's not too big. We can still hear each other."

Ali was right. On his way into Indiana, Teddy saw far larger cornfields than the one behind his house. It was more like a large patch of corn rather than an entire field. Still, he was afraid.

Before Teddy could argue with Ali, she stepped from the yard and backed into the cornfield. She stared Teddy down with a mischievous smile that said, "Come and get me."

The sun barely peeked above the tall green plants. It would be dark soon. The new house made him fear the dark in a way he never had before. And as he imagined the cornfield's openness, the likelihood of getting separated seemed to expand—another one of the house's tricks, like the slamming doors.

Teddy stood on the cornfield's edge, trapped on a bridge between two worlds of terror. He couldn't see Ali anymore. Maybe she'd known the field well enough to go that far, but Teddy didn't like it—no matter how small the field was. His mouth felt dry as the cornfield sucked up each of his breaths.

His stomach churned, and Teddy could taste its after-effects as they teased his tongue.

He threw the baseball into his father's mitt, forgetting he was tossing the ball to himself while waiting for Ali.

When he thought of just turning back to the house and telling Ali later that he got lost and found his way out himself, she called, "You go first! Find me, Teddy. Yell Richard!"

Richard Nixon. It had become their own special game, just like tic-tac-toe or the Polaroid pictures with the shadow.

"Yell Richard!"

She must've been closer than he thought. Teddy cupped his hands around his mouth and again realized he had yet to set down the ball and the baseball mitt. He slid it off his hand and patted the glove before he tossed it and the ball into the yard behind him. He felt more exposed without the mitt, like he was shedding the last bit of familiarity before stepping into the unknown.

The knot in Teddy's throat continued to build, and it was heavier than the sick feeling that was there moments before. Tears built in Teddy's ducts and merged the cream mitt's colors with the green yard, like an artist with too much water on his brush.

He missed his dad.

"Come on, Teddy! I can keep moving until you start, you know!"

Teddy threw his head back, forcing the tears to subside. The darkening sky wasn't blue, but a grey color that seemed to reflect his sadness.

"Still going! Going, going—"

Teddy was beginning to realize the struggle his mother felt of hiding her pain. Kids don't think of their mothers as sad people. But that's what she had to have been, because that's how he felt. He had never known pain like this. A single tear spilled over, but Teddy was quick to wipe it away.

"Not here," Teddy said aloud to himself. "Not now."

You're okay, Teddy.

The shadow could reach him beyond the house, into the cornfield, and at the pond. Teddy liked it. It allowed those moments of lonesomeness to pass more quickly.

"Thanks, Shadow. We'll come to see you soon."

Good, Teddy.

"Teddy? Are you still out there?"

Ali had kept going, just like she teased. Teddy barely heard her. It was more like the wind's afterthought than a shout.

He didn't want to scare her, so Teddy cleared his throat and conjured a single shout, "Richard!"

Ali's voice was then completely swallowed by the gulp of wind the field took in. Without much choice and fear of leaving his friend in what seemed to be a brewing storm, Teddy stepped inside. He wondered if pilots above could see the corn curve into a smile as a willing victim wandered in.

Teddy only took a few steps before he realized why Ali wanted to go just before sunset. They would've been too hot during the day to wear long sleeves. And she told Teddy, "You always wear long sleeves when you run through the cornfield, so you don't get burnt."

As thick corn leaves brushed against the bare part of his neck, Teddy learned firsthand, Ali was right. It stung.

"Richard!"

He didn't like the cornfield. Teddy wanted to get Ali and go. Of course, he had to find her first. Ali wouldn't have come on her own, no matter what Teddy said. She was past the niceties of letting Teddy win. Ali beat Teddy at nearly every game. Teddy still beat the shadow in tic-tac-toe, but the shadow promised Teddy he was simply the superior strategist.

"Richard!"

Teddy took another step and moved behind the final spot that wasn't surrounded by corn. He looked ahead and saw there wasn't much of a path. He had to navigate only by his friend's wind-suffocated voice.

A thick leaf whipped Teddy's hand, hard and quick. He balled his hands into fists and his covered elbows to split the leaves as much as he could.

"Richard!"

Blackbirds, crows Teddy figured, were flying overhead. They shrieked at one another, and he wondered if they were saying something like, "Look at the scared little boy about to be lost in the cornfield."

Teddy shook his head in annoyance. He needed to find Ali.

Teddy took a deep breath and found his release of it shaky. He took a left turn.

"Richard!"

Nothing from Ali. Only the birds answered. One flew down from the group and perched itself on something farther back in the field. It poked its head over the top, like the creator of a maze watching its visitors follow the wrong twist and turns. Its beady eyes locked on Teddy.

"Richard!"

The bird cocked its head and flapped its wings. Teddy hoped that meant there was movement beneath—Ali.

"Richard!" Teddy was getting frustrated and scared as the sky rumbled and darkened. He turned behind him and couldn't see a clear way out. He wondered if he just turned around and ran straight back if he could eventually find the way back to the house.

The leaves swatted Teddy as he turned and moved closer to the bird. "Come on, Ali! Let's turn back!"

The ground was more uneven the deeper he got into the field. It seemed to emphasize the otherworldliness he felt the cornfield to be.

Teddy's foot missed a rise in the dirt, and he stumbled to his knees. Small pieces of rock and littered corn bit into his hands. He flicked them out and turned to study the obstacle that caught him. He was scared. Too scared to stand. Teddy was lost.

The birds shrieked.

"Richard! Richard! Richard!"

Teddy was practically pleading with Ali. He wanted out of the field. Though he couldn't see it, he felt like the house sat behind him, eager to his distress.

"Richard!"

Teddy pounded his fists helplessly into the dirt. "Richard! Ali, please!"

The wind blew through the corn, separating a group of plants. Teddy saw a red and yellow-colored splotch move. He tried to remember what color shirt Ali was wearing.

"Ali! Ali! I'm down here!"

The dirt swelled in front of him as the angry wind began to roar. Teddy covered his eyes, protecting them with his hands. He split his fingers to peek through and look for Ali.

The red and yellow colors were just in front of him. Something cold grabbed his hand.

Teddy screamed and kicked away. He opened his eyes and saw a little girl with dark hair. There was a deep incision around her neck and a mound of purple and green bruises. A worm wiggled in and out of a crater in her grey skin. One of her eyes seemed to sit further out from its socket than the other. This girl was dead.

"Who are you?"

Another voice came.

Come back, Teddy. Come back to the house now.

Teddy closed his eyes, shook his head, and opened his eyes. It wasn't a dream. He was there, and the girl was too, and so was a small violet-colored bag before him. It was coated in dirt, and Teddy noticed a hole in the earth beside him. The girl dug it up.

Teddy pulled on the drawstring loop at the top and emptied the contents. He knew what they were. He knew from years of putting his baby teeth under his pillow in hopes of a trade for a dollar, or in some cases, a new pack of baseball cards.

Teddy looked to the little girl. He figured she was younger than him by at least five years.

"Are they yours?"

The girl, with her pointer finger in her mouth, nodded yes and then no.

"Some?"

She nodded, yes.

Teddy examined the teeth. He had never seen so many at once like that. And a mixture of both little and big teeth.

"Who did this?"

The girl stood. There was still just enough light amongst the grey clouds. She stepped from behind two corn stalks, and shoved them together, dipping them downward and creating a shadow in the dirt.

Teddy, you need to come home, now.

A chill, the same chill Teddy had felt in the house, encapsulated him. The little girl stepped further into the corn, but the two she restructured crumbled to ash and feathered away like dead skin.

"Teddy? Teddy? Can you hear me? We have to go back. It's going to storm!"

Excited to hear Ali, Teddy left the teeth in the dirt and ran for his friend.

"Ali! I'm over here."

The corn shuffled as the two ran toward one another, nearly running into each other. Teddy couldn't help it; he threw himself forward and hugged Ali. She hugged him back.

"I didn't know it was supposed to storm," Ali said.

She pulled herself from Teddy, and they wiped the dirt from their clothes. Ali walked in front of Teddy, pulling him along naturally and with ease, turning to her memorization of the corn's unmarked path.

As she did, Teddy turned back. There was no sign of the little girl. And he couldn't help but notice, Ali was wearing blue.

15

———

Ali and Teddy made their way through the backyard as the thunder in the clouds paired with heavy rain.

Teddy was surprised to see the back door wide open. Ali, as though she had been Teddy's friend for years, stepped right inside the entryway. Teddy's mother was sitting in an old wicker chair in the corner. Her knees were crisscrossed, her long hair fell loosely around her face, and she had a pen hanging out of her mouth. The swelling of her lips had nearly gone down entirely, but there was a deep scar on the corner that Teddy thought his mother would likely carry the rest of her life.

His mother tapped the velvet-covered notepad in her lap, and Teddy could see the bruising on her hands from when she tried to cover her face was lightening up too. She was healing, and she was writing, something she used to love to do during thunderstorms. For the first time, in as long as Teddy could remember, she was at peace, listening to the rain through the open door and humming one of Teddy's favorite songs, "Puff the Magic Dragon."

It was the most comfortable his mother had looked in a long time, not just in the new house. Teddy hadn't seen that journal in a long while. This one wasn't for her news stories or articles she wrote at the Oakhaven Chronicle, but for a story, like the kind she used to read to him before bed. One with gentle dragons, fields of flowers, and children rescued from their homes to live out their childhood in peace and wonder.

Teddy used to believe there was such a place, and there was such a gentle friend who could take him there. But he was learning that some things were too sweet for real life and could only exist in loopy gel ink on a page to fade with time.

Still, Teddy hoped his mother would let him read her next story about the dragons and fields of flowers later that evening. He wanted to see what kind of kid they saved next. Maybe it would be a kid who left his whole life behind late one night after his father went on a rampage. Teddy needed to know what came next for that kid.

He was quiet, waiting for his mother to finish her thought and look up when she was ready. He thought it had been conditioned in him as the son of a writer, but Ali, politely and unusually, was quiet and just watched Teddy's mother too.

After a moment, Ali tugged at Teddy's hand, and his mother looked up from the notepad, still humming. She smiled at Teddy and his friend with such a sincere smile.

"I was hollering for you guys when I heard the thunder, but Mr. Abraham said Ali knew her way back and you two would come along soon."

Ali stood tall and proud because she did just as her father said.

"If you're hungry, there's some chili on the stove. It should be ready in about five. Go ahead and eat without me. I'm onto something here."

Teddy's mother winked at him as she shooed him along.

Teddy and Ali went to the kitchen, and the smell of tomatoes, onions, and chili powder flicked the hungry vibrations in his stomach.

Are you coming soon, Teddy? We could show her the Polaroid trick.

"Shadow." Teddy had forgotten entirely about his secret friend in the basement.

Teddy turned to his blonde guest, who sat at the table and waited politely to be served by her friend. Her long hair was still damp from the rain, and she shivered.

That was Teddy's chance.

"Ali, wait here a second. I'll grab you a sweatshirt or a t-shirt you can change into. We'll put your clothes in the dryer while we eat."

"Thanks, Teddy."

Ali sat at the table, and when Teddy got to the hall, he peeked around the corner to make sure she stayed put.

Teddy took a couple of extra stomps in place for good measure to cover any creaks the basement door might make. The light from the halls spilled down the steps. Teddy leaned forward and whispered, "It's me, Shadow."

Teddy closed the basement door behind him and slowly felt his way down the unlit stairwell. Like Teddy, most people were afraid of the dark because they didn't know what was hiding within it. But in the basement, Teddy knew what was waiting for him—a friend.

As it had each time he came down the steps, the pull-string of the light tickled Teddy's face, except now he responded playfully, as he would if his father was tickling him. He pulled the string.

The shadow wasn't hiding beneath the chair in the dark corner. It was standing, its height barely contained by the damp boards of the basement ceiling. It was taller than any person Teddy had ever seen, like how his mother described the dragons that befriended the children in her story.

The silhouette of one of the shadow's bony hands extended across the floor like it was pointing at Teddy. Then, the hand emerged from the concrete and came to Teddy's shoulder. Teddy only felt a small bit of weight. He wondered if the shadow were able to move its entire being closer, if it would feel less like a projection and more like a person.

Hi, Teddy.

A baseball rolled from the corner.

"I can't play now. I just came to see if Mom put the bag with the records down here. I thought while I looked for them, I would say hi."

Thank you, friend. But where is the girl?

"Oh, Ali is upstairs. I was going to grab a record for Mom and then get her a sweatshirt." Teddy smiled and said, "It's kind of nice, taking care of them like this, I mean. Makes me feel a little less, I don't know—"

Helpless.

The grit in the shadow's voice made it sound more like a scold than an attempt to finish Teddy's thought.

Teddy only nodded.

"Anyway, Mom is writing. So, I wanted to find the Sgt. Pepper's album for her. She likes music when she writes, and she's a big Beatles fan. I don't think I've told you about them yet."

The shadow was quiet.

"You wouldn't know where it is. Would you?" Teddy asked.

The shadow's eyes opened and closed as its head leaned forward from the wall.

Living room.

"Oh, right. Mom didn't want to put them down here. She was worried they'd get wet."

Yes.

Teddy turned to go back up the steps but was stopped by warmth on the back of his neck.

You'll come back. Won't you, Teddy?

Teddy stopped at the top step and said, "Yes."

He hurried to the living room, knowing Ali was waiting on him. In plain sight sat the reusable produce bag he had placed all the records in the night they left.

Having the same thought, it looked like his mother had already set up the record player on the far side of the living room, away from the window that scared Teddy so much when they first got to the house in Indiana.

Teddy flipped through some of the greats—funny enough, one was *Moving* by Pete, Paul, and Mary—until he found the one he was looking for, *Sgt. Pepper's Lonely Hearts Club Band.* He set the record on the Crosley and placed the needle on top. Then, Teddy skipped up the stairs to save his shivering friend from a case of pneumonia, ignoring any creaks on his way.

Teddy could hear the British group from Liverpool singing below. He opened his closet and grabbed a Cubs sweatshirt for himself and an Indianapolis Indians crewneck his grandparents had sent him for Ali.

Excited for chili and to tell Ali everything he knew about The Beatles—after all, she'd gotten to be the know-it-all in their friendship so far—Teddy returned downstairs.

Ali had helped herself to a bowl of chili and had already downed half of it. Teddy laughed at her as he tossed the Indians sweatshirt at her.

"There's a bathroom in my mom's room. You can change in there."

Ali went, and Teddy peeked into the entryway near the back door. He was happy to see his mother was still hard at work. She smiled at Teddy, "Thanks for the music, Teddy Bear. Could you turn it up a bit?"

"Yes, Mom."

As Teddy stood over the record player, he felt heat on the back of his neck. It intensified, and Teddy said, "Ow, ow. Shadow, what are you doing?"

Someone is here, Teddy.

But the pain didn't subside; it continued to grow. Teddy hunched over, as though the heat was an anvil weighing him down.

"Shadow, it's probably just Mr. Abraham."

It's not.

Teddy stood and shook the shadow off in annoyance. Then, he heard his mother's voice from the back. Her voice was firm as she said, "Absolutely not. No, no. No way."

Teddy moved up the hall with his back pressed against it for cover, like in the police shows he watched with his dad.

Teddy could see his mother had her hands on her hips and was shaking her head. Her face was beet red and full of anger.

He took another step.

"Mom?"

"Teddy, I want you to go up to your room and lock the door. Now."

Someone on the other side of her. The man stepped out and said, "Lila, listen to me. Please."

Teddy knew that voice. He would know it anywhere. The shadow was right. It was not Mr. Abraham.

Teddy crept through the hall and closer to the entryway they were standing in. His mother snapped her neck and shouted, "Teddy, no. Not another step. Upstairs. Go."

The man took another step forward, and Teddy couldn't believe it when he said, "My little Bambino. How are you, bud?"

Teddy froze. He felt a wave of energy surge through his body. Only he didn't know what he was supposed to do with it. What was that feeling? Was it relief, anxiousness, anger? Was it possible to be all of the above?

Teddy was almost relieved when his mother stepped in front of him, forcing his father to step back into the rain. "Do not speak to him, Arthur. You've done enough. Now, I want you to leave."

Teddy's father looked rough. His hair was messy, unlike its usual tight and clean style. The circles under his father's eyes were dark. Pairing those with his gaunt cheekbones, his father looked like he had come to them from beyond the grave.

"Lila, please. I messed up. I messed up big time. Things got so out of control. I'm sorry. Please hear me out. I'm so sorry."

Teddy stood behind his mother like a bear cub in the woods. She stood tall and crossed her arms. He could hear the struggle in her voice as she said, "No, Arthur. I don't want to hear anything you have to say."

Teddy's father put a hand over his mouth and released a heavy breath. When he raised his arms and let his hands smack the side of his pant legs, Teddy felt himself jump.

"Lila, you can't be serious. You can't just run off with our son and live in this shitty house. I mean, Jesus Christ, Lila. *This house?* Has the blood even stopped seeping through the floorboards?"

"Enough, Arthur."

His father took in a deep breath, but Teddy knew he wasn't calming down when he exhaled. More rage and less patience filled his father. His eyebrows furrowed, and his nostrils flared in a distinctively animalistic way. It was his father's pre-rampage look. Teddy only needed to see it the one time to recognize it instantly.

Like a little kid who couldn't see at the fourth of July fireworks show, Teddy tugged on the back of his mother's shirt. He didn't know how to tell her, but given his nightmares, Teddy knew it wouldn't be long before the bull kicked out of the pen. And just as it had every time he closed his eyes, and as it had the night they left, the beast would strike her down.

"You haven't even told him. Have you?"

Teddy poked his head out from behind his mother to meet her eyes. She glanced momentarily but couldn't look at Teddy. Something *was* there. Something she knew. Something he had started to believe Ali knew too.

His mother held her ground, strong and silent. Teddy hoped this difference in the defensive approach might lead to a different outcome than his nightmares. Teddy's father took another breath. He raised his palms and pushed them down in front of him as if suffocating his anger's rising energy.

"It doesn't matter. I get it. I get why you left. But that was then, Lila. I'm better now. I'm ready to fix things, to be who you need me to be. I'm sorry it took me so long to understand." Teddy's father reached for his mother's hand and said, "But I do now, Lila."

His mother pulled her hand back, like touching his father burned her skin. Like he was some flesh-eating sickness.

"Lila, please."

Teddy looked back and forth between them, feeling like he was frozen, waiting for the rest of his life to unfold there at that moment.

"No, Arthur. You need to leave. I have company coming back soon—the man who helped my father fix up the house."

In his mother's voice, Teddy could tell she shared that detail as a threat to his father. Someone would be here soon. It wouldn't just be her and Teddy this time.

"Are you fucking kidding me, Lila?" Spit flew from his father's lips like a rabid dog.

As if on cue, the bolt on the pen burst open, and the bull was free. Teddy and his mother watched as his father stepped into the doorway, sending the wicker chair to the ground and smashing small porcelain figures from the last owners his mother had placed in her writing station. He opened his mother's journal and tore the pages right out, sending them flying into the cornfield.

"Stop it! Stop it!" his mother yelled. "Same old Arthur, throwing a big-ass tantrum when he doesn't get his way. Get out, Arthur! Get out now! We aren't coming back!"

Teddy's father shoved past both of them, nearly sending Teddy to the floor. His mother hurried after his father as he stomped into the living room.

Teddy's father grabbed their unpacked tubs and sent the contents crashing to the hardwood floor.

"Stop it, you crazy son of a bitch! Stop it now, or I'll call the police!"

Teddy stood in the hallway, panic taking over his body as his father grabbed the front his mother's shirt like one of the bad boys before a fight from a James Dean movie his grandfather once showed him.

"Fucking do it. I dare you. I'll tell them my wife kidnapped my fucking son and stole all of my shit."

And before Teddy knew it, he was reliving the night they left. He closed his eyes tightly, thinking this had to be a dream, the most vivid, realistic dream he'd had in the arena. But when Teddy opened his eyes, his mother fell to the ground, and her shaking hands tried to cover her face.

His father grabbed her wrist and squeezed hard to pry them to the side of her head. "No, you don't. You fucking take this, Lila!"

Teddy heard a small shriek come from his mother's room. Ali. He had forgotten all about her. He poked his head into his mom's room and whispered, "Ali? Ali?"

Ali's crying face poked out from under his mother's bed. "Teddy, what do we do?"

Teddy swallowed hard, afraid of his father catching him trying to do anything. "I need you to run, Ali. Run home, and get your dad. Hurry."

And without a moment's hesitation, Ali crawled from under the bed and zipped out the back door. Using her momentum, Teddy ran and jumped on his father's back. He hooked his legs around the front of him and clenched his fists. Teddy beat into the back of his father's head, hoping to hit the same spot he had weeks before with the baseball bat. Teddy hoped the knot would still be tender.

But his father, with one quick swat, threw his fist into Teddy's face, *hard*.

Teddy fell to the splintered hardwood floor of the living room. The light was blurring. He couldn't lift his head, and when the train roared by, it sounded like a faint hum.

Teddy could hear his mother whimper. Her cries were desperate and terrified. Teddy couldn't bear to hear them fade out like they had in his dreams.

"Shadow? Shadow, I need your help."

Tell me to come up. Tell me you give me my freedom and you give me my strength.

Teddy watched the distorted image of his father wind his arm up and deliver it to his mother. Teddy wondered if that was it. He sat there, immobile.

Tell me you give me my freedom and you give me my strength.

It was just like the Polaroid. Teddy had to let the shadow speak to him to make it better. It would make it better.

So, Teddy quivered through the words. "I give you your freedom; I give you your strength."

Good. Say, you give me absolute control.

The heaviness of the words… Teddy had never said anything like it. He heard his mother cough, and a wetness splattered the floor. As the pain pulsated in Teddy's head, he shouted, "I give you absolute control!"

Teddy rubbed his eyes and scanned the blurred floor for his mother. She had gone completely silent and still.

Teddy crawled to the basement door. It creaked open before he reached it. Down the steps came a hissing sound. Then, a growing, sketch-like figure. Teddy was afraid, but then he recognized the shadow's golden eyes.

The shadow was a gleaming tower in that old musty basement.

I'm coming, Teddy. Say it again.

The pain in Teddy's head made his eyelids feel heavier. He fumbled through his words, "Absolute power. Absolute control. I give you strength. Strength and freedom."

The height of the shadow folded and stretched over the staircase. It tore through the basement ceiling. Insulation fell on the wooden steps as if shaken free by an earthquake. Then, with inhuman speed, the shadow arched its back and clawed its way up the steps.

The shadow tore through the floor as it towered over his father, who was still beating his lifeless mother.

The shadow didn't say a single word. But as it stretched its skeletal hand around his father's throat, Teddy heard it hiss. Teddy squinted to see through the haze and saw the shadow raise his father in the air as he kicked like an angry bull.

Teddy saw something in his father's expression that he had never seen on him before—fear.

His father turned to Teddy. "Shit! Teddy, help me! Help me!"

The shadow turned Teddy's father so he could see his son wounded on the floor. The shadow set his father down and tore its claws from the back of his neck forward. His father gargled and convulsed as he fell to the floor.

Before the pain carried Teddy into the darkness, that awful copper smell beat into his nose.

16

When Teddy woke up, the smell of copper was more prominent than ever. It wasn't much different from the smell of Mr. Abraham's steel building at the end of the road. At that moment, Teddy put together what happened there. Ali never even flinched when the pigs' squeals would break through the trees when floating in the creek.

Ali. Teddy hoped she was back from getting her father. He lay on the floor, his head heavy with pain as he called for her, "Ali? Are you here?'"

The house was still and silent.

Teddy closed his eyes and opened them again and again. His vision only offered moments of clarity. He was still navigating in a hazy fog. One second he could see. The next he couldn't.

Once it faded in again, Teddy saw two lumps on the floor across from him. He knew one was his mother's body, and the other was his father's.

Teddy heard the gurgling sound again and lowered his head as if the memory triggered a physical pain. He crawled to the first body, the one that belonged to his father. The tan skin around his neck was long gone. Pieces of the skin dangled around his muscle, like feathered strays of white that peeled from the inside of a clementine. His father's throat had been torn away, and it looked flattened among the pool of blood.

Teddy feared that when they carried his father away, his head would detach. Even worse, he feared they wouldn't stop the severed head before it rolled to his feet. Teddy gagged and then felt a pang in his chest. He thought of his mother.

With his vision still fading in and out, he crawled quickly to her. "Mom! Mom! Are you okay?"

His mother's eyes were sunken into her swollen face. It was finally healing, and now it looked worse than ever. Teddy supposed even if she was trying to open her eyes, she couldn't.

"Mom, please get up. Please. Mr. Abraham will be here soon. Please, get up."

Teddy felt a dry knot thickening in his throat. He swallowed, but the knot fought back. He sobbed and beat into the floor beside his mother. "Mom, please!"

Her body shook from the force in the old, weak floors. Teddy stopped and waited for a response but got none. He put his hands to her chest and pushed again and again in a pulsating rhythm. Teddy had no idea if he was helping. As he pushed, more blood pooled from the sides of her mouth. He couldn't help but think *the living bleed, so she has to be alive.*

Teddy drove his palm into his mother's chest as hard as he could. He had seen this done once or twice on television and prayed to God that he was doing it right

When he heard a deep, dense inhale, his eyes lit up. "Mom?"

But it was his own exhausted breath. With the throbbing pain in Teddy's head, every sound felt answered or reciprocated, like an echo. Another thought occurred to him. *Living things make echoes.*

Then it hit Teddy. "I'm the only live thing here."

Teddy looked at his mother's lifeless face. There was no movement, but her face was full of color—pink from the clean smacks and purple and blue from the closed fists. Around her eyes, she had new bloodied cracks in her face that matched the permanent split on the side of her mouth.

A single line of blood fell from her nose. It traced the softness of her freckled face. Then, the crimson strand fell from her chin to her chest. Her body hadn't completely shut off yet, but she had.

Teddy laid his head on his mother's chest, closed his eyes, and cried. He had seen the bull for the first time not long before. As quickly as it had run them out of the home they had always known, the beast trampled the new life they had only begun to build.

"I'm sorry, Mom. I'm sorry," Teddy sobbed.

Teddy looked up and saw the shadow on the wall, back to its two-dimensional form but still as monstrously tall as ever.

Teddy tried to rise to his feet, but the weight of his head pinned him to the floor. He whimpered. Teddy stretched his hand out in front of him and brought one foot up at a time. When Teddy felt stable enough, he pushed his hands from the creaking wood floor and stood.

There you go, Teddy.

The living room looked like it had spun above the state in a wind gust that carried it to Kansas. The unpacked tubs were scattered, and Teddy's baseball trophies, old t-shirts and jerseys, and his mother's notebooks littered the floor. Some of the old sheet-covered furniture was flipped on its side. The edges of the sheets were stained with dust, and now blood too.

Teddy's head immediately punished him for the movement. The pressure beat into his eyes and tried to push him back down. He thought maybe the bull had climbed from his father's body and was now trying to stampede his mind.

He put both hands to the sides of his head and cried, "Stop! Stop! Stop!"

With the energy of building rage, Teddy kept his head down and went to his father's dead body. "It's all your fault. It's *all* your fault." Just as his father had done to his mother, Teddy crouched down to him and smacked his dead, clammy face.

"Your fault! It's all your fault."

Good, Teddy. Release your anger.

Teddy heard a car coming down the gravel road. The noise pulled him from his anger. He looked at his bloody palms—the blood of his parents on his hands.

You did all you could, Teddy. It is his fault. The shadow's skeletal hand released itself from the entrapment of drywall, crawled across the floor, and pointed to his father's bloodied corpse.

But Teddy couldn't bring himself to look at his father. His father was a monster. All this time, his father was the bad guy he had seen in cartoons and *Columbo*. He wasn't the hero or the George Jetson kind of father he had always believed him to be. It made Teddy want to throw all of his baseball cards and jerseys into a fire and watch them burn, just as he did his own illusion of his father.

Instead, Teddy looked once more to his mother. She had been the most beautiful person in the world. She was the one who tried to save him from the bull. And as much as Teddy wished he could've saved her, he knew his nightmares had been realized. The vague, empty arena that burned into his peace of mind as he tried to sleep was this old, beat-up house. Part of him wondered if the vagueness of the arena's scenery meant it could've been a motel in Ohio or his grandparents' house in Florida. Maybe it meant the bull was always going to come, no matter where they tried to run.

Teddy listened for the car, scared out of his mind and hoping he would hear Ali and Mr. Abraham, but the car drove on. He went to the Crosley and lifted the needle to the opening track. He slumped himself onto the creaky staircase and thought the best thing to do was to wait.

Paul McCartney's vocals beat through the emptiness of the home. Its bare walls and hollow doors sat as still as his dead parents in the living room. Teddy listened to the Fab Four sing about a band that would make the crowd smile. The song that had once comforted him took on a whole new meaning. And instead of singing along as he always had, Teddy said, "I didn't enjoy the show."

The blood on his hands was dry and splotchy. Teddy still couldn't believe how much there was. He immediately winced. There was a good-sized knot and wetness that he felt was becoming inescapable. When he took his hand away from the wound, his fingers had a brighter, fresh red, atop the crusty crimson.

Without warning, Teddy's stomach somersaulted. The acidity of that morning's orange juice charged up his throat and onto the floor. The reality that was closing around Teddy made him whimper and cry with every movement. He peeked out of the corner of his eyes at his parents. He was hoping, any minute, his mother would wake up. She would be weak from the beating but ready to take care of Teddy, ready to run if they had to.

"I would take care of her this time. I was still learning how."

Teddy tried to imagine how he would take care of her if she woke up. He could wrap one of her arms around his shoulders and just get her to the creek. He could lay her down by the water and run to Ali's house. Mr. Abraham could call the police while he and Ali took care of his mother. Then, that day would just be an awful day, and they could work again to make that house home.

He would play all his mother's favorites on the record player while she sat in the entryway out back and wrote. He would learn to be less afraid of the house. He would make the most of it, just as she asked him to.

He tried once more, "Mom?"

Teddy raised himself from the steps, and nausea accompanied his every move. His mother was quiet and still.

Teddy? Teddy, listen to me.

Teddy dragged the top of his hand under his nose and wiped his eyes.

"What do I do, Shadow? They're both dead. Ali and Mr. Abraham aren't here. What am I going to do? They are dead. Aren't they?"

The shadow nodded as if agreeing on the price of a train ticket rather than admitting to mutilating his father.

Teddy waited for the shadow to explain, to help him make sense of everything, but it didn't. Still, the way it closed its eyes when it nodded, the way its gold eyes looked at him, Teddy couldn't help but feel as though the shadow was the gentlest thing he had seen that day. The shadow saved him. The shadow was his protector.

Teddy, you have to listen to me. They'll come for you. Soon enough, someone will come for you.

Teddy sniffled. "I know. They'll take me to Ali's house. Or maybe they'll call my grandparents, and they'll come to get me."

Teddy turned toward the shadow, and with praying hands pleaded, "Bring her back, Shadow. Please bring her back."

The shadow's hissing whisper encircled Teddy.

I can't, Teddy. I'm sorry. But the men that will come for you will take you away.

"Take me where?"

They have places for kids without parents—awful places, Teddy.

Teddy began to sob again. He trembled through his words. "I. Don't. Want. To. Go. There. Shadow."

I know, Teddy. That's why we have to run.

Teddy hesitated and scanned the room. It was as if he thought the right answer would jump out at him. As if that was what was hiding behind the curtain in the living room all along.

I'm stronger now, Teddy.

Teddy turned toward the hacked bits of insulation and wood that had caved as the shadow tore its way up the steps. Teddy thought that had to require a great deal of strength.

You made me stronger. Strong enough to protect you, Teddy. Let me keep you safe.

Teddy nodded.

Say yes, Teddy. Say I can protect you. Say we are one.

Teddy swallowed, afraid of what would happen next, of what would happen tomorrow or a week from now, but he said it. "Yes, Shadow. You can protect me."

Say we are one.

"We are one, Shadow."

The shadow grew taller and pulled from the wall, its eyes gleaming with pleasure. Its hiss burned Teddy's ears, like it was sharper than it had ever been before. Sirens emerged from the background. Ali must've finally made it to her house. But why had it taken so long? Teddy didn't have long to wonder as the sirens grew louder.

Teddy panicked and looked to the shadow.

Go. Now.

The shadow didn't wait for Teddy's response. It clawed through the hall, past the bodies, past the kitchen where the chili was still bubbling on the stove, and out the back door. Teddy followed, looking back once more, still in disbelief at how quickly the last bit of the life he had known had been ripped apart and left lying in a pool of blood—soaking up all the gore of that evening.

Gravel churned under fast tires down the road.

When the shadow stood from its slither, it was nearly as tall as the trees outside Teddy's window. Before Teddy could think about its claw like limbs or Bella's corpse stowed at its center, the shadow hissed again.

To the woods. Go to the woods.

And without question, Teddy obeyed.

PART 2

A VILE, MERCILESS KILLER

1

One Year Later...

Officer Jack Burklow was coming off one of his legendary hangovers when the phone from the kitchen rang.

Burklow tossed in his bed and arched his eyebrows in discomfort and annoyance. After five or so rings, the phone went quiet. But only for a moment before the urgency in the ring beat through the hall again. He pounded a fist into his mattress.

This better be good. Real fucking good.

Burklow kicked his musty bedding off and stumbled to the floor. The sunlight tried to peek through the closed curtains, and Burklow's headache noticed it right away. He lowered his head and realized the tube socks he put on the night before didn't match. One was dark green, like the forest, while the other was a bright red. It was the middle of June, and he looked like a fat, grumpy version of one of Santa's helpers at the mall.

The phone continued to ring. Each shrill shriek of it felt like a mighty, painful flick in Burklow's head.

"Jesus Christ. I'm coming."

Burklow held his head in one hand and went to the kitchen's far wall, just down the hall from his bedroom.

As a creature of habit, Burklow answered his phone the same way, whether he was in the office or at home. "Officer Burklow."

Heavy breathing sounded from the other side. "Burklow, it's Finch. We got a call this morning. It's him. The Williamsons' son. The body, brutalized. It's enough to make everyone sick. They're eager to wrap up the body and go, but you need to see it. They won't listen to me."

Burklow rubbed the stubble on his chin, wondering just how many days it had been since he last saw his razor.

"So? Let them wrap it up, Finch. I can meet you at the coroner's. Actually, I'm not even due in today. I'll check it out tomorrow."

Finch exhaled in frustration. "Listen to me, Burklow. Put on some damn pants, take a swig of some mouth wash, pop some Tylenol, and get out here."

Burklow smiled. "You don't get to call the shots, rookie."

That would've intimidated the boys, but not Finch. It only ignited her edge. "I do when I'm at the scene. I do when I'm looking at the body. Get to Warren Woods. *Now.*"

Before Burklow could argue further, the phone on the other side clicked. He wished he knew exactly where Finch was calling from so he could call her back and tell her to shove it.

Instead, Burklow did as he was told. He groaned as he got ready for work on his day off. He hated taking orders from that high-strung newbie. Burklow figured she was all worked up over nothing. He knew he wasn't supposed to think things like that, but he guessed that nurturing thing that women had made her so hysterical. The Williamson boy wasn't quite a kid anymore, twenty-three years old, but he knew the boy was just a baby in the eyes of a woman.

"A bunch of bull shit. A huge load of bull shit."

Burklow pulled on his pants and tied the laces of his boots. When he looked down, he was reminded of his headache once more. It was as if a pack of coins slid from the back of his head and slammed into the front. Then, the pressure split into two and pulsated behind his eyes.

"For fuck's sake." Burklow rubbed his temples and then threw open the drawer of his nightstand. There was just a splash of whiskey in the glass above the drawer. He grabbed four Tylenol, placed them on his tongue, and threw the whiskey back. The warmth of the alcohol carried the painkillers down.

Burklow grabbed his gun and his pack of cigarettes. He lit one of the Marlboros and went out the front door of his beat-up house.

Why wouldn't she just let them take the body? This better be good.

2

_____

Burklow pulled into the eastern edge of Warren Woods—no more than two miles from the Williamson kid's jogging path each morning.

Call it a hunch, but Burklow figured he was taken further into the woods, in that same direction. He opened the door of his white and brown squad car, rocking his body forward and to the side as he tried to shimmy out without letting his headache split him in two.

A subtle rustling of leaves and snaps of discarded, weak branches sounded at the woods' open mouth. The steps were soft, but Burklow could tell they were moving quickly. The sun beat into his eyes and pulled his focus from the woods. He lowered his head to his hands and took a long drag on his cigarette with his eyes closed.

"Looking good, Burklow."

Burklow scowled and released a foul puff of smoke. He saw the petite rookie stomping toward him.

"Ah, Finch's sarcasm. It's like a warm hug."

"Uh, huh. Put that nasty thing out and take these," Finch said as she shoved sunglasses at Burklow.

When he didn't move, Finch knocked the cigarette from between his fingers to the ground, stomping on it for good measure.

"Ma'am, don't make me arrest you on the intent to start a fire in Warren Woods."

Finch shot Burklow a look that he knew meant, "Can it."

Burklow cleared his throat and spat nicotine and phlegm into the mud.

Finch cringed. "Charming."

"Let's hear it, Finch. What has you all upset about this one? What was so important you had to drag me out of bed on my day off?"

Finch's stern expression softened, almost saddened. "Wait and see for yourself."

The further they got into the woods, the less light spilled from between the trees above. The ground was soft, which lightened the pressure in Burklow's head.

Finch's petite body led Jack through a fading trail in Warren Woods. Her black, tightly wound bun hit the top of her upper back. After a few minutes, Burklow could hear mumbling voices. Some of them were mocking what he assumed was something Finch had said. "Hold it right there. I have jurisdiction here too, and you're not taking it anywhere."

A roar of laughter followed the high-pitched imitation. Then one of them said, "Honestly, what the hell is she even doing here?"

Another answered, "Yeah, honey. Be sure you didn't leave anything on the stove when you came out here to play dress-up."

Burklow eyed Finch, waiting for her to react, but her determination and stubbornness carried her forward, seemingly unfazed.

When they rounded a row of trees, a cluster of four men stood in a circle. They laughed at the one who had his hands on his hips, stomping as he said, "I mean it, boys. You better listen to me. All four feet of me will kick your ass."

Finch broke through first, and the men cleared out of her way. Burklow turned to the men, grinning, and said, "I'd put good money on her. Now, shut up and get of our way."

They straightened up and nodded to their boss.

Finch knelt to the ground, and Burklow saw the body.

"What do you think?" she asked.

Burklow rubbed the prickly hair on his chin. The body on the ground had yellow-green stains here and there and even looked a little bloated. The eyes sent a chill through him—the stillness of them. He winced and turned away. His tough facade was fading.

Burklow struggled through the words, "How long has he, it, the body I mean, been out here?"

Finch pointed to the puffing on the side of the man's stomach. "We're guessing two days. It's just like the others, Burklow. Look at his hands."

Burklow didn't have to get any closer to see the bloodied mess at the tips of the Williamson boy's fingers. The last two victims had the same thing. Their fingertips weren't a soft pink, but a blend of red and white splotches with bloodied strings feathered around the edges. Burklow figured those were the pried-up roots of the nailbed.

Finch sighed. "Burklow, a kid found him. And I mean a *kid*, younger than him." She pointed to the body. "Someone reported an odor out this way. The ranger assumed it was a dead animal, so they called the groundskeepers to remove it. Their summer help is a kid, fourteen years old."

It was freaky, it was foul, Burklow could understand that. Still, the nurturing thing, he thought, was beaming through Finch.

Burklow clapped his hands together, signaling they were finished there and said, "Okay, Finch, I'll get the kid who found Williamson in touch with a trauma counselor or a shrink. How's that?"

One of the officers in the circle behind them laughed. Burklow waved them away. "Go on, boys. Get out of here."

They obeyed, pleased to be off the hook from any work that morning. They piled into their squad cars and would likely go back to a leisurely day of staking out traffic lights.

Burklow nodded to the coroners, and they unfolded a large white-toned zip-up bag.

"Burklow! What are you doing? We don't have all information yet! Something could be different here. We have to check it out."

Burklow raised his hands to his forehead and dragged them down to his chin.

"Finch, come on. I'm supposed to be off today. There's nothing more we can do. I know he was just a kid. It's awful. It is—"

Finch rose and stomped closer to Burklow. She pointed her finger in his face. "That's not what this is about."

The coroners lined the body bag with a preservation mist as one gave Finch a look of annoyance. "Miss, we need to begin the autopsy. We have a family to inform, and to do that, we have to have a certain identification of the body formally."

Finch shot a look at the man. He was quiet.

"Burklow, we owe it to the Williamsons. We owe it to the Byers. We owe it to everyone else this guy might have gotten before he came here."

Burklow sighed. The new officer had heart and resilience—two factors he reminded himself were key to being a good cop. He had fallen lazy. He knew it. Everyone did. But Finch was the first who expected more from him.

"Fine. I'll humor you." Burklow looked to the men in front of the hearse, "We'll be a few more minutes."

One of the two men began to protest. The other, looking at Finch's sternness, nudged him. They returned to their vehicle and cracked the windows. Soon the smell of cigarettes blended with decay.

Burklow felt the Tylenol easing the pressure in his head. He removed the sunglasses and got closer to the body. Finch dug into one of her pockets and pulled out a round, blue container of Vick's Vapor Rub. She dipped two polished red fingers inside and wiped the spread in two lines under her nostrils. Finch shoved the container at Burklow, and he did the same.

"Come around to the back. It would be best if you saw it from the right angle."

Burklow followed her instruction and squatted next to the top of the man's distressed Levi jeans.

"I know we can't move it, but try to look under him," Finch said.

Deep oozing incisions started on the man's side and, seemingly, went clear across his back. The marks were a blaring crimson color with patches of dry purple surrounding them. Torn flesh hung loosely from the wounds where the skin was separated by what appeared, at first glance, to be claws.

Burklow raised his eyes from the body to find Finch staring at him, waiting for him to catch on. "The cuts?"

Finch nodded, but her eyes said, "And?"

Burklow didn't see what Finch wanted him to see. She called to the coroner, "I need a cleaner and cloth."

Burklow stopped her, "Wait a minute. Did they already take photos?"

Finch nodded, seemingly insulted that Burklow would even suggest such carelessness from her.

The man handed Burklow the cloth, bypassing Finch. She snatched it without apology or explanation, which made Burklow grin.

With her gloved hands, Finch swiped the cloth in the arch of the man's back.

"Come here."

Burklow moved to the other side of the body.

"See here. There are several marks. Several cuts. Going up the back. You can tell on the sides here," Finch's fingers followed the man's hips to his shoulders. "The cuts get bigger, deeper even."

Burklow got what she was saying. The cuts, the fingernails, the swollen joints—like the two others they had found in the last month, the Williamson kid had been tortured. The open rawness of the wound likely accelerated the decay.

"Finch, how long was this boy missing?"

She stood and removed the gloves from her hands. "Seventy-two hours."

Burklow wondered exactly how much of that time the poor Williamson boy, the one who had taken his daughter to her first dance, had spent suffering.

He snapped out of it. *Jesus. Finch's empathy is contagious.*

Still, the shock was there, and it melted away the fatigue from the night before.

"I think we need help," Finch said. "I know a guy. He's been out of the game for a bit, but he's dealt with something similar and is really good at putting things together. We were in training together here."

Burklow nodded, pleased to hear the workload on this case would be divided even further. "Great. Let's call him in."

Finch shook her head. "He'll need some time to get here. We'll have to call his station to get his information. I don't have it, but I'm hoping he's still around." She looked to Burklow, "Do you remember the Warren and Blackwood cases?"

Burklow nodded. "Yeah. In that little township."

"Yes. The one in Indiana. It wasn't quite southern, maybe central. Not too far from Indianapolis."

Burklow remembered that one. The murders with the missing kids.

"That officer has quite the reputation, Finch. As I understand it, he's not working much anymore."

Finch balled her gloves into a fist. "We need him. I need him. This isn't going to stop, Burklow. We need his help."

Burklow sighed, "Pain in the ass." He raised his hands, admitting defeat. "Fine, fine. What's his name again?"

Finch smiled, "Strode. Officer Strode."

3

Strode knew he was only one more outburst from handing in his gun and badge. He felt the anxious beats pulsate through his body.

He saw her again yesterday. It was a routine traffic stop, but when Strode approached the car, little Jackie Warren stood before it, her short frame barely visible through the fog.

Strode tried with all his might to close his eyes, look away, and tell himself she wasn't there. When he looked back, in the center of the road, a few steps closer, Jackie Warren still stood there. He couldn't see her face, but he knew the red and yellow colors of her Winnie the Pooh pajamas.

No matter how many times he looked away and looked back, she was still there. And every time, Strode followed her. He had to know if it was really her, or if it was an informative illusion, luring him to an answer, to closure.

Strode had stepped right past the vehicle he'd pulled over, ignoring the complaining high school speedster. Strode stepped into the fog, his arms stretched before him, ready to embrace the lost Warren girl. When he closed his arms around her, he was only hit with the weight of his own hands and disappointment.

He was getting so tired of the unyielding sense of defeat he carried from not finding Jackie Warren. It was ruining his life.

Strode fell to his knees and beat his hands into the pavement, yelling, "Come back, please! Come back!"

No one was there to hear his cries except for the teen who called from his car, "Hey, man. What the hell are you doing? Are you tripping out?"

Gravel was churning behind them.

It was another squad car. It pulled up slowly alongside the kid and cranked the far window down. The officer inside said in his deep, grumbling voice, "Get to school, Fletcher, and slow your ass down, or I'll call your father."

The smart-ass kid laughed and said, "Aye, Aye, Captain," before he pulled away.

Strode couldn't pull himself from the road ahead. Instead, he buried his head into his hands and felt himself quiver in regret and frustration.

Sergeant Lantz's heavy steps stopped behind Strode. "Come on, man. Let's get you home."

"I saw her, Lantz. I see her everywhere."

Sergeant Lantz rested his hands on Strode's shoulders and turned him away from the empty road before them. "Easy, Strode. You're alright."

But Strode went on, too far into his own thoughts.

"I see her everywhere, and then she disappears."

Lantz sighed, looking away from the sorry son of a bitch before him. Finally, he turned Strode to face him. Strode's eyes hung low, examining the road at their feet.

"Look at me, Strode." Strode hesitated but then brought his eyes to Lantz. "You're a good cop. You saw shit that no rookie should have seen. But you have to let it go, man. It's not your fault."

Strode shook his head. He didn't argue, but he knew it wasn't as simple as letting it go.

"I want you to take some time off, Strode. Talk to your therapist, play some golf, or whatever the hell you do in your free time. Then, when you come back, I need you sharp, okay?"

Strode was too worn to protest.

So, there he was, day two of his leave on account of multiple mental breakdowns.

He raised his particularly thin and frail shoulders and rolled them back.

Breathe.

Strode reached for the notebook on his coffee table. His ex-wife, Maggie, had put him in touch with the therapist who had given it to him.

But what was he supposed to do? Keep a record of his own insanity? Share his feelings? Strode rolled his eyes and gave the notebook a toss. "Give me a break."

Strode dragged his worn moccasin slippers to the coffee machine and flipped it on. He had used the same filter three days in a row. His mind was too deep into other thoughts to notice the ever-weakening strength of recycled grounds.

The coffee machine groaned as it tried to circulate the worn grounds.

Strode had to meet his therapist that afternoon. It had been a year and a half since the Starling house nightmare. That's what his ex-wife called it.

Strode spread his hands out on the counter and took a deep breath.

Thud. Thud.

Strode stayed as he was, hoping the noise would cease.

Thud. Thud.

"I can't. You're not here."

Thud. Thud.

Strode tightened his grip on the counter. Unwiped jelly stuck to his palms. "Please, go away."

Then came the smell of bleach. He immediately visualized the overturned bottle in the Warren's living room. Had Mr. Warren planned on getting rid of the bodies before taking his own life? Had he succeeded somehow with Jackie? Those questions had haunted Strode ever since the night he responded to screams at the Starling house.

The thuds stopped, but when Strode peeked over his shoulder, she was there—Jackie Warren.

The bleach burned into his nostrils and stung his eyes. Strode rubbed at them frantically.

"She's not here. She's not here."

But when Strode turned again, Jackie Warren was swinging her head back and forth, humming. She kicked the cabinet again with her bare feet.

Thud. Thud.

If Strode and Maggie had ever been able to have the daughter they wanted, he always thought she might look like Jackie. Jackie had dark chocolate-colored hair with big brown eyes to match, just like Maggie.

Strode had only seen Jackie's olive-colored skin in pictures and a few times when she was playing outside of the Starling house. He would drive by every few days just to check on the two houses at the township's edge.

Only now, as she sat on Strode's kitchen counter, Jackie's skin wasn't warm-looking. Instead, it was a ghostly pale, and her eyes were anything but calm and beautiful. They bulged. They said fear and extreme, wicked pain. They said, "Evil was here."

A deep incision wound around her neck, accompanied by a mirage of green and blue. She hummed and bobbed her head, and one side of her neck gave way. Her head hit the top of the opposite shoulder. One eye sat further out than the other. Her innocent Winnie the Pooh pajamas were marred by slices and bloodstains. One pant leg exposed what appeared to be a broken ankle. It twisted in a freak-like contortion.

She hopped down from the counter, her head barely hanging on. Her feet gave a final thud as her heels hit the floor. Then, there was a snap. It made her bend at the knees, but her face stayed the same—dead-cold.

"I'm sorry, Jackie. I couldn't find you in time. I'm so sorry, sweetie."

Strode heard his therapist. "Separate the painful from the imaginative."

He turned to the little girl, "You can't keep doing this to me. I have to get better. I lost Maggie. All I have is my job."

An invisible force threw something over Jackie's head and around her neck. Her eyes bulged wider and wider as she gasped for air. Her feet kicked as her breaths became shallow, more like croaks. Blood poured from her neck, down her pajamas, and onto the kitchen floor. Strode watched the front of his tan slippers absorb the red, making them a deep purple color.

"No, no. Stop. Stop." Strode felt the weight of his head lighten, as if it were a balloon on a string, inevitably blowing away into the clouds.

He couldn't take it anymore. "Enough!"

Strode reached for a spatula and swatted just above Jackie's head, hoping he could take the invisible force harming her. Jackie's limp body fell to the floor. As he thought he might have done if he had ever found her body, Strode knelt to Jackie's side and took two fingers to her eyelids, closing them.

His stomach turned—both from the gore and the ever-growing weight of the Starling house nightmare.

"It's not real. It's not real," Strode tried to convince himself. He rose from the dusty and blood-covered kitchen floor and grabbed a coffee mug from the cherry-colored cabinet.

He carried his coffee to the back porch and shut his mind-made manifestation of horror inside. He hoped in the time it would take to finish his cup, the bloodied scene would clean itself up or disappear or whatever the hell it did to go away.

Strode fell into the ragged armchair he substituted for appropriate outdoor furniture and brought his palms to his face as he tried to breathe. His hands shook.

Less than two years ago, Strode thought he would make a good cop. Now, he was a man with a gun and a badge who, on a good day, didn't have a breakdown.

Strode put his hands out in defense and spoke to the empty yard. "I know. I know. We don't call them breakdowns. We call them," he raised his fingers to create air quotes, "bad brain days."

Strode sighed. This time mostly with exhaustion. Whatever the hell he had, whatever had buried itself deep within his brain since the night he found the slaughtered Warren family at the Starling house, and the Blackwoods not long after, was wearing on him more and more each day. Some people knew it. And that's why some people wanted him to hand in his gun.

He wasn't sure a simple reclassification of his upsets ("bad brain days") per his therapist would be enough.

The sound of the red telephone, the one Maggie had picked out to match the red laminate-decorated kitchen, rang through the glass of the sliding door. It was soft but enough to let Strode know someone needed his attention.

He ventured inside, pausing to ensure the Warren girl's corpse was gone, and answered the phone.

"Hello?"

Strode circled his head and inhaled, smelling for bleach.

A woman on the line asked, "Is this Officer Strode?"

Strode peered up again, double-checking for Jackie or his mind-made remains of her. The coast was clear, and the smell was gone.

The woman on the other end was patient. She waited a moment for Strode's response.

"Yes," Strode said. "I'm off today, though. Did you need the number of the station?"

Strode felt his anxiousness pick up the pace. He hated shoving work off to other officers. Trying to cope with every-thing without being a burden to everyone else was sometimes enough to send him over the edge.

The woman maintained her patience as Strode's mind derailed.

After a moment, he remembered someone was still on the other side of the line. Though Jackie, or the illusion of her, was gone, Strode was no longer alone with his thoughts.

He cleared his throat. "Excuse me. Could you repeat that please? I'm afraid you cut out a bit."

The woman paused and then said, "Oh, sure. I said I don't need the number to the station. I'm actually looking for you, Officer Strode. We went to the academy together."

Strode thought her voice sounded familiar. She wasn't hard to place. Only one woman was in the academy when he went. He couldn't remember her name, but her grit, ferocity, and keen attention to detail were unforgettable. One word, not a name, came to mind when Strode reimagined this woman—badass.

"Ringing any bells, Officer Strode?"

Damn it, Strode thought. *I did it again.* He could hear his therapist, Dr. Evers, say, "Remember to be present. It's not enough to exist in the background."

His ex-wife had said something similar toward the end of their marriage.

Strode bypassed the woman's name, hoping it would come to him, and said, "You climbed the rope faster than half the men. They didn't think, as tiny as you are, that you could do it. Remember that?"

The woman on the other end laughed. "Explicitly." Then, her laugh, her energy, cut off, like it had suddenly run out, like an hourglass. "Officer Strode, I'm afraid I'm not only reconnecting with you to relive our academy days."

It was humorous to Strode how she made it sound like ancient memories rather than only a couple of years prior.

She continued. "I'm calling from Michigan. I joined the police force in a town not too far from the academy. Have you seen what's going on here?"

Strode eyed his office door around the corner, trying to remember if any of his research, his newspaper clippings, had come from Michigan. Either way, given his state, Strode thought it best not to admit an obsessive pastime willingly.

"I don't believe I am familiar with the situation, ma'am."

The woman's tone on the other end of the phone dialed back even further, past low energy, and into chilling. "We found a body. In the woods. He was a young man. The guys wouldn't call him a kid like I do, but he was only twenty-three."

Strode felt his breath bury deep within his chest. It hung suspended. The victim wasn't as young as Jackie Warren, but yes, Strode would agree that twenty-three years old was a kid.

"Well, I heard your name when I visited the training camp recently," she stopped.

Strode could only imagine what the officers-to-be at the academy had to say about the unhinged rookie. He hoped the next time they ran laps in Michigan, it was humid as fuck, and their trainer took them to the park to run uphill.

Strode laughed into the phone, which turned out to be a more fitting response than his sarcastic mind could've conjured if he'd tried.

The woman on the other end offered an awkward giggle and said, "What's important is, I think I could use your help. I heard you were on leave, and I just thought with your, er, um, experience with this sort of thing, you could help."

Strode rubbed his face, reminding himself to shave before he went anywhere. He wasn't sure he was in a place to help anyone. He had a feeling Dr. Evers would agree.

Strode waited for the woman to continue. After a few moments of shared silence, she went on.

"The body we found here, the kid, he's our second victim in two weeks. The cuts, the indications of torture, just the extent of mutilation, reminded me of—"

Strode winced. She didn't even have to say the names. That's how fragile he was. Strode tried to say it, and found his voice cut off. He cleared his throat and tried again. "The Warrens and Blackwoods."

She answered in a near whisper, "Yes. I've heard about your—"

"Delusions," Strode supplied.

"Questions. I was going to say questions. Like you, I can't let these go. Yours had missing teeth, and ours have missing fingernails. I wanted your help because I think you're right. There's more here, and we need to figure out what it is."

Validation. That's what she was offering Strode, even before the investigation. Validation in her own belief in him. It felt so foreign to him Strode didn't know how to accept it.

The woman went on, "I mean, to make someone suffer like that, to create so many incisions, to remove each fingernail, I would say it's barbaric, animalistic, but none of them feels like the right word. It feels—"

Strode interrupted her, "Personal."

"*Exactly*. Personal. Is that how you felt with your cases?"

"Yes. In the Blackwood case, we believe the mother was beaten to death by the father. There was so much bleeding and swelling of her brain. But the man, his injuries were monstrous. It was a different kind of suffering. It was like the goal wasn't to immediately kill but to make him bleed, really bleed. Still, it was less patience than we saw with the Warrens, and less so than what you're describing now. It was like the killer decided Arthur Blackwood just wasn't worth it. It had to be done to get him out of the way."

"Like he was somehow competing with the true killer?" the woman asked.

"Exactly, yes. That's what I thought."

Strode felt a dryness in his mouth, and it hit him that this was the most he had spoken with anyone in a long time. Even his hour-long sessions with Dr. Evers were quieter.

Strode nervously scratched the bottom of the phone's receiver; Maggie hated it when he did that. The red paint lifted from the phone easily and nestled under his nails.

"I didn't know about the domestic situation. You believe the mother was beaten by the father? Wasn't there a witness? I read about it. The boy? Theodore, I think it was."

"Teddy. He liked to be called Teddy," Strode corrected.

Strode heard the woman's chair squeak as her eagerness prompted readjustment. "So, there must be something there. Did he see the man who killed his father? Did he see how he was killed?"

The scene tore into Strode's mind, and the gore of the Starling house where Teddy and Lila Blackwood had moved to replaced that morning's torment of Jackie Warren.

Her patience had faded. "Strode? Strode, are you there?"

Strode sighed. "We don't know exactly what happened because we never found Teddy."

Strode expected shock, maybe even hysteria, not because she was a woman, but because the details were wicked and disturbing. They had haunted Strode ever since.

But the woman stayed calm. "I see. Well, I want you to come take a look at the body we found today. I want to see if it looks anything like what you've seen. I think you might not be so crazy after all."

Strode laughed. "Gee, thanks."

"How far of a drive will it be for you to Michigan from Starling?"

"Starling was the name of the house."

"I'm sorry?"

"Starling was the name of the house where both families were killed."

"Oh. Of course, Starling was the mother's maiden name."

Strode, again forgetting to be more aware and present, nodded as if the woman could see him.

But she didn't press him.

"Well then, can you come right away?"

Strode hesitated. "If it's not too much trouble, could someone from your office report it to mine? Just so the sheriff doesn't think I've lost my marbles again."

"Of course. I'll take care of it." The energy, the pleasantness, had returned in her voice. "It's going to make one hell of a story, the cop off his hinges solves the murder of the Starling house and Warren Woods."

Strode froze. "Where did you say you found the body? Where in Michigan?"

"Oh. I said Warren. Warren Woods."

It was funny. Wasn't it? How calmly she could let *Warren* pass between her lips. The name was a pest laying eggs in the corners of Strode's brain, biting, tearing at his peace of mind, and calling the havoc home—an invasive intruder that no number of pills or sessions with Dr. Evers could exterminate.

"Yeah, Warren Woods is a big one, but someone called in about the smell of the body," she went on.

Strode didn't even realize he was holding the kitchen telephone between his pointer finger and thumb. The other three fingers, not a thought but a reflex, hung in the air, counting how many times the woman said "Warren."

She filled the gap of silence. "Well, great. Can you be here in the next few hours? I'm going to make them hold the body for you as long as I can. I don't want to move it, just in case."

"I'll hop on the interstate in thirty minutes. Should be there in two hours."

"Perfect. What kind of car will you be driving? I'll have someone meet you at the entrance of the hiking trails."

"A red Ford Pinto."

"Got it. Well, Officer Strode, we'll see you in a bit. And don't forget, Warren Woods."

Strode slid the phone back on its base on the kitchen wall and said to the empty room, "How could I?"

Strode pulled the plug on the coffee machine. He went down the dim hall and folded some old t-shirts into a bag. He realized then that he needed new clothes. He stepped into faded and slightly distressed Levi jeans and kicked his bedroom door shut behind him.

He was packed and in his Pinto in under five minutes. He did another quick shoulder roll and took a deep breath. If he was going to help the police in Michigan, and maybe, just maybe, clear his name, he needed to focus.

Strode put a cigarette between his lips, thanking the little devils for keeping him thin, and realized he forgot all about his appointment that afternoon with Dr. Evers.

He smiled, shifted the car into gear, and said, "Sorry, Dr. Evers. Duty calls."

4

As Strode exited I-65 and steered the red Ford Pinto to I-94, he thought of Dr. Evers sitting in her ridiculous, cliché shrink leather chair. She would tap her foot and check her watch. When she started to lose patience, Dr. Evers would poke her head into the waiting room, as if her trusty receptionist had neglected a patient sitting in the corner.

Strode supposed he should feel guilty, but he couldn't stop that mischievous grin from spreading on his face. He threw his head back and laughed. *Maybe I am out of mind.* He laughed louder.

A convertible with a man and a woman and two kids in the backseat zipped past him. The pair up front, who Strode assumed were the parents, gave him a concerned look. Like a scolded school kid, Strode hushed and straightened himself up in his leather seat.

He mumbled to himself, "Yeah, you're definitely losing it."

Strode wondered if part of his laughter came from the fact that he was walking right into the very thing he had spent the last year and a half trying to escape. Something was terrifying about the idea that going into this would cause irreversible damage, and the only way to prevent himself from sinking into the blackness of true insanity was to laugh it off. Maybe that was true insanity in itself.

Hell, at least I'll go out smiling.

With his nicotine-stained fingers, Strode turned the radio up and hummed along to a soothing Peter, Paul, and Mary song about a dragon. Without a doubt, the radio host would come on after to discuss whether the song was really about drugs and not a magic place called Honahlee.

Before Strode could hear the big debate, a peeling wooden sign pointed him to Warren Woods. He pressed on the brakes, and the Pinto hummed as it drove down the gravel path. When he saw a squad car through the break in the trees, he turned right where a petite police officer was waiting with her arms crossed. That specific stance was quite familiar to Strode. He remembered her standing like that at the academy, scowling at the dipshit men chasing each other around the dirt track or arguing who climbed the rope the fastest. The woman didn't smile or wave. She just waited for Strode to pull in.

Strode got out of the car and offered her his hand. "Hello—" Strode still couldn't remember her name. "Long time no see."

The woman looked at Strode's hand with only the slightest hint of a smile and said, "Good to see you again, Strode."

Again, without offering her name or much direction, the woman turned and headed for the woods. Strode followed.

The woman's dark hair was collected tightly at the nape of her neck. Not a single piece was out of place, even in the humidity. Strode thought of Maggie, who would throw her dark hair on top of her head and then tug at the pieces. "If it's too tight, I'll get a huge headache," she would say. Maggie's ponytail always hung high and sort of lopsided. Just the thought made Strode smile.

"Strode, did you hear me?" the officer asked.

He'd done it again. *Be present. Exist as more than a two-dimensional figure in the background.*

"Sorry. Lost in thought. What did you say, ma'am?"

The woman shoved a circular container at him. "If you can't smell it yet, trust me, it only gets worse."

Strode dipped two fingers in the container and rubbed the mixture under his nose. The smell of peppermint tingled up his lip and into his nostrils. "I'm familiar with the smell. It haunts me to this day."

With a heavy look of empathy and analysis, the woman nodded to Strode. "Of course."

Strode was surprised how far into the woods they were before he saw the caution tape, another squad car, and the van marked Haddonfield Coroner.

"Haddonfield? I thought we were in Three Oaks?"

A deep voice came from behind the police car. "You are, Officer Strode. Haddonfield is a family name. They've run that business for three generations now." The man extended his chubby hand and Strode accepted it. "Officer Jack Burklow."

The man raised his flabby arm, revealing a great deal of underarm sweat in his corpse-grey-colored uniform, and pointed to a cart in front of the van. "Finch, grab us all some gloves. Would you?"

Finch looked at Strode as if to say, *Now you know,* and came back with three pairs of bright purple gloves.

Below them was a sheet-covered body. The cloth's once pure whiteness was stained with traces of something wicked and vile, the aftermath of something hungry for blood—a feeding. Finch started to crouch down and pull the sheet back, but she rose to her feet and turned to Strode, "Actually, why don't you take a look? We all know what I think. I'd like to hear what you think."

Strode nodded. He immediately thought of the Warren family, of Jackie, and then of Teddy Blackwood. He hoped to God they weren't somewhere torn apart like this man. He hoped if they were dead, they went quickly. It was wishful thinking, and he knew it.

Strode settled his boots into the dirt, took a deep breath, and held it. The nerves were trying to battle it out with the smell, fighting for the satisfaction of making Strode hurl in front of his new acquaintances. He hoped his nerves would settle so he could be the bright-minded outsider rather than a confirmed whack-job.

Strode pulled the sheet back. It was like slowly peeling the bandage off a wound. There's a reason it's recommended to do it quickly. But if the body were torn up as badly as Strode expected, pulling too hard would make loose skin come up with it. It turned out that was inevitable. The skin made a rubber band flicking sound as it tore from its base and stuck to the sheet. Burklow turned his head to gag.

Finch paled but held her composure.

Just like Arthur Blackwood's, the body had dangling pieces of skin that decay would soon claim. What was left of this man was stained with a deep purplish-red color of dried blood. There was a faded pinkish color in some spots too, almost like a piece of salmon gone bad.

Torn down to the muscle, just like Arthur Blackwood.

Finch elevated on her tiptoes and rocked back on her heels. "Any thoughts?"

Burklow still had his head turned.

"Let me check one more thing."

Strode turned his head to take a small gasp and regretted it almost immediately. The contents of his stomach readjusted, and their movements crept up Strode's throat.

No. No. No.

He fought it down.

Strode lifted the sheet from the victim's feet, noticing the bloodied shoe nearby. The hole and blood spray on the top suggested a quick stab through the shoe. He lifted the sheet again and noted the deep stab wound on the right foot. There were even cuts on the heel, deep cuts, that showed the whiteness of tendons.

The toes were bent in inhuman contortions and were twice their usual size, like packs of sausage links that had laid funny in the fridge while they were defrosting.

Strode looked at Finch. "Miss Finch, did they notice the broken toes?"

Finch's eyes shot at him. "Officer. Officer Finch."

"Excuse me. Officer Finch, did the coroner notice the broken toes?"

She shook her head. "No, I did. Did any of the Warrens or Blackwoods have breaks like that? It just looks so obsessive. Like a 'getting every last one' mentality."

Finch was right. The precision, the details, it was obsessive behavior. Tactful. There's a method to the madness, as Maggie used to say.

The toes reminded Strode of the thing his mother used to do when she tucked him in at night. She flipped the blanket up, just exposing his toes, and one at a time she'd pinch them between her fingers saying, "This little piggy went to the market. This little piggy stayed home," until she was squealing and tickling his feet. But whoever did this didn't tickle each little piggy.

"Strode? Are you with us, man?" Burklow asked. "What are your thoughts?"

Even before the paranoia, Strode easily lost himself in thought when on a case. It made him a good cop, the way he could tune out everything else. Now, it just piled onto his oddities, and people credited it to his insanity.

"Sorry. I was just thinking how methodically this was done, as Finch said. Like someone had to get every toe. Can you imagine the agony of that? It's like the nursery rhyme about the piggy that squealed all the way home."

Burklow had this *Are you out of your fucking mind?* stare, but Finch lowered herself beside Strode. "Is this anything like you saw in Indiana?"

Strode nodded.

"In part. The others, they had small indications of physical pain, but it wasn't straight torture. The Warren girl, the one we found, the older of the two daughters, was missing teeth. So was the mother. But the wounds seemed older. There were a few like this beyond the Starling house, a few miles out in each direction. But we credited those to Mr. Warren, and he killed himself. We were sure of it, but now—"

Finch nodded, signaling for Strode to go on.

"There was another body found in the woods outside the Blackwood's home. It was a man. His toes were broken, his fingernails removed, and deep incisions from his face to his inner thighs, and—"

Strode moved to the side of the man's body. His "Tri-County" t-shirt was torn to hell, with bloodied, fringed pieces of cotton smashed into the dried wounds. But at the center were two deep gashes. The man was either stabbed with a long object or, worse, impaled.

Strode surveyed the area. Nothing immediately pointed to the double-impaled wounds.

"What is it?" Finch asked.

Strode shrugged. "How long did you say—" He pointed to the ground.

"Williamson. Well, Nate Williamson," Finch said.

Strode nodded, and he hoped his eyes showed his condolences for her. The kid's death pained her. Twenty-three is a kid. He agreed with Finch, and he was all too familiar with the helpless feeling of not being able to save them.

Still, he went on, "How long since Williamson's time of death?"

Burklow stepped in, flipping through some papers, but Finch knew on the spot. "Roughly forty-eight hours ago."

Strode scratched his beard. "There are definite similarities to the bodies we found back in Indiana. Murders we thought ended with Mr. Warren. But, when I saw the brutality of the slaughter of Arthur Blackwood, I wondered if we missed something."

Finch nodded, hanging on his every word. "And now, Officer Strode, what do you believe?"

Strode hesitated. Part of him felt conflicted. Was this good police work or an illusion that carried him right back to Dr. Evers's couch for an "intervention session"?

He had caught Burklow's attention too. The way the two of them looked at him, Burklow with curiosity, maybe a personal bet on how nuts Strode really was, but Finch was different. Strode wondered if Finch already knew what he was thinking.

And that was enough. So, Strode went on, "I think whoever did this in Indiana... I think it's connected to the Warrens like we thought, but I think it somehow connects to the Blackwoods too. And now, I think that person is moving."

Finch nodded. "But, Strode, if I may. The families, their deaths weren't prolonged as I understand it, other than the one Warren girl. They were all killed in a matter of minutes. There may have been instances of aggression between the wife and the husband, but that night, he slit her throat before his own. Correct?"

Strode winced. The night of the Starling house nightmare, or the Warren Massacre as the papers called it, Strode found the family. He had been camped out at Abraham's Abattoir because teens had been sneaking onto the property after dark.

But Strode didn't hear teens laughing or disturbed pigs that night. Instead, he heard screams. Agonizing, horrific screams. When he responded, he found one of the Warren girls dead in the living room, her head smashed to oblivion and smeared on the rug. The mother was in the hall. Her eyes were wide and expressionless as a pool of blood drained from her throat. When Strode went up the stairs to check for the others, he saw Mr. Warren in the office. He was arguing with himself. When he saw Strode, he said, "You! Get out of here before it takes you too!"

Strode drew his gun on him, seeing his words as a threat, but then Mr. Warren grabbed an already bloodied letter opener, turned his eyes to the sky, and dragged the blade across his throat.

Strode learned later that the youngest, Jackie Warren, was nowhere to be found. And while Strode searched for her for the next year, he saw her in his dreams and his home. Each time Jackie was branded by new injuries as a fresh reminder of her likely death—and worst of all, Strode's inability to save her.

And after the disappearance of Teddy Blackwood, Strode only saw Jackie more and more.

Finch put a hand on Strode's shoulder, causing his body to jolt. She raised her hands in defense. "Hey, easy. Are you alright?"

Strode nodded. "Sorry. Yes."

Strode tried to refocus. He cleared his throat.

"You're right, Finch. The Warrens' deaths weren't prolonged. With the Warrens and the Blackwoods, I believe the person was simply out for death, or pushed into it with a sense of urgency. But it's different now. Now it's like the killer needs more. He needs lasting fear; he needs pain. He needs to play with his food before he's ready to take a bite."

Finch was following. "Now, they're torturing them. Savoring their kills."

Burklow turned to Finch. "They? You mean a group of people did this to the kid?"

"No, I'm saying it could have been a man or a woman."

Burklow shook his head. "I don't think a woman could do something like this, the physical brutality of it. The grisly wounds."

Finch rolled her eyes and gave out a big puff of annoyance. "Evil is nonbinary, Burklow. It nestles and builds in whatever host it deems fit. Young or old, beautiful or ugly, and yes, man or woman."

Strode rose to his feet and removed his gloves. "I'd have to agree, especially since we can assume the victim was weakened with injuries that held him. Trapped like a fly in a spider web, the fly knows it's the main course, but it's stuck. Still, no matter the spider's strength, or lack of, that makes the fly an easy and filling kill."

Finch looked back and forth at the two men. Burklow looked like he was going to be sick. Strode was too deep in thought to let nausea steal the stage.

"So, we all agree then? We have something here. Something the two," Strode stopped and motioned to Burklow too, "the three of us, should pursue?"

Finch stood straight and, as those being asked by a commanding officer at war if she was proud to serve her country, said, "Absolutely."

Burklow shrugged his shoulders just as the chief had back home when Strode suggested a connection between the Blackwood massacre and the Starling house nightmare. Strode thought of little Jackie Warren and Teddy Blackwood again. They deserved more.

The thought enraged him. If he was getting back into this, he was going all in. Strode stomped to Burklow and shoved his face right at the chubby officer. "If we're going to find this sick son of a bitch, if you're going to help us, you have to get off your ass. I'm sick of small-town officers like you, who don't want to put in the work that comes with asking questions, so you write it off as some commonality and let criminals go. Free to roam with immense blood on their hands as they drive off, giving us the finger."

Burklow put his hands up. "You're right. I'm sorry. I'm sorry."

"I don't want to hear you're sorry. I want to hear that you're going to help. That you're going to carry some weight."

"I'll help… in any way I can."

Strode stepped back and took a deep breath. "Good." He tried to let the anger fade so he could think. He had to put all of his energy into this. He had to, for little Jackie Warren and Teddy Blackwood.

"Okay. How long was this guy missing?"

Finch stepped in. "Three days. Maybe more. But the coroner thinks he's been dead for two."

Strode nodded. He was putting it together. He thought the killing still began quickly, but it was drawn out over twenty-four hours, give or take.

But before Strode could fill the others in, Burklow surprised him. "At least one complete day of torture." He looked to the shape of the man under the sheet. "That poor bastard."

5

———

Finch and Strode sat in a crappy diner drinking coffee that tasted as stale as the place smelled. Strode rolled his neck. The hotel he'd stayed in, one of only three in Three Oaks, didn't grant him a good night's sleep. It had offered the hardest, maybe dirtiest mattress he had ever slept on. Then again, he didn't think he'd have slept any better in his own bed. Too much was on his mind. Too many questions that he couldn't answer.

Burklow stood on what was left of the splitting sidewalk out front. He held a thick cigar between two fingers and was taking deep inhales, smiling after each one like a man celebrating his daughter's wedding day.

Strode supposed some men woke up with a cup of coffee, others with a big fat cigar. He studied the oversized officer out front and wondered how much help he was really going to be in all this. Part of him wished Finch was older, and that he was, well, not thought of as a mental case. Then they could just handle it on their own.

Finch caught Strode watching Burklow and said, "He used to be good, you know. Burklow moved around from city to city, really whenever they needed him."

Be present, more than a two-dimensional figure in the background.

Strode turned to Finch to show he was listening, but then she seemed to be the one floating away. She stared at Burklow. He was fat, thick-skulled, in Strode's opinion, and he already saw him as more of an obstacle than any help.

Finch spoke without thought, as though the words themselves fell out of her mouth. "Burklow was a detective back in the day."

Strode gave Burklow another look. He guessed he did look older than Strode initially thought. Certainly older than him and Finch. Burklow had strong lines across his forehead and a small bald spot on the top of his head that Strode hadn't noticed before.

"A damn good detective too."

Finch's eyes pulled from the window but fell to the sticky table between her and Strode. "Now I'm stuck with him. It's like having a child for a partner. I call him when he's over-slept after a long night with Mr. Daniels."

Strode gave her a blank look.

Finch raised her hand and closed her fingers like they were hugging a glass. "You know, *Mr. Daniels*."

Strode did know. Conversations like this, this one-on-one thing, weren't his strong suit anymore. But still, he tried. "Well, then, if he was so great once, what happened?"

"His daughter. His *only* daughter. She got hurt. And Jack—Burklow, I mean—blames himself. I think he drinks himself to sleep every night because he can't bear to be alone with his thoughts. Alone in a house that used to be full of love and laughter that now sits quietly."

They both looked to Burklow outside to make sure he

wasn't coming in. The cigar between his fingers was only halfway gone. They still had a little time.

Finch went on. "They got into it one night. You see, Burklow's wife died. She got pneumonia a couple of winters ago and just never bounced back. I was still in training then." Finch stopped and smiled at Strode. "Well, as you know." She shook her head. "Anyway, last summer, only about a year and a half since Sarah's death, Burklow began to see another woman. A married woman. And a mother of one of his daughter's closest friends."

Strode adjusted in his seat. The only thing more uncomfortable than a one-on-one conversation was one about others' indiscretions.

Still, Strode tried to remain present. "Did his daughter confront him about it?"

Finch nodded. "But I don't think he was willing to stop seeing the woman. So, his daughter stormed out."

Strode's interest was piqued. He leaned in. "Did Burklow go after her?"

Finch's eyes shifted. This wasn't a juicy drama. It was a tragedy. "No. No, he didn't."

Finch took a deep breath, with her heavy, pained eyes on Strode, and went on. "It was storming bad that night. There's a backroad not far from here, and when it rains really hard, the water sort of collects. Drivers forget and speed along. Distracted and angry drivers are even more careless. The water built up so quickly. She turned—"

Finch put her hand under her nose, and her eyes were glossy. "And she lost control."

"Hydroplaned?"

Finch bit into her lip, fighting the tears. This woman had

heart. Strode knew many men would call that an unnecessary emotion, but he would call it a "heightened empathy" that allowed Finch to catch details others would only skim, or miss entirely. It made her an intelligent and thorough investigator.

She waited for a moment until she could speak without letting a tear fall. "Yes. Hydroplaned. Right into the lake. The station's team thinks she couldn't get her seatbelt undone when the car hit the water. By the time they got there, everyone, even Burklow, knew the team was going in not to bring Jack's daughter home, but to give him a body to bury."

Strode figured he was supposed to say something, but Finch went on.

"Jack," Finch's eyes widened, "*Burklow* just hasn't been the same since."

Strode tasted blood. He had been gnawing away at his lip without even noticing how hard he was doing it.

Strode lowered his head. He wondered if he could open up to Finch. If he *should.*

"I can't say I blame him. I always wanted a kid. My wife and I, my ex-wife, we tried for years. Then, that night, when I responded to the screams at the Warrens, I saw Laurie Warren. The first thing I thought was if I was that girl's father, how destroyed I would be."

Strode sighed. "Then, when I saw in the photos that there were two little girls, I searched everywhere for the younger one."

"Jackie," Finch whispered.

"Yes, Jackie." Strode let her name hang in the air before taking a deep breath and moving on. "But I couldn't find her anywhere, and it turned out I didn't need either of the girls to be my own for it to ruin me."

And then Teddy on top of it all. He didn't want to say it. People already thought he was out of his mind. Strode thought it best not to help guide them there when people began empathizing with him.

Finch gave Strode an even better version of the consoling look he had tried to offer her in the woods. He gave her a weak smile.

"I don't think you're ruined, Strode. Changed, maybe a little scarred, of course, but not damaged. Everyone else, they see the horror of this job sometimes and think it's simply that, part of the job. They all shake it off because that's what gets them home in time for dinner and a game show."

Strode said, "But for us, there can't be anything else after something like that."

Finch shook her head, disagreeing. "No. We know there's something else. We know there are more pieces to put together, and we can't walk away from a puzzle left unsolved."

She said the exact epiphany that unboxed itself in Strode's mind, "And that is what makes us good cops, and I'm willing to bet, one heck of a team."

Strode nearly felt himself blush as he realized the growing expansion of his smile. It was more reassurance than he had gotten from anyone in a long time.

Strode and Finch didn't notice Burklow come into the beat-up diner. His sweat was visibly noticeable in the woods the day before, but in that compact space of the leather booth, Strode couldn't tell which smelled worse, the stale food or Burklow. How was that possible first thing in the morning?

Burklow stuffed a packet of spare crackers on the table into his mouth. Strode wondered how long that packet had been there. It was sitting there when he and Finch sat down.

The thought made him realize he was the guy who "recycled" coffee filters and grounds.

"Is that right, Strode?" Burklow asked.

Shit. I did it again. Be present. Cover this one and pay attention.

"Uh-huh. Yeah." Strode nodded and tried to hide the confusion on his face.

Finch and Burklow looked at one another and back to Strode, as if Burklow's rejoining had made him the outsider again.

"Is that what they said, exactly? And what about the boy? Did anyone look for him?"

Strode hurdled over the first question. "Of course, we looked for Teddy. After what I saw the first ti—"

Strode stopped himself, a thick welt building in his throat that made the diner's stale air feel thinner. "I just didn't want to see the kid get hurt. We looked everywhere."

Again, Strode removed himself from his present company and dove into his inner thoughts—the personal ones.

"Hell, my wife and I would've taken the little guy ourselves. He had some Yankees cards in his room. But I could've made a real Cubs fan out of him. I know it. And Maggie, she would've loved that little boy so much. No woman ever would've felt good enough."

Strode laughed and beat his fist into the table, startling the other two—a failed attempt at smoothly breaking the tension. Strode took a moment to compose himself. Looking at his lap, he said, "I need a look at those other reports."

Finch nodded. "Burklow, we can follow you to the station and work in your office."

"No," Burklow said. Strode was surprised to see the man arch his eyebrows and narrow his eyes.

By god, the man has a thinking face.

"Not my office. If we're going to be on our own with this investigation, as I think we'd be better off doing, we can't draw attention to ourselves. Let's keep this between the three of us as much as we can. Whoever is doing this is still in town. Hell, they could be from here."

Finch nodded like a diligent protégé of Burklow's.

Burklow slapped his hands on the table. "Alright, you two. Let's get to work. And let's—" Burklow put his hand to the side of his mouth, as if that was a useful sound barrier. "—get a decent cup of coffee at my place. I'll stop and get the files and meet you two there."

The waitress, who seemed to have forgotten her table until Burklow's loud dig, scoffed and pushed her way into the kitchen. Burklow threw a five from his worn leather wallet on the sticky table and said, "Okay, let's move."

Finch rose from the booth and ran her hands over her thick, black hair to smooth any pieces astray. There weren't any.

Strode followed Finch outside, and he couldn't help but feel hopeful. Hopefully, Finch and Burklow were the real deal, and they'd see this through with him. And hopefully, along the way, he could unveil some truth behind the disappearances of Jackie Warren and Teddy Blackwood.

6

There was a worm inside Strode's brain. One that wiggled around and occasionally gnawed at his memory center. *Think, think,* it demanded. But think about what? What was he missing?

Strode hated that feeling. Every cop, or every *good* cop, did.

Strode and Finch walked to the red Ford Pinto, and Finch climbed in. Strode raised his elbows to the top of the vehicle and brought his hands to his face. He was beginning to think that damned worm had the answer. But every time his train of thought got closer to it, it hopped off the tracks and sought shelter in the darkness of the unknown.

"What are you trying to figure out exactly? What *exactly* do you need to know?"

Maggie was always so good at getting his thoughts rolling. She organized them. It was as if she could flip open the top of Strode's head and bring what mattered most front and center. Every time he talked to her about a case, he eventually reached that a-ha moment.

But the Starling Nightmare, the missing Blackwood boy—those had to be different. Strode hadn't known how to begin thinking about those, so Maggie had been unable to help. When she tried, another cinderblock stacked in the ever-growing wall Strode was building in his mind. It pushed her farther away.

He then realized how Maggie felt. Every time he tried to see what he couldn't, his brain threw him back, flat on his ass. And when his mind felt like really burning Strode bad, it carved open a new gory corpse manifestation of the little girl he saw in the family photos but never found. When Jackie Warren came around, Strode would do anything he could to get out of his head. And it only got worse with Teddy.

Strode felt paralyzed by the thought of Jackie and Teddy. He stretched his arms out and put his palms on top of the driver-side door. When he leaned his hips back to take a deep breath, he saw Finch sitting inside the car. Lately, Strode had spent so much time alone, he was having trouble remembering how to behave in someone else's company.

He realized how insane he probably looked to Finch. Strode took a deep breath, opened the door, and lowered himself into his seat.

His mind raced as he tried to think of what to say when Finch asked for the hundredth time that day if he was okay. But Finch didn't ask. Strode wondered, after their talk, if she knew what he was thinking. Or if she didn't, maybe she understood why his mind carried him away here and there.

When Strode started the car, Finch pointed ahead. "You're going to take this road for about fifteen minutes, and then you'll turn left into the first neighborhood."

Strode nodded, turned the radio dial, and was pleased when the car filled with one of his favorite Beatles tunes. He nodded along, focusing on the words and the smoothness of the sitar, and tried to let it carry some of his tension and anxiousness away.

Then Strode remembered that he needed to continue to try to be present, especially with the first person who had truly taken him seriously in months.

He turned the volume down and turned to Finch, "Do you like The Beatles?"

Finch pulled her gaze from the small shops passing by. "I'm sorry, what did you say?"

Strode smiled. He had a feeling that someone as smart as Finch also struggled with being both physically and emotionally present. He wished that was his problem, just too intelligent to do both at once rather than too broken.

Strode started to ask again but saw Finch had already slipped away. He turned the volume up and let Lennon's voice fill the Pinto. He followed the road for about fifteen minutes and felt overwhelmed by the number of trees in town. Rather, the way they were all clustered together, masking whatever lay amongst them.

"The turn."

Strode stared into the trees, hoping whatever he felt he was missing would jump out at him. Or at least give him a sign.

"The turn."

Whatever they were tracking could hide so easily amongst all the trees. Strode thought their killer had used the leaves and twists of the branches as cover to move through the town.

"Strode. Strode. The turn."

Strode cranked the wheel to the left. Finch let out a little sigh when the curb elevated her side of the vehicle and then slammed back to the pavement.

Strode cringed. "Sorry about that."

Finch smiled. "It's okay."

Finch didn't need to give Strode any further directions. Burklow had beat them, and his car was in the drive.

They got out of the car, and Strode smiled as he heard Finch humming "Norwegian Wood."

Burklow's house wasn't what Strode expected—at least not on the outside. The egg-shell colored paint was crisp, as were the navy double front doors. It reminded him of the home in the sitcom *The Brady Bunch*.

Finch nodded to the house and said, "Don't give him too much credit," she said. "Sarah did it all. She liked things a certain way. Even a single chip in the paint would've had her out here in one-hundred-degree weather, repainting the whole thing."

Finch stood back with Strode, looking at the house and seemingly speaking beyond it. "I always liked her. I met her when I was training here. She told me every time I saw her that if the rest of the country could keep up and put women in roles like a police officer, we'd all be better off." Finch smiled. "The world needs a woman's touch, Sarah would say. I think that's why Burklow wanted me with him, to commemorate Sarah."

"Sarah sounds an awful lot like Maggie. Warm and kind, but capable and strong-willed. I can see why Burklow took to her, just as I did Maggie. No matter how long you're around women like that, you'll always underestimate them. As, I know, people do you."

Finch seemed taken back by the compliment. Her eyes widened and she cocked her head before saying, "Thank you."

Part of Strode wished there were more officers like Finch back in Indiana. He couldn't find the perfect words, but he thought she was incredibly decent.

Burklow came barreling out of the double doors with another cigar hanging from his mouth and a glass of a warm honey-colored drink. Strode wondered how anyone could toss whiskey like that so early in the day. But he stood there, drink in hand, with a big-ass grin on his face. It was like a fat, redneck Jay Gatsby.

Finch laughed. "Good God. You'd think he was hosting a barbecue instead of investigating a murder."

Strode was just glad to see he had changed. Hopefully he had taken a quick shower too. Strode wondered how long his thoughts carried him away at the diner. It had to have been longer than he thought.

Again, he was thankful for Finch's understanding and patience.

With the cigar wagging between his lips, Burklow yelled, "Come on, fellow man and woman of blue!"

Strode and Finch went up the drive and to the blue doors. It felt like another dimension, one that countered the one on the outside of the house. The inside of the house was a somber reminder of Sarah's death. The weight of it seemed to hit Strode as soon as he stepped inside. From what Finch told him, signs of Sarah's absence were everywhere: peeling wallpaper, a potent odor of cigars and alcohol, piles of news-papers, and what looked like baseball scorecards on the table and counter.

Strode realized he was staring. Burklow caught his wandering eyes, and Strode straightened himself up, trying to think fast.

"I noticed your scorecards. Who's your team?"

Burklow raised his glass, again reminding Strode of a loose imitation of the high-class party host from the 1920s. "Yankees all the way, baby."

The Blackwood boy liked the Yankees.

Burklow went on, "My dad was a huge Joe DiMaggio fan. He was born in New York."

Strode wondered how Teddy, born in Oakhaven, New Hampshire, became a Yankees fan. He supposed it could simply be geographical.

As Burklow told a story about one of the best games he went to growing up, Strode continued to eye everything in the home. The place was without what Finch had said was Sarah's touch. Maggie would've called the mismatched floral and brown leather furniture in the living room sickening.

"Drink, anyone? Coffee?"

Bypassing the coffee pot, Burklow went right to his nearly empty alcohol shelf. Below it was a trash bin filled with Jack Daniels and Jim Beam bottles.

Finch shook her head. "Just the files."

Burklow grinned and pointed to Finch. "All work with this one."

He carried the Jim Beam bottle to the kitchen counter and grabbed a stack of four thick files. He tossed them on the dining room table. "Here's everything we have."

Strode grabbed the top one labeled "Byers." The first of the documents was the basic template with the detail of the event, actions taken, and a summary. It looked like a half-assed job. Both the details and descriptions were vague.

Strode flipped the first page aside. Underneath was a grotesque photo of the victim. Her hair stuck to the stickiness of the open wounds in her chest. The ends were stained with a darkness that stretched to the gash on her head.

Strode turned to the other officers. "Was she hit with something?"

Burklow shrugged his shoulders. "It could've been anything. She could've fallen. Hopefully, she knocked herself unconscious before the guy got to her."

Strode tried not to be infuriated that no one looked for the weapon that could've created a wound like that to the poor girl's head. Strode was thankful that Finch shared Burklow's background with him. And now, he could see why she did. A comment like that would've otherwise had him in Burklow's face. She was sparing Burklow another outburst.

Finch came from behind Strode and reached for the file. Finch grabbed the photo and held it up to the light. Then she set it on the table, giving it an angled turn. "Burklow, where is the evidence report? I need to see what you found."

Strode raised his eyebrows. They kept Finch out of the loop on this. She was learning some things alongside him.

"Wait," Strode said, "*you* found this girl, Burklow?"

Burklow, with that same shoulder shrug and clueless look on his face, said, "Well, I was the responding officer."

"And you didn't bring Finch along?" Strode felt the edge in his voice. It emphasized "didn't," stressing the first of several errors Strode was sure he would uncover in this conversation.

Strode's heart pounded as he clenched his sweaty hands. He tried to let it go, to keep all the contents inside, but like a careless child, he spilled the glass, and his rage poured out.

"*You* let them write this off." Strode turned the photo so it was facing Burklow.

Strode's finger stabbed the picture of the battered corpse and then pointed at Burklow. "You didn't want to help this girl? You didn't think she deserved your attention?"

Burklow's shit-eating grin withered away so all that was left was hurt. "There was nothing left. She was gone. I called it as I saw it." Burklow, not sarcastically but in a defeated manner, raised his hands and turned the picture back to Strode as he said, "Hopeless."

Finch ignored them both. Strode realized she was studying the photo as the men turned it back and forth toward one another. She had something.

Strode turned from Burklow, trying to focus instead on what could move the case forward. "Finch, what is it?"

She pointed at the bottom of the picture. "Do you see her shoes?"

The Byers girl was wearing platform shoes. The black and white photo indicated that the shoes' soles were a darker color than the white on top. This time, Finch was the outsider. Strode and Burklow looked at one another, both without a clue.

Burklow took another swig of his drink.

"And her pants. Don't you guys see?" Finch held the photo in front of the men.

Burklow turned away and murmured, "Your point, rookie. Find it before my stomach finds the floor tile."

Finch looked back and forth at them with a wide-eyed eagerness. She was waiting for it to click.

It didn't.

Finch pointed to the photo, standing beside it like an instructor to a blackboard. "These are fashion pants. Look, they have a high waist with the long zipper and flared bottoms."

Burklow laughed. "Solve this case, Finch, and you'll get a nice bonus. Then you can go get yourself a pair."

Finch held the picture in front of her chest and turned to Strode. It hit him. He saw it too. "She wasn't dressed to go hiking or running."

Finch nodded and smiled. "Yes. She was going out."

Then what the hell was Marlene Byers doing in Warren Woods?

Burklow took another swig of his drink, and Strode noticed the overweight officer swaying as he spoke. "We tried to get people to steer clear of the woods. But things like this just don't happen here, so I think the locals just thought it was this freak thing and tried to move on. People only avoided the path for a day or two."

Strode wanted to say, "*You* let them believe it was 'some freak thing.'"

Instead, his curiosity called him to another file. The tab read, "DEREK RUSSELL."

The photo of him looked an awful lot like how Nate Williamson did. Except, Russell, like the Byers girl, didn't seem dressed for the woods. He was wearing long pants with a cardigan sweater. Glasses lay above his head, cracked and coated with a mix of dirt and blood.

There was no sign of the shoes.

Strode turned to Burklow. "What kind of shoes was this man wearing?"

"Uh. I'm not sure what they're called. They looked like slippers to me, except they were leather.

Strode wasn't sure what the hell those were either, but he was willing to bet those weren't durable outdoor shoes. This man hadn't planned on going to the woods either.

"Mules," Finch said. "Those shoes are called mules."

"Why aren't the shoes pictured, Burklow?" Finch asked.

Strode flipped through the DEREK RUSSELL file. A date was highlighted, three days after they uncovered the body. That's when they found the shoes, more than a mile from Russell's body. Strode handed the sheet to Finch.

The next sheet indicated that some of the cardigan's fibers had stuck into Russell's skin. Wool. Strode thought wool might be fine in a well air-conditioned home, but certainly not outside in June.

Finch peered over Strode's shoulder. "I knew Russell. He was a writer. He had a fancy place in New York, but he came back here in the summer to write."

Strode put the picture down and bit his lip, a bad habit but a sure sign he was thinking. "Finch, where was Russell staying?"

"The old cabin just behind the main entrance of Warren Woods. It's quiet, so he always liked wri—"

Finch stopped. Her eyes zipped back and forth and then up to Strode's. "I have an idea. I think I've got something, but I need to go to the cabin first. I'm hoping something there can prove me right."

Burklow came to the table and examined the images himself. "Well, shit. We do have something. Let me get ahold of the cabin's keys somehow."

Strode nodded. If Burklow wasn't going to bring any brains to the case, at least he supplied resources.

Burklow shoved his cigar into what looked like a cereal bowl on the counter. "So, we go to the cabin. Then what's next?"

Strode followed up. "We have to walk the woods. See if we missed something."

Burklow shook his head. Strode and Finch could tell it was more thinking than Burklow had done in a long time.

Finch's eyes were wild with avenues of thought and the satisfaction of moving one step ahead in the case.

That rush had become a stranger to Strode. But it surged from the petite cop to him, and he welcomed it back like an old friend.

"Well, Strode, what do you think? Are you sticking around for this?" Burklow asked. Finch watched Strode with concentrated, hopeful eyes.

Strode twirled his keys around his scrawny fingers and said, "I'm in."

7

_____

Burklow made another trip to the police station to grab the cabin's keys. Strode and Finch took notes of things to search for at the cabin and reviewed the files to see if there was anything they should be looking for in the woods.

Strode rubbed his eyes. Despite the anticipation and adrenaline rush he felt moments ago, his eyes were heavy.

"Finch, I could really go for that cup of coffee now. Do you think Burklow would mind if I—"

Finch rose as Strode reached for the cabinet door above the coffee pot. She waved him away.

"I can do it," Finch said. "Go sit down. I can tell the day has worn on you. You look like you're about to keel over."

Strode laughed. "Between you and me, this is probably the most I've done out of the house in a while."

Finch raised an eyebrow. "But in the house, what do you do?"

She was good. Strode left the door wide open for her to catch on to his at-home investigations. He imagined the bulletin board in his office, the newspaper clippings, the red thread, the notes he took from radio reports throughout the country. He tracked everyone, the guy who was moving through the Seattle area and killing college girls, the guy who sent cryptic letters to the *Chronicle,* but more than anything, Strode tracked disappearances of children.

Above all the thread and all the crime scenes, at the right of his bulletin board were two pictures: one of Jackie Warren and the other of Teddy Blackwood.

Strode's head suddenly felt like it weighed a ton. The pressure filled his ears and throbbed in his eyes.

He stood. "I'd actually love to clean up a bit. Which way is the bathroom?"

Finch answered fast like it was a reflex. "Go straight down the hall. There's one in Burklow's bedroom."

She turned from the counter smiling. Strode tried to smile back, but the pressure was building in his head.

"On second thought, why don't you use the bathroom in the basement." Finch laughed. "Trust me, I'm sparing you from ungodly terror."

Finch covered her mouth as if she had let out more energy than she meant to. Her smile faded as she straightened her top and smoothed her already tamed hair. There weren't many policewomen, no matter where you went in the country, so Strode understood why Finch worked as hard as she did and always tried to maintain a level of professionalism.

The opposite side of the kitchen had a wide mouth and spiral tongue of stairs. Strode went down and around the steps. The motion collided with the pressure in his head and made him feel nauseated.

But the surprise of the basement, how clean and cool it was, pulled him from it. The basement was furnished with shag carpeting and a ping pong table. Various framed jerseys hung on the walls from all sorts of New York teams.

So, it wasn't just the Yankees.

A framed Knicks jersey displayed a neatly laid out net in the corner. Strode would have to remember to ask Burklow the story behind that. On the other side of the ping pong table were two couches and a television. There was a basket in the corner with spare pillows and blankets, all a purple-pink tie-dye pattern. Strode figured this must've been the perfect spot for sleepovers. Burklow's daughter probably had many growing up. Maybe the reminder of his daughter was why Burklow left this area untouched.

Strode followed the tan shag past the spiral steps and toward the back room. He could hear Finch opening and closing cabinets and rattling glassware.

There was a tall step into the back room. The room was painted a soft blue with a big chalkboard wall at the farthest end. The front had a mirror and a leather chair that stood on a round metal base. Outside of the bathroom was a picture of Audrey Hepburn with her hair done up, wearing an elegant black gown and holding a long and lavish cigarette between her gloved fingers.

Suddenly, the pressure in Strode's head returned. This time, it was accompanied by a potent smell that stabbed into his temples.

Strode turned, trying to find the source and the bathroom. He stumbled to the wall and used his upper body to hold himself up. Bottles were spread out on the countertop, and beside them lay a pair of scissors, a spray bottle, and a large sink with a handheld hose.

The pain lifted for a moment, allowing Strode to put it together. This was Sarah's. Sarah was a beautician.

The smell was getting stronger. Strode felt the inside of his nose become inflamed with irritation. Then his eyes followed. That's when he knew that smell was bleach.

"No, Jackie. Please, please. Not here."

At the back of the home-salon was a small closet door. Strode hoped that was the bathroom. He hoisted himself up from the counter, knocking several beauty supplies to the floor.

The bleach smell was nauseating, and he felt as though his feet were otherworldly. He commanded them to move but looked down to find they were still. His feet looked as though they were stories below him.

Strode closed his eyes, counted to three, and moved as quickly as he could to the chair at the center of the room. His hand tried to use it for balance, but the chair spun and sent him to the floor.

Invisible fingers drilled into the sides of his head. He closed his eyes and, like a soldier at war, crawled to the bathroom door. His limp legs hung behind him as his core and arms tried to carry the weight.

Strode found yet another step and threw himself over it. With his eyes still shut, he felt for the toilet bowl. When he was sure he found it, he threw his head to the opening, and bile splattered the hard-water-stained residue. His stomach dug for more and burned when it pulled up only saliva and a bit more bile.

Strode coughed into the toilet bowl. When he was sure he had nothing left in him, he brought his hands to the toilet's side and inched his way up to his feet. With his hands still in place and his ass waving in the air, he looked above the toilet into the eyes of a white-faced clown. The artist gave its teeth a sinister point and a grin far too wide to be human. Its eyebrows reminded him of images he had seen in religious art, warning of the temptations of the devil.

Creepy ass clown.

Strode tried to push off from the toilet, but nausea held him in his position. Then, he heard a chuckle.

"Had too much to drink. Have you?"

Strode closed his eyes and began to turn his head. His body immediately punished him for the movement, and he coughed up more chunks, this time missing the porcelain toilet.

"You're falling apart, bud. Coming completely unraveled."

Strode's eyes moved to see the broad grin of the clown opening and closing. Its eyes flashed a hellish red at him. Its face began to blur, and the colors of the bathroom swirled together. He was going to faint. Or maybe he already had. He couldn't decide.

"What if you're having a stroke? Sudden numbness. Dizziness. Confusion. Poor guy. That's what this seems to be. Imagine what they'll say, 'Strode had a stroke.'"

The clown's jaw fell beneath the photo as he roared with a booming laugh. The bathroom walls shook, and the hand soap holder crashed to the floor causing pieces of glass to spread around Strode's feet.

The clown's mouth stretched and showed rows of leech-like teeth—the teeth of a monster. The clown continued to shriek, and its high-pitched laughter teased the possibility of blowing a fuse. The lights in the basement wavered, and the bars of the striped wallpaper shook as if the clown was imprisoned behind them demanding its freedom. But it only laughed and laughed.

"Strode had a stroke! Strode had a stroke! Strode had a stroke!"

A choir of invisible children began chanting with the broken jawed clown.

"Strode had a stroke! Strode had a stroke!"

Strode tried to stand again, but it was no use. The pain beat into his head and only worsened with the cries of his tormentors.

Strode bowed his head and closed his eyes. *When I open my eyes, this will all go away.*

Strode waited a moment and opened his eyes. The clown was still there. It had climbed from the picture frame and was crouched on top of the toilet. Its jaw hung open, and when it spoke it brought its hand to the bottom of its mouth to help it open and close—the cost of its teasing.

The clown began to kick its feet one at a time as it danced on the fragile toilet and let it slam into the water-stained wall. The clown's tiny yellow-paper hat bounced on the top of its head as it chanted, "Strode had a stroke. Strode had a stroke. Strode had a stroke."

Strode shook his head, counted to three, and tried again. Then, the clown stood face to face with him.

It turned its head to the right until it nearly touched its shoulder. It laughed again and allowed its jaw to fall to the floor bloodied and torn.

The clown spat through its razor-sharp teeth. Strode could hardly understand it as it said, "Oh, but Officer Strode, if you have a stroke, who will bring that little girl home? Who will find that little boy?"

Strode shouted, "How do you know about that?"

The clown laughed back at him and did its maddening little dance again. Pieces of its face, beefy and wet, fell to the floor.

Strode rose to his feet and grabbed the clown's blood-soaked cotton candy-printed shirt. "How do you know about Jackie and Teddy?"

Even with half of its jaw in a gooey mess on the floor, Strode could tell the clown was smiling again.

Strode, his passion reinstating some of his strength, slammed the clown into the bathroom door. Pieces of its face flailed as it dangled and drooped toward the floor.

"Listen, you creepy fucker."

The clown giggled. "Tsk. Tsk. Oh, Strode. You naughty boy."

Strode smacked a hand upside the clown's face. His palm burned from the contact.

"How do you know? Tell me where they are!"

The clown brought its white-gloved hands to Strode's face. Strode's head bobbed as his vision tunneled. The clown hooked its two pointer fingers in Strode's mouth and said, "Oh, my sweet boy. You really ought to smile more."

The clown tugged its two fingers up.

And Strode hit the floor.

8

"Put it over his head," Finch ordered Burklow.

Strode opened his eyes only to find a brief moment of light swallowed by the dark. Something wet was on top of his head.

Finch's patience thinned. "Ugh. Not like that. Move. Move. Let me do it."

Strode's eyes fluttered as he fought to hold them open. Burklow threw his hands in the air and moved to the wall opposite of him. He leaned against it and lit a cigarette.

Burklow inhaled and blew a puff of smoke down on Finch and Strode. "This is Mommy stuff, Finch. I don't know what the hell to do for him."

Finch's dark eyes were on Strode, and he could see the annoyed expression on her face shift to anger.

"It's not 'Mommy stuff.' If some low-life hit you upside the head and knocked your ass unconscious, wouldn't you hope your partner would do this very thing for you? And I'll tell you another thing, if you're telling me only women are capable of doing this, then the whole damned department just crossed over to completely useless."

Strode felt a tickle in his face. He felt like shit, but listening to Finch tell Burklow off made him want to smile.

Finch noticed and put a hand to Burklow as she asked Strode, "Are you with us, man?"

She folded the rough, wet washcloth and held it over Strode's forehead. The coolness of the cloth was bringing him back.

Strode raised a hand and held the cloth himself, taking over for Finch. "What the hell happened?"

Burklow pushed off the wall and said, "I came in, and Finch was yelling. She said you were down in the basement screaming at someone. She said she went downstairs, gun in hand to see what was going on, and the door was closed."

"I came down the stairs as you yelled, but when I got closer to the bathroom, you went quiet," Finch said.

Burklow, not seeming too disturbed by what happened to Strode, took another long drag on his cigarette and again blew it without a care of whose face it was beating into. Finch waved the smoke from Strode's face and mumbled, "Jackass."

Finch smoothed the hair on her head. Again, not a single curl strayed out of place.

"I tried to open the door," Finch went on. "I could tell it wasn't locked, but there was something against it. It was you. I called your name, but you didn't answer. It took nearly everything I had to push the door open. No thanks to my partner."

Burklow gave an insincere chuckle. "I didn't know what the hell was going on."

Finch rolled her eyes. "It doesn't matter. But, Strode, do you remember seeing someone down here? What happened?"

Strode held the washcloth to his head and tried to sit up. He was queasy and still a bit out of it.

Finch grabbed his shoulder and said, "Easy now. Just stay put and tell me what happened."

Strode's eyes investigated the bathroom and found pieces of the soap dish on the floor. He reached for a piece and held the sharp glass between his fingers.

"He made this fall while he was laughing at me."

Finch arched her eyebrows in question. "Who did?"

Burklow pushed through. "Strode, was there someone in my house? In my wife's shop?"

With a new sense of care, Burklow became upset. His fingers shook around the cigarette he was holding. He held it tighter between his middle and pointer fingers. "The fucking nerve of some people." Burklow locked his lips around the dwindling Marlboro and blew the smoke directly onto Strode. "The fucking nerve."

Strode only coughed as renewed pain slammed into his head. The intensified pressure took him back to the moments before the ordeal.

What the fuck happened?

As if she received a telepathic cue to explain, Finch said, "You were yelling, Strode. I was making the coffee, and you yelled at someone."

Burklow smacked the back of one hand into the palm of the other. "A name. We need a name. Or anything to indicate who might've been in my fucking house!" Burklow's eyes spotlighted Strode. "Well?"

Strode was still confused and trying to piece it all together. "I really can't remember. Did I say a name, Finch?"

Finch bit into her dark lips and ran her palms over the top of her head. "You didn't say a name. But he upset you. You asked him how—"

Finch gave Strode a similar look to the one she gave the Williamson boy, filled with empathy.

"What is it?" Strode asked.

She sighed. "You asked him how he knew Jackie and the Blackwood boy, Teddy. You told him to tell you where they are. You called him a 'creepy fucker.'"

Strode remembered. "The clown."

Burklow was taken aback. "A clown was in my house? What clown?"

Strode saw splotches of yellow and blue dance around the room. His stomach burned from vomiting, and his head felt like it weighed a hundred pounds. He pointed to the picture that hung above the toilet and saw lettering that he hadn't recognized before.

Burklow stepped into the bathroom. Strode felt pinned to the back wall, with all three of them huddled in that cupboard-sized space.

Burklow looked to the picture, "What about the clown?"

Strode's eyes were tiptoeing back and forth across the line of present and long-gone.

"It was him. He knew about the kids," Strode said.

Burklow and Finch turned to one another. Strode's eyes allowed him a peek at how crazy he truly was becoming, and he watched his new partners eye one another. Neither of them was sure what to do next.

Strode knew he needed to fix things, or just as he had back home he would be sent home and off the case. He grabbed onto the bathroom sink, finding it was a bit lower than he expected. He overshot his hand, and it felt like it was free-falling to the surface. With minor gagging and a bit of headrush, he pulled himself to his feet.

Strode could see it then. There wasn't a Gacy-copycat with a bloodied face with him that afternoon. The clown was a picture. He had blacked out.

A complete 360 from how Strode felt just moments before, his body was surging with energy, one that he felt he couldn't pinpoint as it moved through him. He supposed he had been more upset about the body earlier than he initially thought. It was probably more triggering than he had allowed himself to think. But what did he feel then? Shame? Embarrassment? He imagined anger too. That had to be the explanation for the unrest in his ailing body.

Too many feelings unchecked make your episodes even more manic, Dr. Evers would say. Strode hated that she was probably right. The last two days had been more stop-and-go than Strode had been in months. He had to fix it.

Finch and Burklow stared at him like a wild animal, whose next move could be worse than the last, maybe even catastrophic.

Strode shrugged his shoulders. "I think I'm still feeling the drive, and I haven't eaten much."

Finch said, "You're right. You did look a bit pale when you asked where the bathroom was."

Finch turned to Burklow. "I was making him coffee. Why don't you go throw a pizza in the oven? We can eat before we go to Derek's cabin."

Burklow's face lit up like a kid at Christmas. "I'll get one delivered. Everyone good with pepperoni?"

Burklow was already headed out of the beauty parlor and pounding his feet up the spiral staircase before they could answer.

Strode found a clock on the wall to the left of the mirror at the center of the salon. It had been nearly three hours since they had arrived at Burklow's. The morning had gone and afternoon was upon them.

Strode shook his head. His anxiousness, his "fits," had always cost him time, and he hated that it may have cost others too.

With shameful eyes, Strode turned to Finch, ready to apologize.

But Finch didn't seem to even notice him. She was looking at the picture on the wall.

"It was this clown you saw? And he was talking to you?"

Strode's cheeks flushed. "I know. I know. I'm out of my damn mind. Right?"

Finch ignored him. She went right up to the photo and smoothed her hand over the clown's face. "I've always hated this clown."

Strode stared at the clown. The little yellow hat. The particularly pointy teeth. Strode remembered how the hat had bounced while torments spat through its teeth.

Finch crossed her arms and said, "The Clowns. It was a negro team. Did you know that?"

Strode swallowed and couldn't help but feel awkward. He wished he knew what to say, but she went on.

"My grandfather played for them. You know?"

Strode curved his lips in an upside-down U shape. "Really?"

Finch's eyes locked on the clown. "Yes. He wasn't too good, and only played a few seasons, but he used to tell my brother and me what it was like traveling around the country as a negro team. He said negro players were welcome to play ball in the sunny afternoons, but if their bus wasn't out of town before sundown, there was hell to pay."

Finch bit her lip and narrowed her eyes.

"People celebrate it but never talk about the way the players were treated, especially on the road."

Strode saw her eyes soften as she sighed.

"So, yeah. I've always hated that clown." She threw her hands up. "Although, some good came from that team. In the fifties, the Clowns signed a seventeen-year-old kid. My grandfather said he was like the John Henry of baseball, worked hard day and night, swinging the bat and getting stronger every day."

Finch turned to Strode, grinning. "Do you know who that kid was?"

Strode shrugged. No idea.

She stepped from the bathroom, "Hank Aaron."

The cold, frail look fell from Strode as excitement took over. "Wow. On the Clowns?"

Finch nodded and waved for Strode to follow her as she headed to the bottom of the steps.

"I know what it's like. To have so much weighing on you, I mean. Our minds play tricks on us. That creepy clown is bad for a lot of reasons, more than people would like to admit, but there's some good there too. From the Clowns came one of the best baseball players of all time. Giving Black kids like my brother and me a little more hope."

Strode nodded, trying to be present and follow where she was going with this. Doing it all at once was difficult for him.

Finch put her hand on the railing of the spiral staircase and one foot on the bottom step. She started to head up, but she stopped and looked back at Strode.

"There's been a lot of bad with this case, Strode. People, good people, innocent people, have gotten hurt. Police officers in higher positions than yours and mine have called us crazy for looking into it. For asking questions. There's always going to be bad associated with this case when people look back on it."

Strode couldn't help but feel a bit defeated, and he let it pour out. "That's *if* they look back on it. *If* we can find something that could make anyone believe us that there's more here."

Finch nodded.

"We have the bad: the clothing samples, the photographs, the victims, the disappearances. We're still learning the bad, and I'm sure worse is yet to come. But I think it's up to us to put the good in it too. To figure it out and maybe stop something like this from happening again. To show people that things aren't always as they seem."

* * *

Strode and Finch climbed the final steps and smelled a cigarette Burklow had lit along with the coffee Finch made for Strode.

Strode went to the files at the table and began picking them up, stuffing the battered bodies' images and reported evidence found at the scene back in their files.

Finch put a hand on Strode's wrist, stopping him. "What are you doing?"

Strode turned to Finch to see a genuine look of concern on her face. Burklow was sitting in an ugly brown leather chair with his legs spread far wider than necessary in the corner of the living room.

Strode looked to him for a clue, but Burklow puffed out a cloud of smoke and smiled. The saying "ignorance is bliss" ran through Strode's mind.

Finch sat at the dining room table and tapped the empty spot next to her at the head of the table.

Strode sat.

Finch gave Burklow a stern look that brought him to his feet. He dragged himself to the table and sat next to Strode.

"Burklow, what time will the pizza be here?"

Burklow pulled the cigarette from his lips. Strode wondered how his chubby fingers didn't smash the damn thing.

"Should be here in the next fifteen."

Finch nodded.

"Strode, are your belongings in your car or at the hotel?"

Strode didn't understand. "Uhm, in my car. I just had one bag. Why?"

"You're staying here. You can sleep downstairs on the pullout couch, and Burklow will take down the picture in the bathroom."

Strode rubbed his palms together as he tried to figure out what to say. "That's okay. I'm fine at the hotel. Besides, we don't know how long I'll—"

Finch raised a hand. "That'll do."

Burklow turned to Strode and said, "I'm afraid Finch has spoken. I'll get the bed made up."

Burklow looked at Finch, and Strode couldn't help but smile at the way the old officer seemed to be asking his trainee if he was free to go. She nodded, and Burklow poured himself a drink, emptying the Daniels bottle before pounding his feet down the steps.

It was just heading into the late afternoon. What were they doing?

On top of one of the open files was a single note in scribbled handwriting, "You can solve this."

Strode pulled it toward him and raised his eyes in suspicion. "What is this?"

"It's my note. When I was tearing through the early details of these files, we got some of the information right as it came in, and some I still learned later just in the past few days. I made that note for Burklow."

Strode closed the file and slid it to the side. "But why?"

Finch brought her hands together and gave Strode a look that demanded his undivided attention.

"He was hesitant and wasn't sure we needed to bring anyone else in. But then we found Nate Williamson."

Strode nodded.

She lowered her chin so her eyes seemed to level with Strode. "Then, I was certain you could solve this. I was certain that if anyone could do it, you could."

Strode sank in his chair and hung his head. "Because I was the one who found the Warrens and the Blackwoods."

"Right. But it's more than that. You found *some* of the Warrens and Blackwoods, and you kept looking for the rest."

Strode smiled. Validation. Was it possible for someone to offer so much of it in such a short timeframe?

Finch gave Strode a reassuring nod.

"But, if you're going to help me, I need you to be on top of things. Now, I don't want to hear it. You're sleeping here, and we're going to spend the night studying these files. We'll have our dinner at three o'clock like retired folks, and hell, we'll order another if we have to."

"But what about the cabin, Finch?"

She closed her eyes and exhaled. "It will be there tomorrow."

Strode felt as though she was trying to convince not only him but herself too. She really was trying to take care of him.

"But I think we should go—"

She raised her hand, cutting him off just as she had before with an unwavering sense of authority.

Strode couldn't help but think, *If this woman is a rookie, I'm a minnow.*

She repeated, "It will be there tomorrow. We'll go first thing in the morning."

Strode admitted defeat and grabbed at one of the files. He looked over his shoulder, checking for Burklow, and whispered, "Thank you," to Finch.

9

Burklow had driven Finch to her car around eleven the night before. She and Strode had studied the pictures and reports of the case files for hours. He could still feel the strain in his eyes, but Finch was up-and-at-'em first thing the next morning.

Using the spare key under the mat, she woke him and Burklow up, started the coffee pot, and had them both out the door in twenty minutes.

Finch did a quick look at her reflection in the car's window and smoothed any loose hairs. Strode wondered what the hell that woman could've possibly seen. Every hair was in its place. He was beginning to think if that ever weren't true, he'd be suspicious. Like there wasn't any way a woman with a few loose strands of wind-corrupted hair could be *the real* Finch. *If her hair was ever out of place*, Strode thought, *it would be my first run-in with a doppelganger.*

Finch looked to Burklow in the drive and gave him a nod as if to say, *We're all set.*

Burklow twirled the cabin key above his head and hopped in the squad car that read Three Oaks Police on the side in an off-putting brown color. Strode began to feel anxious. In the off chance they could run into the deranged maniac who had mutilated those poor people in Warren Woods, a police car might be too telling. If the guy was working from the woods, or even just revisiting the scene, he would run or hide at the sight of them.

"Burklow!" Strode called. "Come here for a second."

Burklow's cheeks jiggled as his feet stomped down the driveway. He raised his eyebrows. "What is it, Strode?"

Strode eyed the police car in the drive. The sun was coming up quick.

"I think we should take two cars. You can come in the back way, and Finch and I can take my Pinto to the cabin."

Burklow cocked his head, not following.

"If this guy is still in the woods, if he's *anywhere* near the cabin, I don't want him to take off when he sees your car."

Finch agreed. "He's right. We'll check out the cabin. You keep your distance and come up the other way. Give us twenty minutes to walk the cabin, and then we'll meet you at the far entrance, near the housing subdivision. Okay? Only the neighborhood kids use that entrance anyway."

Strode felt his anxiousness ease. It was reassuring. For the first time in a while, he wasn't told he was overthinking everything. Instead, he was treated as though his thoughts, his concerns, were part of his skilled and tactful police work.

"Alright, then. I'll grab one of my fancy cigars from the house to keep me busy."

Burklow shot finger guns at his partners, tossed the cabin's key to Finch, and then carried his jiggly body up the drive and into the house.

Finch climbed inside of the Pinto, and the grace period of no questions began to fade. She eyed Strode, and he then realized how much he was sweating. He pulled the neck of his shirt up and wiped his face dry.

"You're nervous about this. I get it. And there's something here, Strode. I know it too. But I need you to do something for me. Okay?"

Strode was taken aback by her tone. It was soft and gentle, but her face showed conflict like she was battling whether to say what she was about to.

Strode swallowed and wiped his face again, ready to be in the woods so everyone would begin sweating as much as his anxiety had made him. "What is it?"

Finch grabbed a stack of folders from the floorboard. Strode hadn't even noticed she was carrying all the files. She raised them and said, "We'll start with the cabin. Then, we can go back to the rest of these. Right now, we're looking into Derek Russell."

Strode said, "Right. I remember the guy's name."

Finch shook her head. "I know you do. That's not what I mean. I mean, we need you, Strode. I need you to take things one step at a time. I need you to focus as best as you can."

Strode looked at his new partner and couldn't decide if he was thankful for the talk or embarrassed that he needed it.

Finch repeated, "One step at a time."

One step at a time. Maggie used to say the same thing.

As Strode thought about it, Dr. Evers mentioned something like that too. "You build a wall in your mind. And not a sturdy one. It's as if it were made of toy blocks, wobbly and destined to collapse. You take everything around you, every interaction, every worry, every task, and stack them on top of one another. Then, when you've got them all collected, and you try to pull at one, you get worked up and pull too fast. The tact of the game is lost in your hurry, and it all comes tumbling down."

"And I panic," Strode answered.

"And you panic," Dr. Evers echoed.

Finch's face softened into a reassuring smile. "One step at a time, Strode."

Strode knew Finch meant well, and her worry and belief in him were unmatched by anyone else. So, he figured if she felt the need to say it, he needed to hear it. It would be the mantra he would carry with him as he worked this case.

Strode turned the key, and the engine hummed. He repeated Finch aloud, "One step at a time."

Burklow had made it back to his car, and the brake lights lit up. "We better go, Strode," Finch said. "We've got a lot of work to do."

Strode was fairly certain he remembered how to get back to Warren Woods, but he let Finch direct him. She reached for the radio dial and turned it to a reasonable volume, saying, "The clavinet and percussion opening of this song is perfect."

Strode had no idea what a clavinet was, but he knew the song and the group. Then he remembered seeing a vinyl somewhere with the five members on the cover. The album was yellow with gold and orange psychedelic letters. Where had he seen that? He liked vinyl records but never really started his own collection.

The Blackwoods. They had quite the collection of vinyl records. Sgt. Pepper's Lonely Hearts Club Band was playing when I got there. The Spinners were on deck.

When Strode entered the Starling house the day the Blackwood husband and wife were killed, "Being for the Benefit of Mr. Kite" played through the murder scene. It danced its way from the Crosley record player, over the gore, and to the hairs on the back of Strode's neck. The carnival sounds made the whole thing feel like a bad dream, like some dope trip where he imagined a freak show. Then Strode remembered the smell of the bleach. The combined thoughts burned the clown from Burklow's bathroom into his mind. He could hear it.

"Strode had a stroke. Strode had a stroke." The clown's laughter clawed into his ears and suffocated all other sounds. Then, in its manic cry, the clown said, "Who will bring that little girl home? Who will find that little boy?"

He turned at the wooden sign that pointed to Warren Woods.

Then, just to Strode's left, he saw the clown amongst the open mouth of the trees. It was waving at him. It hopped from one foot to the other, its yellow hat bouncing atop its head, and stringy strands of its bloodied jaw moved with it.

Strode slammed on the brakes, and Finch caught herself on the dash.

"What the hell are you doing?"

Strode unlocked his seatbelt and dumped himself from the car. Tiny pebbles ate their way into his palms as he vomited onto the worn pavement. He had only had a cup of coffee, but the claws in his stomach dug it up. It seemed as though he could feel it carry away the coffee, then the creamer, and then the sugar. He flung his head up, pinching a nerve at the bottom of his neck.

The shock lingered, but the clown was gone.

Finch came around the side of the car and put a hand on Strode's back as his body thrashed and the acidity of his stomach emptied once more.

Strode wiped his mouth and beat his fists into the ground. "God damnit."

The woods were quiet. No laughing clown, just the sound of rustling leaves.

"I'm sorry, Finch. I just—the kid—Teddy. And Jackie. Both of them. I can't stop thinking about the kids. They can't just be gone, right?"

Strode felt defeated as he failed to recite and follow his mantra less than twenty minutes after declaring it.

Finch nodded, and as a mother would, she continued to rub his back and hushed him, "You're okay."

Strode shook his head. "You don't understand. That's the good, Finch. That's the good I'm supposed to bring from this godforsaken case. I *have* to find him. I *have* to find them."

Finch only nodded, letting Strode get out whatever he needed to, whether it was mid-digested dark roast coffee or angst about the kids.

When Strode was quiet, Finch stood and reached a hand out to him. "Ready?"

Strode nodded and took Finch's hands. He was surprised. For how small she was, she tugged him up with ease. Part of him was surprised at how weightless he felt too.

"I know you're thinking about the kids, especially the boy right now. Theodore."

"Teddy," Strode corrected.

"Right, Teddy. But Strode, you're putting too much on yourself at once. For over a year, you haven't had anyone believe you, or in you, but you do now."

That was true, and Strode supposed he failed to realize how much things had changed for him in just a day and how much could change if he didn't mess it up.

Strode smiled at Finch, who was beginning to feel a bit like a savior to him. "You're right."

"Now that there's three of us, Strode, maybe we'll get more answers, and maybe faster. But we have to be patient and vigilant, or we'll miss things. We all have reason to be here, but we have to focus or we'll screw this up, and more people will get hurt."

Strode's eyes narrowed, and he did a shoulder roll, trying to reawaken his sickly body. "You're right."

Finch smiled, letting her guard down a little more and more each time she was with Strode. "You know, you've got more heart than any other officer I've ever met. There's something about you. A—"

"A total loss of my fucking marbles." He laughed.

Finch ignored Strode's interruption entirely. She was still searching for the perfect phrase. She found it.

"A heightened empathy." Finch snapped her fingers. "That's what it is."

She stole his own phrase. Strode felt like it was a lesson in reflecting his compassion and understanding onto himself, even better than Dr. Evers was able to do.

Strode knew he felt things differently from all the other officers back home, and at the end of their marriage, it was different from Maggie too.

She went on, "And you know what that does?"

Strode shrugged his shoulders. "Makes me a nut case who sees clowns and nearly throws his partner through a windshield?"

Finch straightened her top and smoothed her hands over hair, as if even discussing something that would cause their displacement had rearranged them.

"A good cop, Strode. I haven't met very many."

Strode wasn't sure what he felt. He supposed it was comfort. He couldn't help but smile—not his usual sarcastic grin but a reflection of genuine warmth.

Finch returned the smile and then clapped her hands together. "We better get going. Here, give me the keys. I'll drive the rest of the way."

Strode waved her away. "I'm okay."

Finch didn't have to repeat herself. She gave Strode a sharp look, and her dark eyes narrowed. He tossed her the keys.

Finch settled into the Pinto and drove it just above the speed limit. The precision, even in her speeding, amused Strode. Exactly five over. Not once under or above.

Strode watched the trees begin to envelop the car. They looked a lot like the cluster of trees between the Blackwood and Abraham home back in Indiana. Even a section of them seemed far more withered than the others, just like back home. Before his mind could tiptoe into dangerous territory, Finch said, "Burklow is parked by now. So, we're on the clock."

Finch parked the Pinto at the bottom of the path. The cabin was just a ways up. She turned to look at the rising sun. "Let's get this day going. Let's move."

And as they climbed the hill, Strode repeated, *One step at a time.*

10

When they came upon the cabin, they heard a quick rustle to the side of it.

Strode reached for his gun and rested his hand on the holster.

Finch noticed and raised her hands as she said, "Easy, Strode."

He supposed he was feeling a bit antsy. He didn't think he would fire if the clown came back, but who was to say? And who knew who or what he might hit instead.

He took a deep breath and tried to focus.

Finch climbed the steps, and they groaned under pressure, suggesting their age. Still, the cabin was well-kept. It looked like a life-size version of the building Strode built from Lincoln Logs as a kid. Only it was stained with a nice cherry oak color.

"This place is nice," Strode said.

Finch shrugged. "Yeah, well, it's not used much. It's technically city-owned, but the mayor rents it out to high-profile visitors. And in Three Oaks, that pretty much just meant Derek Russell."

"So, he was local too. Right?"

Finch dug for the key in her pocket. "Yes. Grew up here and then moved to New York."

Strode remembered nearly everything in Russell's file. But he needed to keep his mind occupied on Russell so it didn't wander to the clown or the kids. So, he replayed the information.

"And he came here during the summer to write?"

Finch held the key before her like it was a prize. "There it is. And yes, he wrote mystery novels, crime thrillers, that sort of thing."

Strode couldn't help but catch the irony. He refocused.

"Has anyone been here since Russell was found?"

A rustle came from behind the house just as Finch began to open the front door.

The noise came again. Something was moving inside. They could see straight through the living room to the back door. It was open.

Strode looked down at Finch and pulled his gun from the holster. "I'll go first. Stay behind me."

Finch cut Strode off. "I certainly won't."

Strode didn't argue but followed closely behind Finch, checking each of her blind spots. She signaled for him to go left into the kitchen, as she began to turn past the living room into the bedroom.

She was following the sound. It moved into the house. The rustle turned into a thud as something in the room, maybe a book, hit the floor.

She turned back to Strode, who was disobeying her order to go left. Her eyes narrowed, the way they did when he protested her driving to the cabin.

She pointed to the kitchen, and Strode shook his head

and brought his hands together. Finch rolled her eyes but then nodded and waved him over to her.

Keeping quiet, they went into the bedroom, a simple cream color with navy striped bedding. Finch stepped toward the bathroom, and Strode moved the bedroom door and shoved his gun in the corner. Nothing.

Finch moved into the bathroom. Strode heard her push the shower curtain aside behind the bathroom door. She came out and shook her head. Nothing.

Aside from the bedroom, the cabin had an open layout. Strode and Finch were alone. They gave one another a concerned look, mirroring one another's arched eyebrows and pursed lips.

Strode reverted to his first order from Finch and checked out the kitchen. Nothing.

Old houses make noise. That's what Maggie used to say when Strode would wake up in the middle of the night, swearing he heard something downstairs.

Strode and Dr. Evers began to think it was yet another paranoia-induced sensation. He hoped that this old cabin, and the woods around it, had simply been settling.

Finally, Finch broke the silence. "We look around here, and then we walk the woods."

Finch pulled a plastic bag from her jacket pocket and tossed Strode a pair of latex gloves. She spread her fingers open and slid a pair on too.

Finch walked to the kitchen counter. "Okay, so let's go over the scenario again. The report said they'd found the stove on when they arrived, the kettle empty."

Finch then pointed to the counter. A mug sat with a green tea bag in it and a glass container next to it missing its lid.

She came beside Strode and, lost in thought, gave him a pushy nudge to get out of her way. He grinned and obliged.

Finch opened the tea kettle on the stove.

"It's empty."

Strode studied his partner. "So?"

The thread hung relaxed over the moon-patterned mug. "So, the assumption is he was making himself tea. And then left the stove on. The water boiled out," Finch said.

Finch went to the desk across from the kitchen. A stack of papers lay beside a leatherbound notebook. The first sheet of paper read, "To-Do List." Each day had writing goals, mostly chapter writing and research to collect.

"Russell had been here for about a week and a half, Burklow said. If you look at his to-do list, it stops on day eleven. According to the date scribbled in the corner here, that would've been Tuesday. They found him on Friday."

"Three days, just like the others," Strode said.

Finch picked up the notebook and flipped through its yellow-tinted pages. "The chapters, his writing, they stop three days before we found him."

"Any chance he would give himself a few days off?"

Finch shook her head. "I don't think so. He came here to write. He clearly had some momentum. I'm no Fitzgerald, but I don't think anyone would walk away from a project that was going well. He was writing a chapter a day. On Tuesday, he meant to write chapter eleven."

Finch flipped through the pages further. "And he started it."

She turned the notebook so Strode could see the few paragraphs written. Scribbled across the top of the page in loopy lettering was "Chapter 11."

Finch's eyes lit up. "It's the one day he didn't finish his chapter, and the to-do list stops there."

Finch hurried from the desk and back to the kitchen counter. She stood at the stove and said, "Russell put water in the kettle and turned it on to boil. He came over here, put in the teabag, and grabbed a spoon for the sugar. Then he sat down to start chapter eleven, but he never ended up making the tea."

Finch walked back to the open back door and raised her hands to rest on the sides of the door frame. She looked into the woods, "Something called him away."

Finch closed the back door, but it wouldn't latch. The wind grabbed ahold of it and pried it open again. She followed it and examined the latch.

Strode's head felt like a cook was stirring around the contents of his brain, whisking them into scrambled eggs.

Finch ran her finger around the edge of the wooden back door. "This should've snagged my glove. The wood is old and rigid. It used to fit perfectly into the frame, there, but now it's too smooth."

She pulled a hand free from the glove and ran her finger alongside the door's frame.

"It's been sanded," Finch said.

Strode was confused. "But why? Why would anyone do that?"

Finch went back to the desk, and with her gloved hand, shuffled the loose papers. At the top of one, in Russell's handwriting, it read, "DISTURBANCE LOG."

It was organized by date and time, over eleven days.

DISTURBANCE LOG

Monday—9:00 a.m.
Monday—1:00 p.m.
Tuesday—9:00 a.m.

Tuesday—7:00 p.m.
Wednesday—11:00 a.m.
Wednesday—10:00 p.m.

... And on.

Then they saw a business card for a locksmith.

Finch held it. "Something was bothering him. To the point where he logged it, trying to decide if the sounds were rational or—"

"Paranoia," Strode interrupted.

Finch pursed her lips. "Right."

She turned to Strode. "Do you know what this means? Something was calling him. Something that wanted him to leave the cabin."

Strode looked at the open back door and said, "Something that wouldn't take no for an answer."

Strode stuffed the gloves in her pocket and hopped outside the open door into the dirt of Warren Woods. She turned back to Strode, determined.

"And neither will we."

11

Strode and Finch heel-toed into the woods. The sun lingered midway into the horizon, creating a dim, golden glow between the trees.

It was cooler in the shade of the trees, but the sweat on Strode's face was still active. He was fighting off the familiarity of the chilled perspiration from when he woke up late at night and saw Jackie Warren's corpse standing at the end of his bed.

Strode tried to repeat his new mantra, *One step at a time. One step at a time.*

Finch and Strode headed through the woods to the main path, as planned. But just after Finch pointed ahead, saying, "It's just a little further this way," she took a sharp left, further off-path.

"Finch? Where are you going?"

She didn't have to answer. Strode saw it too. The golden light was merging with a nightly purple and spotlighted a row of crippled, decayed trees. Despite the others having full, bright leaves, the row of trees was grey and rotting—like a corpse.

Strode grabbed one of the limbs, and it disintegrated. Its remains fell to his muddied work boots.

Strode turned to Finch. "I've never seen anything like this. Have you?"

Finch shook her head. "It doesn't make sense." She pointed to Strode's shoes and then raised her own, to show matching muddied soles.

Strode started to say it, but Finch beat him to. "It's rained in the last few days."

"And rained hard enough that the ground is still wet," Strode answered.

Strode folded his lips into his mouth and moved them from side to side, thinking. He knew Finch wasn't going to like his new plan.

"Here's what I'm thinking. You know the main trail. You know the whole damn woods. You go find Burklow and come back this way to meet me."

Finch put her hands in front of her and pulled them apart. "No way. No way. We have something here. We need to follow the decayed trees."

Strode smiled at her expected stubbornness. "And we will. But if something or someone is at the end of this, we need to be sneaky. We can't have Burklow running through the woods wearing a police shirt and calling for us."

It was an extraordinary feeling for Strode to be so confident that he was making the right call.

Finch kicked her boot into the mud. "Fine. You're right. But follow these trees, exactly as they line up, so we can find you. No turn-offs. Follow the trees."

Strode gave a salute and said, "Yes, ma'am."

Finch started down the main path and looked back at Strode. For her sake, he repeated her instructions, "Follow the decayed trees, no turn-offs."

It was enough to send her on her way.

Strode looked to the ground at the ash pile, which was a decaying branch only moments ago. It made him feel nauseatingly fragile. Maybe even insignificant.

Strode shook his head. *Focus. Focus.*

He looked past the first of the decayed trees and saw the line was continuous and straight. Strode wondered how far it would go. Another part of him feared it wouldn't go too far, and whatever had killed the trees was opening its jaws as a willing victim blindly strolled into its mouth.

It didn't matter. Strode had to go on for the Blackwood boy, for Jackie Warren, and the people of Three Oaks.

Strode continued down the unofficial path of sickly trees. He noticed that some had exposed roots, as though they were diseased right down to their core. They were like bony fingers, trying to escape being buried away—like the living dead.

Then Strode heard a whisper.

"Pretty lady couldn't have a baby."

Strode felt his shoulders rise as he stopped. He turned his head slowly, looking behind him and hoping there wasn't a bloodied, talking corpse behind him.

Not here, Jackie. Please. Not now.

The voice crept through the leaves, up Strode's back, and into his ear.

"Pretty lady couldn't have a baby."

Strode pulled a flashlight from his back pocket, though a fair amount of light was still left in the evening. He was hoping that even if he couldn't catch the speaker, maybe he could find their shadow.

Did he dare speak to it? The clown, Jackie, what good ever came from engaging with them?

But what if this isn't an illusion? What if this is real?

Dr. Evers had told Strode hundreds of times that he needed to work to separate illusions—he was certain she wanted to say delusions instead—from reality. But as Strode stood in Warren Woods, searching for a sign, he realized Dr. Evers's advice was simply that—advice. It wasn't instructional. How the hell was he supposed to determine if the whisper was in his head, or if it was real, hiding somewhere within the trees of Warren Woods?

"Pretty lady couldn't have a baby."

Strode closed his eyes, took a deep breath, and said, "One step at a time."

He continued following the trees.

The further he got, the dryer the ground became. The path became an uphill slant. Strode noticed spots in the dirt where moisture held. The rest was bone dry. And rather than being that rich soil color, it was a light grey.

"Pretty lady couldn't have a baby."

The voice was dry, cracking as if whatever killed the trees was circling through that being too.

"Pretty lady couldn't have a baby."

The voice no longer sounded like it was behind Strode but calling from ahead.

The whisper was like a gnat. It tiptoed around him, from behind, to each side, and then back in front of him, repeating, *"Pretty lady couldn't have a baby."*

The icy breath with its cunning spider-like legs crawled into Strode's ears and across his brain. Once it got inside his head, it must've found the clearly marked command center for his paranoia.

"Pretty lady couldn't have a baby. Pretty lady couldn't have a baby. Pretty lady couldn't have a baby."

The voice became louder. It spoke quicker, with an alarming sense of urgency.

Strode threw his hands to the sides of his head, covering his ears. He ran forward, following the trail of death and decay.

The voice boomed in front of him, *"The pretty lady couldn't have a baby. The pretty lady couldn't have a baby.*

And then Strode saw a baby's head pop off.

Strode envisioned a strangled Jackie Warren, just as he did in his kitchen days before. There was a thick, rusted wire hanger around her neck. It circled tighter and tighter.

Jackie cried out for him, "Please, help me."

Strode reached out to the little girl, and when he did, the girl disappeared.

But the voice remained.

The whispers were no longer dancing in circles around Strode. They tunneled straight at him. They echoed as they reached him, as though the path ahead was a cement hall rather than open woods.

"The pretty lady couldn't have a baby."

Strode called, "Stop it!"

The voice's splitting sound surged through the path, *"Then Strode tried to save a little girl."*

Strode's feet pounded into the barren hill. Lifeless twigs snapped under his feet, and he jumped at the sound of each break. His mind tried to convince him that they were the sound of his body breaking down, bone by bone, just as his mind had, illusion by illusion.

"Strode tried to save a little girl."

Snap. Snap.

"But Strode and the pretty lady who couldn't have a baby couldn't save the little girl. And the little girl's head popped off."

Strode winced. He had seen the aftermath of Jackie Warren dying a thousand different ways: starvation, strangulation, a slit throat, asphyxiation. But never had Jackie Warren come to him headless.

He turned behind him, hoping he would see Finch and Burklow, but the path was bare with just fallen branches and littered leaves. Strode's first thought was to turn around and find the cabin, to wait there for his partners, but he pushed that thought away.

The voice remained in front of Strode.

With a newfound sense of strength and tact, that had no doubt been given to him by Finch, Strode stared dead-ahead.

The voice isn't moving. The voice is trying to keep me from going straight.

Strode thought maybe the voice was trying to push him off the path. It was trying to separate him from his partners.

Without them, illusions could freely feast on his sanity.

Strode had to take a stand.

He shook his head, repeated his mantra, and ran through the shrill voice as it sang, *"Her head popped off. Her head popped off."*

The trees took a sudden turn and Strode followed their guidance.

Then the line of death and the voices stopped. Strode had made it to the end of the line, and before him stood a massive tree, nearly one hundred feet tall. Near the bottom, splitting roots with a strand of black spiraled into a break in the bark, was an opening.

At the top was a human head.

Bloodied and battered.

12

———

The cutout of the tree where the head poked out was like a scary story Strode had heard growing up about a poor woman who was left to rot in a tree.

What was her name? Becca? That doesn't sound right.

Just beneath the hollow trunk were engorged roots. Strode steadied himself atop one of them and reached for a thick branch above him. The branch scuffed his hand but Strode held it tighter. His heart pounded. He hoped to God that this person was still alive.

Strode put one of his feet on the side of the tree for stability. Then, he peered into the top of the cutout. All he could see was this poor person's head. A maroon stickiness stained the person's white-blonde hair. Strode was familiar with this sight. It turned his stomach. He had seen an injury like that before, only the previous was far worse. Laurie Warren's smashed-in head produced the same dark gelatinous thickness. Only her father hit her harder and far more times.

Strode realized Marlene Byers suffered this same kind of injury. She and the older Warren sister had wounds on their heads that showed bright chunks of a stringy-worm-like texture. Brain matter.

Strode had to get that person out of the tree before they ended up like the girls. He bent at his back and let his hands fall around the sides of the person's head. His foot slid and nearly had him in the splits.

"Fuck."

Strode had to take his hands out of the tree's open mouth to readjust. This time, he bent at his knees, putting more weight against the tree as he leaned into the head. He felt something on his fingers, wetness, and rubbed them together. It balled on his fingertips and feathered away as he continued to roll it, between his thumb and pointer. It was blood.

Strode had no other choice; he would have to begin lifting this person out by their head. The tree was too narrow, and the stretch was too far to do it any other way.

Strode cupped his hands around the head like a hawk's claw locking around a prey. He was so relieved when he heard a faint groan.

"Hello? Can you hear me?"

The groan answered.

"My name is Officer Strode. I'm going to get you out of here."

Please let this be real. Let them be alive.

"If you do it that way, the baby's head might pop off. Pop. Pop. Pop."

The voice returned. And this time, it sounded as though it was right behind Strode. He turned to look over his shoulder, and his foot answered the fast motion with a slide.

"Fuck. Fuck."

Strode closed his eyes. *Them. Not Teddy. Not Jackie. Whoever this person is. Them. It has to be about them. Don't let the delusions carry you away.*

Strode tugged at the head and used the tree as he shoved his weight into. He was surprised to find the resistance eased, and he could see the person's face.

It was a little boy. Strode pulled harder, and the boy groaned again.

"Not too hard, Strode. You don't want his head to pop off."

Strode shook his head and took mental inventory. *Real— this boy. He is alive, and he needs my help. Not real—the voice trying to stop me.*

"Ahhh!" Strode released a heavy grunt, and the boy's shoulders emerged from the wych elm. Strode grabbed the torn bits of the boy's shirt and dragged the body down to him. He flipped the top half of the boy over his shoulder and hopped down from the puffed tree root.

Strode laid the boy gently on the ground. The injuries were more than his head. The boy had cuts around his lips. The small, bloodied tics looked like fabric stitches that could create a smile with the tug of a thread.

On the tips of every other finger the skin was far darker than the rest of him. He was a ghostly pale, but his fingers were a scorched red color. They were blistering burns.

"I wanted him to understand the heat."

Strode put his hand on his gun and rose to his feet. His eyes scanned the woods.

Nothing.

He pulled the gun off his belt and pointed it, doing a small circle around the boy's body.

"I needed him to understand the heat. To know why."

The voice was soft, almost sweet, despite its cryptic words.

"Who's there?" Strode shouted.

The boy on the ground winced and groaned as he tried to lift his head. He couldn't, nor could he open his eyes.

But when the voice said, "Come find me," the pommeled boy parted his swollen lips and whispered, "Don't."

Strode stepped back with his gun still raised. "This isn't real." He looked to the boy on the ground, whose head was still bleeding. "This is, and this boy needs my help."

Strode could hear Finch's mantra again, *One step at a time.*

Then, a boy stepped from behind the trees. "Of course I'm real. Can't you hear me talking to you?"

The kid was smiling, an innocent-looking smile. He had dark hair and grim grey-colored eyes. His skin was pale and showed every trace of dirt. He was wearing a blood-stained New York Yankees t-shirt.

"I need your help."

Strode blinked, waiting for his vision to clear and the boy before him to disappear, just as Jackie Warren had all those times she haunted him.

But the boy was still there.

"Teddy?"

The boy nodded. "Now, I need your help. There is someone here in the woods. Someone who wants to hurt me."

Strode looked back to the boy on the ground. "Like they hurt him?"

Teddy nodded. "Maybe. I've been out here even worse. Follow me, and I can show you where he's hiding."

Again, quiet enough so only Strode could hear, the boy on the ground whispered, "Don't."

Strode began feeling irritated. He had tried to find Teddy for a year, and there he was right in front of him, but something in his gut told him to stay put just as the injured little boy said.

"What are you doing out here, Teddy?"

Teddy took another step back, "He's going to come for us if we don't go now."

Strode stepped closer to Teddy.

"Don't."

"Please, I've been lost for so long," Teddy said.

Teddy grabbed on to the tree to the side of him.

Strode stepped closer.

Then, the tree's leaves darkened from a bright green to a burnt brown and crumbled to the ground. Teddy's eyes widened.

Strode pointed his gun at Teddy. "How the hell did you do that?"

Teddy raised his hands. "Please, it's not me. It's him. I need your help. Please help me."

Then, Strode heard the boy on the ground whimpering in pain. There were fresh cuts under his eyes. Strode saw a figure on the ground slither around it. Without a moment's thought, Strode fired at it, sending leaves and dirt spewing into the air.

"Please, don't do this. Help me!" Teddy cried.

Strode turned to Teddy, and the boy on the ground whimpered again. Strode turned back, and blood dripped from the widow's peak and down his forehead.

This boy is going to die.

Strode turned to the boy, piled leaves around his head, and pushed to slow the bleeding.

A hiss erupted through the woods and burned Strode's ears. The shrill shriek surged through Strode and pinned him to the ground. He tried to cover his ears. Then, Strode felt like someone had tipped him upside down and let all his inner fluids leak out. A pain far worse than his usual headaches beat into his right eye. The trees above him seemed to interlink, and their leaves became a continuous loop of green.

Strode heard someone shout, "Stop! Stop where you are!" It was a woman. It was Finch.

Strode heard rustling beside him.

Someone's feet shifted in the dirt and pounded away.

A second shot, this time not from Strode, fired. It jolted Strode's adrenaline, and his eyes cleared a small patch of vision for him.

He saw the whiteness of Teddy's t-shirt, now with a growing bloodstain, move into the trees. He was running.

Strode shoved himself off the ground, taking down Finch who rushed to his side.

Without explanation, Strode yelled, "The boy. Save the boy. I have to go after Teddy!"

Strode felt like a horse rounding the final curve of the track and kicked into the dirt. A hammer tapped into the sides of his head and skewed his vision, but he could hear Teddy running too. Strode could hear the pounding of Teddy's feet, the panic in his breath, and the hurry in each of the branches he tossed aside.

Teddy weaved on and off the straight line. Strode was stumbling down. Then, just as Jackie had all those times, he vanished.

Strode continued to run. "Teddy! Teddy Blackwood! I know you're real! I know you're alive!"

Something hit Strode in the throat, cutting off his speed and sending him to the ground gasping for air. Skeletal fingers tickled up Strode's throat. The gold eyes hung just above his own and didn't blink. Strode noticed they were flickering, like a bulb that needed replacing.

The eyes brightened by a single hue as claws penetrated Strode's throat and wrenched back out.

Strode's head fell to the side as blood spilled from his neck.

The hiss came again. Muffled and shaky this time, it spoke, "Go, Teddy. Get out of the woods."

Strode's adrenaline burnt out, and he tried to excavate any bit of fire left in his being to watch the boy he had searched for over a year stumble away.

The blood on Teddy's shoulder spread down his back. That Yankees shirt was a goner.

Strode's final thought was, *So am I.*

13

Strode awoke to President Richard Nixon discussing progress in peace negotiations. Even in a daze, he didn't buy it. He knew the kids wouldn't either.

His eyes felt heavy. Holding them open long enough to see where the hell he was felt like Jimmying a safe open with a nail file.

"Hey, man. Can you hear me?"

Strode was hit with a strong odor of whiskey, nicotine, and sweat.

Burklow.

"Hey, man. It's Jack."

Strode wondered if Burklow had said his first name in their day together. Maybe Finch had said it. Burklow seemed to say it in a way that made his first name sound nearly foreign to him too.

Little flicks of water hit Strode's face, and he realized how much he was sweating. Maybe he was the one who smelled like body odor.

The coolness of the water was enough to help him divide his eyelids. Sure enough, Burklow stood over him with a cigar hanging out of his mouth as though he'd come to visit a friend whose wife had just delivered twins instead of a bat-shit-crazy officer from out of town.

Strode smiled. He was glad to see Burklow.

"Wha—"

Pain choked Strode and pushed him to a foam pillow. He wondered if he was in a panic-induced trip.

Strode tried again, "Wha—"

Burklow put his finger to his lips. "Shh. Doc says it shouldn't cause permanent damage, but you shouldn't push it."

Strode brought his hands to his throat.

There was a thick layer of gauze with a cotton puff at the center. He could only imagine the pain killers pumping through him. He turned to Burklow, hoping he would continue to explain. Strode was still trying to piece together what had happened.

Burklow smiled his shit-eating grin. "You gave us a good scare. I thought you were heading to the grand salvage yard in the sky. But doc was able to get you all closed up again. Finch will be in soon."

Strode started to sit up and immediately regretted it. He felt as though someone had opened the top of his head and filled it with a gallon of water. As he adjusted, it sloshed back and forth and made each of his movements feel as choppy as a sea storm.

"Whoa. I didn't say you could run a marathon."

Burklow stepped closer to the bed, carrying his array of scents along, and pushed Strode to the bed.

"Here. I think I can find the right button."

Burklow readjusted his cigar, scratched his head, and pressed the button shaped like a downhill. Strode's legs sank lower, and his back straightened. He felt like he was being carted away on a utility dolly. "Hmm. No that's not right."

Burklow paused to exhale the cigar smoke. He pressed the one at the top of the panel shaped like an "L." Strode's feet elevated, and his abdomen folded in.

Strode could see Burklow and the room better. The wall was an irritating bright-blue color that made his head feel even more atmospheric. A small cut-out window in the door reminded him of the slots correctional officers used to pass stale crackers and lard-loaded chili to inmates. And one of the lights above him flickered, not entirely, but just a single row of the three rod-shaped bulbs. It was enough to make fuzzy green and purple dots leap across the artless walls.

Strode wiggled his fingers and felt a tug in his wrist where they nestled the IV needle.

"Bu—"

A harsh weight squashed Strode's thought.

What the fuck?

Strode lifted one hand and stretched his fingers out. He watched them shake as though electricity was pumping through his veins.

He noticed a shadow outside the square window. Strode pointed to it and then waved forward.

"Settle down, Strode. Finch will be in in a minute. She's talking to the doctor."

Strode nodded. He was certain his panic was taking over his eyes. He probably looked like Vincent Price before he fell into his boiling vat of molten wax.

The thick, steel, prison-like door to his room opened. Finch came in with a tall man who wore his glasses at the bridge of his nose. He looked above the square frames and said, "Without speaking, giving me a thumbs-up or down. I need you to answer a few questions. Okay?"

Finch nodded, concern smeared across his furrowed eyebrows and tucked lip.

The confusion was making him anxious. Underneath the blanket, he curled all of his toes as hard as he could.

The doctor pulled up a round-topped swivel chair with no back to Strode's side. He pulled a pen from his pocket, put it in his mouth, and pulled it free from the cap. He tucked the cap on the end of the pen.

Strode flexed his toes up as far as they'd go.

"Okay, can you confirm for me, is your name Leonard Allen Strode?"

Finch and Burklow turned to one another. Strode wondered if they thought Leonard was weird, or if they had just expected something simpler like Ron or Barry.

Finch gave Strode a thumbs-up, with an encouraging nod that reminded him to be present. But the more he sat through Burklow fixing his damn chair and the doctor's question, the more impatient he became.

Strode returned Finch's thumbs-up, and the doctor said, "Good. Good. And were you born on the twenty-ninth of September in nineteen forty-eight?"

Strode gave a thumbs-up.

"You were born in Indianapolis, Indiana. Correct?"

Strode gave a thumbs-up.

"Okay. Good. Something harder now. Is George McGovern our president?"

Strode gave a thumbs down.

Come on, man.

The doctor asked a few more no-brainer questions and Strode proved his head wasn't full of goo.

"Okay. So, I think we got pretty lucky today here, Leonard."

Strode cringed, and Finch smiled, shaking her head like saying, *Let it go.*

"You were in your carotid sinus. It's a reflex of the carotid artery."

Strode raised his thick eyebrows and shook his head.

Meaning?

"Your throat will be sore for a few days, but we stabilized your blood pressure. There doesn't appear to be further bleeding on the brain. Some rest and resting your voice for the next week should help."

"Tha—"

The doctor wagged his off-putting, long finger at Strode.

Strode smiled and hoped it hid how bad he wanted to hit the guy.

"Thank you, doctor," Finch said.

* * *

Finch and Burklow laid it all out for Strode. Burklow went first.

"When Finch came to find me, I was already wandering through the woods. She heard me yelling for the kid."

Teddy.

"I got a message radioed in that said the Byers boy was missing. He rode his bike home from a friend's house yesterday and never made it," Burklow continued.

Byers?

Finch leaned into Strode. "The kid you found, that was the Byers boy, Marlene's little brother. He had some bleeding on his brain, but he was able to pull through. It'll be a long recovery, physically and mentally, but he should be okay."

Burklow wasn't calling for Teddy.

Strode began to wonder if the part about Teddy had been real at all.

But Finch put a hand on Strode's. "And the other boy, the one I—"

Burklow finished for her, "The other kid she shot."

Strode opened his mouth, and his partners both hushed him like crotchety librarians.

He needed to know where Teddy was; how much of what he saw was real. Was he even alive? Though she had only known Strode for a few days, Finch was already becoming incredibly in sync with his thoughts.

"You didn't imagine it, Strode. He's alive. He was in the woods."

Burklow pointed to the top of Strode's head. He raised his hand and cringed upon contact. There was an ultra-tender wound up there.

Then he remembered right as Burklow said it, "And the Blackwood kid damn near crushed your skull with a rock. Finch says he was winding up for the next pitch when she shot him."

Finch exhaled. Strode knew, no matter if that kid had killed him, Finch would always be sorry she shot him.

Her eyes were still as she said, "And then, Strode, you just got up. Your head was bleeding, but you kept going. The doctor said your adrenaline probably gave you more juice than even you thought you had."

Strode pointed to his throat.

Finch shrugged her shoulders. "I don't know. We were going to ask you. Could a kid do something like that?"

The light above no longer flickered.

Instead, it was as though there was a drain beneath him, and it was slowly emptying its illumination.

Strode remembered the golden eyes—how they seemed faded.

Whatever tried to rip out Strode's throat was too weak to do it. So, it nicked at him instead. That was why there was so much blood at the Blackwoods. Whatever had taken Arthur Blackwood's life that day at the Starling house had tried to do the same to him.

And Teddy tried to lure him to it.

Strode scribbled a signature in the air, and Finch hurried for a pen and paper.

TEDDY TOLD ME HE NEEDED HELP.

Strode turned the paper to Finch. She read it, her eyes widened, and she said, "It was him. What called Marlene, a girl ready for a night out to the woods. What called Derek Russell and wouldn't let him ignore it. What called Nate Williamson."

Burklow tugged his pants up and was trying to keep up.

Strode drew a cluster of trees and then a house sitting outside of it, and put "*SUBDIVISION.*" He drew a bike going through the woods and pointed to Burklow.

Finch turned to her mentor. "You said only the neighborhood kids went through the far entrance near the housing subdivision. Byers must've taken that path home and then Teddy—"

Burklow followed. "And then Teddy called him away too."

Strode gave the most inappropriate response to putting together the pieces of a multi-murder case—a thumbs-up.

Teddy had lured Marlene Byers, Derek Russell, and Nate Williamson. Russell had even logged it. Teddy had told them he needed help, just as he did him. And people responded to the poor boy in the woods.

The pain medicine was playing tug of war with Strode's ability to stay awake. He had questions. He wanted to talk to the Byers kid, though he probably couldn't. He wanted to get in a car and start tracking Teddy.

Strode closed his eyes and shook his head in disbelief. He was right. There was more to this case. But Strode was learning that being right wasn't always a rewarding thing, despite what marriage taught him. Being right burned a lot more than his pride.

Teddy, the missing boy from Indiana, was the cause of the disappearances here and God knows where else.

Before the Grade-A pain meds carried Strode into a restless night of nightmares and cold sweats, he tried to summarize the key point of their day, of their finding: *Those people didn't just disappear. Teddy Blackwood was a murderer. A vile, merciless killer.*

PART 3

THE MAPLE STREET MASSACRE

1

Teddy fell against a tree, and sweat dripped from his hairline. The air felt thin and bent on building in his lungs without exiting.

The shadow's golden eyes stood above him.

We have to keep moving, Teddy.

Teddy's head felt like an air balloon floating into the sky.

People are searching the woods. They'll find us.

Teddy knew the shadow was right. The cop got away. And that stupid woman who shot him. They would, without question, spill the beans about the lost boy from Indiana in the woods.

Teddy kicked his feet into the mud, but he couldn't lift his body. He groaned in pain. "It hurts so bad."

The shadow's hand stretched from its flat figure to a three-dimensional shape, reaching for Teddy. It was as though its complete form was conveniently tucked under a veil until needed.

The shadow's hand rested over Teddy's shoulder, and Teddy could feel the blood clot. He sighed a breath of relief.

"That feels better."

You're still hurt. I need more strength to heal you. We have to move.

Teddy dug his sneakers into the mud and used the tree to lift himself. He pushed on his side with the gunshot, and the wound became enraged. Teddy locked his jaw and gasped. "It stings."

I know.

"I need more, Shadow. It still hurts too much."

It had been a few hours since they had seen a waving flashlight or heard the shouts of Three Oaks police officers. But they couldn't be sure they weren't still out there.

We have to move now.

Teddy nodded and obeyed the shadow. They stayed away from the paths of the woods and wandered through the trees. It was getting dark. Teddy had lost track of time with his injury, but he knew if it was getting dark, they had been in the woods too long. Too long after being found.

Faint hints of the sunset shone between the trees, and within twenty minutes Teddy knew the woods would be dark. Since he had been with the shadow, his only sense of time was through the sun. So, he followed it through the woods, looking up at the sky between the green.

Then, Teddy brought his good hand to his nose, too afraid to raise the other. Something smelled awful.

"Ew, what is that?"

The shadow's eyes seemed to brighten.

Our lifeline.

"What do you mean? It smells li… uh. It's just awful."

The smell reminded Teddy of a time when he was younger in Oakhaven. He woke up forty-five minutes early for school because his mother screamed. Teddy ran to see what was wrong, and she had the back door wide open, standing in her underwear and a Beatles t-shirt, shooing an animal away with a broom. It sprayed this yellowish-green liquid, just missing his mother. The smell lingered for a week.

This was the same smell.

The shadow took the lead, and Teddy followed closely behind.

Your wound is too open, Teddy. Too tender. It could tear, and you could bleed again. I have to save you.

Teddy and the shadow had had many conversations about what the shadow had to do. And he was becoming less and less prone to arguing it or feeling too guilty. He wasn't sure what the shadow's plan was with the skunk, but he thought it best just to be appreciative.

Teddy nodded, "I know, Shadow. Thank you."

They followed the smell, and with each step the shadow came into its fuller form, growing four feet and giving some of the younger trees a run for their money in stature. Its hands emerged from the shadowed veil, and its fingers grew to inhuman lengths. Then, they curved and sharpened into claws.

The smell was stronger, and Teddy pinched his nose. He heard laughing. It sounded like two, maybe three younger guys. One shouted, "And I'm telling you, no matter how many dinners you buy her, or how many romance movies you sit through at the drive-in, Melissa is never going to give it up, man. She keeps her package tightly wrapped up in corduroy slacks and librarian sweaters."

They laughed.

Teddy could see the guys just on the other side of a brush of trees. The shadow was right. He was still hurt, badly. The light-headedness clung to him and made each step feel like his head was drifting away.

"Yeah, you're probably right. Maybe I'll try Annette. Here." The smaller of the two guys passed what looked like a home-made, fat cigarette to the other.

Teddy watched the burly guy give the other a nudge and said, "Don't worry, my sweet Danny boy. We won't let you leave high school a virgin."

Teddy turned to the shadow. "I can call them here one at a time. If one hears the other getting hurt, he may be afraid. Won't that keep you fuller longer?"

The shadow closed its golden eyes and shook its head. *No time, Teddy.*

The shadow put a skeletal hand to Teddy, as though it was telling a dog to stay. Teddy obeyed.

He watched from behind the tree as the shadow stepped into view. The burly one dropped the rolled "cigarette" to the ground, and just before he could scream the shadow took its claws and tore into the guy's throat.

When the other tried to run, the shadow slithered across the ground and then rose before him, standing nearly twenty feet tall. He repeated the motion.

Teddy came from behind the tree. The gurgling sound the boys made reminded Teddy of his father. Blood squirted between their fingers as they clutched at their torn throats. Though the shadow's throat swipe had been much cleaner then.

He lowered himself to the thicker guy, whose eyes were full of terror. Teddy pitied him only for a moment until he heard his friend stop choking on blood. This one *had* to die too. They couldn't risk someone else saying that Teddy was still in the woods.

Teddy searched the wooded floor and found a fallen branch. It was thin but sturdy. He snapped it in half and

took the jagged end. With his good arm, he shoved it into the guy's throat. He didn't raise it to stab again. Instead, Teddy grabbed the end that stuck into the air and twisted it. He turned it round and round as the guy made cut-off choking sounds until he felt it split through that back layer of skin and out the other side of his neck.

Blood spewed across Teddy's face and into his mouth. It tasted like pennies.

His hand went limp, and the wide eyes froze.

Teddy turned to the shadow. "Does that get us a little more?"

The shadow's golden eyes closed and opened. It was pleased.

It set its hand on Teddy's shoulder, and Teddy could feel the heat that was burning the shadow. The heat of hunger. But the beating pain of his wound rested. And Teddy wiped the guy's blood from his face, moving his injured arm just a little more than he could before.

2

———

Teddy and the shadow made it from the woods to the neighborhood that sat just outside it. They paused behind a house in a backyard when they saw a squad car rolling through. A chubby police officer with a cigar hanging from his lips crept along by himself. He shined a light on each house and in between them.

We need more, Teddy. Fast.

Teddy nodded. "I know. I have an idea."

Teddy waited for the police vehicle to reach the end of the road, and for the first time, he took the lead.

Before they moved away from his father, Teddy's mom always forgot to lock the back door at night. The next morning, his father would say, "Lila, the back door was unlocked all night."

His mother would laugh and say, "We live in sweet, simple, little Oakhaven."

Teddy had a feeling that in this town, surrounded by woods with just the one housing subdivision immediately nearby, people forgot to lock their doors too.

The first door Teddy tried was locked. He hopped down from the back patio and went next door. In the back was a well-kept garden with tomatoes, zucchini, and more vegetation that Teddy was careful not to disturb. His mother used to like to garden.

Teddy tiptoed up the cement steps from the back of the house. He opened the thick white screen door, and it didn't screech like the back door at the house in Indiana.

Teddy reached for the golden handle of the white-painted wooden door, and it proved his theory about people in small towns. It opened and showed a dark kitchen. A collage of pictures hung on the teal-green refrigerator across from the back door. Teddy stepped into the kitchen, eyeing both sides of it as he peered into the living room. The suede sofa was empty, and a knitted black blanket lay neatly across the back of it.

Teddy couldn't help but smile at the shag carpet. The familiarity of a home, something he hadn't known for the past year.

We have to get on with it, Teddy. Your pain will come back.

Teddy nodded, embarrassed by the way the reminder of home had distracted him so much.

They crept up the stairs, and Teddy noted the clock on a stand at the top pointed to 9:47 p.m. The day had gotten away from them. Teddy's dad always said, "Time flies when you're having fun." He wondered what the right word would be for the way time moved when you helped kill to stay alive. "Fun" wasn't fitting.

At the top of the stairs a dark green carpet split into three bedrooms and what Teddy assumed was a bathroom. The two rooms on the right were empty. They were neat in a way that felt as though their owners hadn't been there in a long time. Teddy wondered if that's how his bedroom in Oakhaven looked—clean but untouched. Or, if some other kid was in it now.

The last bedroom had a massive bookcase against the far wall, and just beside it was an open door that led to the master bathroom. Teddy could see the shadow's golden eyes reflect off the bedroom window. His eyes merged with the yellowed street lights outside.

Teddy stood back and waited for the shadow to move, but the shadow shook its head.

You can do it quickly. It has to be you. I don't have the strength.

Teddy noticed the spare, decorative pillows thrown to the floor. On the edge of the bed, just feet from Teddy, was an older man long into his retirement days. He snored with a croaking sound that reminded Teddy of his own grandfather falling asleep on the couch after his mother's Thanksgiving feast.

It's just like all the games we play, Teddy. I go, and then you go. It's your turn. Take your turn, Teddy.

Teddy grabbed the pillow on the floor and prayed to God that it would be quick, just as the shadow said. He placed it over the old man's face and put as much weight as he could onto it. Teddy used the other hand to hold him down if he started thrashing.

He felt movement underneath the pillow. The man's head tried to turn back and forth, and Teddy pressed harder, turning away and biting his lip. The shadow was right; the more he used his shoulder, the more the pain came back. It shot through Teddy's arm, and he began to feel feverish again. The person on the other side of the bed was still.

Almost, Teddy. Just a little longer.

Teddy waited until the movement beneath him ceased.

Just another moment. Just to be safe.

Teddy obeyed the shadow, though he felt worn out and nauseated.

Then, when Teddy removed the pillow from the man, he saw his lifeless eyes, just like the man's in the woods. Killing—whether watching or doing it himself—was hard. But something was satisfying in the way the eyes seemed to freeze at the peak of the person's fear—at the moment when both the body and the person knew death was just moments away.

Teddy turned toward the shadow and gave it the thumbs-up.

The shadow's arm stretched across the floor, onto the bed, and pointed to the other turned body.

That one too.

Teddy whispered, "Can't you do this one? My arm hurts so much."

Someone else spoke in a frantic hushed voice.

"I will be a better woman. I will sing in church and help at the soup kitchen. Grant me the means, and I will grant you my word. My soul. Please, God, don't take me yet. I'm not ready to go."

The woman kept her back to Teddy. Teddy knew what it was like to freeze in fear. The slamming doors in Indiana had done that to him several times.

You can do it, Teddy.

The shadow's eyes beamed into the window, and the woman shrieked, burying her head away.

"Please, you son of Satan, stay back. I have nothing for you. Stay back." The woman's hand fumbled around her nightstand until she found what she was looking for.

As Teddy came around the side of the bed, the woman thrust her fist at him. Dangling from it was a silver cross.

"Please, Lord. Can you hear me? Spare me. I grant you my word."

Teddy grabbed the coral-colored ceramic lamp beside her. Wincing in pain and grunting in agony, he raised the light over his head and smashed it into the woman's skull.

It took just the one hit for her calm.

Her hand fell beside the bed, and the cross fell to the floor.

For good measure, Teddy threw the shade from the lamp, used the smooth ceramic's edge, and beat into her tight curls once more.

He turned her on her side.

Yet again, he couldn't help but feel a rush when he saw the lifeless eyes.

Creating that stillness, just moments after frantic praying and pleading, made Teddy feel invincible, like a god.

3

___

Teddy felt torn. He had this rush, an energy, that he couldn't define. Was he proud of himself? Or did he feel extreme guilt? Was it satisfaction? Or was it anger?

You did well. We have to move.

The shadow placed a hand on Teddy's shoulder, and again he could feel the warmth of the shadow's hunger. The pinkness of the wound began to fade to scarred white. The blood felt less like it was orbiting the bullet and went on about its business elsewhere.

Teddy did a shoulder roll and was pleased that he was getting the rotating mobility back.

He patted the sweat on his forehead with his blood-doused shirt. The wetness smeared across his face.

He peeled the shirt off his back, and the pain in his arm reminded him it was still with him, though it was better.

Rotating it continuously was still tricky. Part of him was starting to hate the woman who shot him.

She cared about the other kid more than Teddy. People had always cared about something or someone else more than him. Maybe not his mother. And maybe not Ali. Teddy balled his fists. But everyone else. His dad cared more about

Amber, Amber cared more about his dad, and his grandparents cared more about their retirement home. Teddy wondered if Amber or his grandparents even missed him. He felt tears forming in his eyes. They blurred his vision as the wave of them built higher and higher to the center of his eye.

What is it?

Teddy shook his head. "Nothing. I guess—" A tear tried to fall. Teddy stopped, brushed it away in annoyance, and straightened up. "I suppose I miss my mom."

Teddy said it as though he was analyzing someone else, someone not in the room, rather than himself.

He thought of the little blonde girl who showed him through the woods and floated with him in the creek. "And, I guess, Ali too."

Teddy threw his bloodied shirt on the green carpet and opened the accordion closet doors. All the clothes in there were sweaters, sweater vests, and button-up shirts.

He went past the shadow and into one of the other bedrooms. One had a rocket poster on the wall that Teddy hadn't been able to see from the hall. It was on the far side across from the bed. Behind those closet doors, he found t-shirts just a little too big for him. Teddy grabbed a black one and held it up. On the front was a yellow and red graphic of a man's face. He had gusty hair that Teddy thought was perfectly rock 'n' roll. It was Jimi Hendrix, one of his mother's favorites.

We have to go.

Teddy nodded and went into the bathroom. He looked in the mirror, surprised by how much blood had stuck to his face. The way it grabbed onto the tiny hairs of his eyebrows made them look like part of a Halloween costume. Teddy wetted one finger under the water and dragged it across the side of his cheek. The dried blood parted like the Red Sea did for Moses. *Miraculous power,* Teddy thought. *Shameful, yes. But miraculous.*

Teddy scrubbed the rest of the blood off his face. It was under his nails and in his hair. He was surprised at how fast the stuff dried. It didn't want to drip off Teddy, like it wanted to stay with the person who had freed it from its skin entrapment. He watched the pink color spiral down the drain's mouth and felt accomplished. Then, he remembered the wound in his shoulder. It was better but still scabbed and bloody, so Teddy dipped his shoulder in the sink and washed it too.

Teddy grabbed his old Yankees shirt from the floor and went down the stairs. He tried not to look at the photos on the fridge. He didn't want to know anything about the people he had killed. His moods, his thoughts on what he and the shadow did, were too wishy-washy as it was. Teddy wasn't sure he could handle any added complexity.

Teddy knew the shadow still needed more and fast. *Think of it as a game,* the shadow had said. Well, to win a game, you had to have a strategy. You had to be creative.

Before Teddy went out the screen door at the back of the house, he grabbed a jagged-edged bread knife sitting atop a Bundt pan on the stove.

Attached to the back of the house, just beside the back door, Teddy noticed a green coiled garden hose. He went to the edge of the yard and saw the neighbor had a nearly identical red garden hose, though it seemed to be far longer. He tossed the breadknife aside into a row of shrubs for safe-keeping. He had an idea.

With the shadow's watchful eyes behind him, Teddy went through the backyards of the houses on Sycamore Street,

right where the Byers boy had ridden his bike, and pulled the garden hoses around to the front. Each of them let running water pour into the streets. It puddled well, with only one storm drain at the end of the road.

Teddy turned to the shadow. "Sometimes in games, like poker, you use other people's hands to help you win. Maybe even take out one of their opponents too."

The shadow's eyes opened and closed as it nodded.

"Do you have enough in you to get those power lines down?" Teddy pointed above at the double wiring that connected post to post down the quiet, little street.

Teddy stepped up to the porch of his first kills of the night, knowing they wouldn't come down if they heard him outside the front door.

He couldn't help but feel giddy when the boom of the first fallen powerline hit the pavement. The shadow slithered like a snake to the top of the wooden pole and tugged at the wires, spreading them out in the pooling water.

Another fell, just missing the siding of a two-story home. It slammed into a plastic slide in the front yard, and the burnt smell suffocated the nighttime air. The cables spread like eels. *Electric eels,* Teddy thought.

He watched as windows throughout the line of homes on both sides of the streets illuminated. He inched back toward the house he had already entered and screamed as loudly and hysterically as he could, "Help me! Somebody! Please help me!"

Teddy tucked into the shrubs next to the porch. The cables coiled along the far side of the street's sidewalk and the center. One of the electric eels even slithered into the edge of a yard.

A young man with sleek and bright blond hair responded to Teddy's cries. He came running into the street, his eyes alert and desperate to find the source of the cries. He opened his mouth as he took another step, but whatever he was prepared to shout was lost to the most horrific scream Teddy had ever heard.

The shadow's eyes beamed brighter in the shrubs. It kneaded its claw-like fingers into Teddy's shoulder and suffocated the soreness.

Two more neighbors came rushing to the aid of the first fallen. One man ran ahead of the other, dodging a strand of cables, while the other ran right into the downed line at the end of his yard, his bare foot splashing into the water. Teddy could smell how fast the jolts cooked through that neighbor's fatty frame.

The other man, slightly older than the rest, his ponytail swaying with each step, was still going. Teddy wondered if this was what it was like for hunters, watching the animals scramble after the first kill.

The men screamed in unison as their skin broiled and their hair fizzed, but the ponytail guy kept going. Teddy couldn't tell if the man's strategy was admirable or plain irritating.

Garage doors slid open, windows opened, and people from the nearby streets flooded the electric avenue. One woman convulsed, wailing her arms and twisting her neck as the electric surge shot through her body. Her marshmallow-shaped foam rollers in her hair blazed with sporadic flames. She ran in circles, screaming before ultimately falling beside a man in a stained tank-top.

The smell was unlike anything Teddy had ever smelled before. It was a mix of melting skin, burnt hair, and smoking grass. Before Teddy knew it, he counted a whopping nine people either convulsing or roasting on the street.

Just as Teddy began to feel nauseated by that part of him that tried to imagine what dying like that would be like, the shadow pulled Teddy toward it.

Its eyes were brighter than Teddy had ever seen before. Their golden hue was nearly a brilliant white.

Well played. You are a worthy opponent.

Teddy smiled, beaming with validation.

The shadow's hand traced the site of Teddy's gunshot wound, and Teddy felt something roll down his spine and to the top of his pants.

Teddy reached for it and found a warm piece of metal laced with his blood's thickness.

It was the bullet. His game worked. His turn worked.

The smoke cloud grew and lurked into the edge of Warren Woods. Sirens echoed on the far side of the trees.

We have to move, Teddy. Through the back. Move.

With a proud smile on his face and the breadknife in hand, Teddy obeyed.

4

Teddy and the shadow used the chaos to blend in. The screams were horrific and uninterrupted, and the noise fueled Teddy's rush.

He and the shadow maneuvered through the backyards, over the fences, and just barely past one territorial German shepherd. Teddy could see its sharp teeth as it snarled at them. He wondered if the dog could see the shadow, or if it could only sense it.

It had been a while since Teddy had seen a dog. The shadow saw it as an immediate threat and raised its hand to the dog's throat, ready to claim it just as it had Teddy's father. His father had hurt his mother, stampeded her with his rage. The dog was guilty only of doing its job.

Teddy yelled, "No, Shadow!"

The shadow froze, its long bony fingers already curved and prepared to use its recharged power.

"Just hurry up. We can get past it," Teddy said.

The shadow's hand fell within its two-dimensional form. *Alright.*

The German shepherd growled and tried to take a bite of Teddy's foot that dangled on its side of the fence. He pulled it up too quickly and fell flat on his back in the neighboring yard.

The shadow's blaring white eyes looked down on him.

"I'm fine." Teddy sat up and brushed the dirt from his shirt.

"Let's get back into the woods. Who knows how long these fences go on."

The shadow hesitated, hearing the sound of sirens mixed in with the agonized cries, and Teddy understood. How could they be certain those sirens weren't separate from those responding to the electric madness? How could they be certain the cops from the woods weren't in there at that very moment, walking the trails and searching for him?

"We have to move fast. I know. But it's been a few hours. Hopefully, if they did search the woods, they've gone by now."

The shadow's eyes closed and opened as it nodded.

They turned away from the line of backyards and instead clung to the edge of the woods. They continued past the housing subdivision, and Teddy peered through to see that the storm drain was obstructed by a fat woman in a neon green robe.

The sirens made Teddy feel a little uneasy, but nothing could trump his new sense of validation and righteousness.

Then, just a few feet on the other side of them, Teddy heard the crackling of dry leaves further into the woods.

Teddy's heart hammered. He hurried to a towering tree and pressed himself against it, hiding the moonlight's glimmer against his bread knife.

A guy came from one of the main trails that he and the shadow had "hunted" on. However, this guy had to have gone off-path a turn or two to reach the housing subdivision. He was wearing the tiniest red shorts Teddy had ever seen on a grown man. Down the sides were two reflective silver strips. Teddy pressed his back harder into the rough bark of his hiding spot.

The guy took another step forward, and Teddy could see he was alone. His first instinct was to charge at him using his new knife, but the shadow was right. They needed to move.

"What the hell is going on?" the man in the itty-bitty shorts said. The flames grew toward the sky, and Teddy imagined one of the houses had caught fire.

A piercing scream followed an enormous puff of smoke, and the man took off toward the commotion. Teddy grinned. If they were lucky, still being so close to the killing field, the shadow would get to feed on the energy of that man's death too.

The shadow's bright white eyes mirrored the moon as it broke through the leaves toward the end of the row of trees. Teddy stopped, nearly tripping over himself when it appeared as though the shadow's eyes had fallen to the ground.

He turned and found the shadow's white eyes still beaming behind him. Teddy reached down and used his thumb to wipe the dirt from the round, white rock. He continued through the edge of the woods with his find in hand when he stumbled on another. And then another. And then a whole pile of the white rocks.

Another scream split through the trees and then a chorus of them. The sirens made the growing tragedy sound theatrical.

Teddy picked up each of the rocks he found and stuffed them in his pockets.

Do they mean something to you, Teddy?

They reached the woods' edge and stood on top of a hill, looking over an ill-lit curved road. Teddy pointed to the tattered welcome sign, which read "Welcome to Pricetown" with the sharp end of his bread knife.

With hungry eyes fixed on the town, Teddy said to the shadow, "The rocks don't mean anything to me, but soon, they will to them."

PART 4

COUNTING CASUALTIES

1

_____

Strode jumped when he heard what he could only imagine was a nurse's supply cart slamming into his door. He had no idea how long he was out, but the pain in his head had died down. He wished he could say the same for his throat. The previously exposed inner flesh still felt raw and seared, as though he'd swallowed a shot of bleach.

He sat up in his bed and was relieved that he could do that too.

The voices outside grew louder with panic in them. They spoke in frantic commands, and he heard one phone ringing, answered only by another ring further down the hall. The yellow lights in the hall were flashing in a tense series, suggesting panic from patients calling on their nurses to explain.

Radios flicked on in the nurse's station and migrated down the hall with a speed that felt as manic as everything else. Strode only caught every few words from the broadcaster, "Fire... smoke... Warren Woods... missing... dead."

The kid. Teddy.

Strode climbed from his bed, tugging the clear tube from his forearm, and nearly fell to the floor.

The pounding in his head returned.

Strode allowed his knees to fall to the cold tile floor and felt his hospital gown flare open in the back. He hoped he was wearing underwear; otherwise, he was guaranteeing anyone who walked in a good look at a full moon.

On all fours, Strode crawled to the radiator. He tapped the white-painted iron to make sure it wasn't going to burn the shit out of his hands and add to his injuries. It was warm, so he pressed on it, waiting for the heat to intensify. It didn't. Strode wrapped his hands around the radiator, and the grooves dug into his palms.

Strode lifted himself to the window and twisted the rod to open the blinds. The sight below took his breath away. Above the trees in the distance was a haunting, orange haze. Was Warren Woods on fire? The smoke seemed to emerge from the further side of the trees.

Trying to make each of his steps calculated but quick, he scrambled to his clothes. He sat on the edge of the bed, held his jeans in both hands, and shimmied them over his thin legs. Strode managed to get them just under his thighs and flexed his legs to hold them in place while he threw his cotton tee over his head.

He flinched at the shock of his soreness but kept going. Gritting his teeth, he looped his fingers in his belt loops and did a small leap into his jeans. He almost didn't stick the landing, but he caught himself on the edge of the bed.

Pausing only a moment to regain his stability, he grabbed the pain pills on his nightstand and hurried out of his room.

The frenzy outside reminded Strode of his high school after the news of President Kennedy's assassination. Only half the people running around looked like Strode feared he did when climbing on the radiator with flowy gown in the front and bare ass in the back.

Nurses were trying to calm patients while others were hysteric, listening to the broadcast. Strode used the chaos to blend in. He wasn't sure how far he was from his car, but he would figure that out. First, he just had to make it out unseen. He pulled his shirt up, attempting to conceal the bandage on his neck. A nurse ran past him in a hurry and did a double-take before moving on. He remembered he had a large chunk of gauze on his head.

He peeked into a room where the door was wide open. An old woman sprawled on the bed, an array of cards on the nightstand behind her. He had a feeling that if she didn't wake up to all of this screaming, she wouldn't at all.

The nurse's station was at the end of the hall, just before the front door. Strode moved quickly through the commotion, knocking over trays full of little cups of pills. He saw a bottle of hydrogen peroxide and some cotton balls and stuffed them in his pocket. He could feel his body telling him that he was moving too fast, too soon. But he had to get out there. He had to see what was going on because, in his gut, Strode knew it had something to do with Teddy Blackwood.

A nurse spoke on the phone at the nurse's station. She was young, maybe a little younger than Strode, and her dark hair was tucked neatly under her nurse's cap. As she placed her hand over her bright, red lips, Strode saw her fingernail polish matched. She screamed into the phone and then let it dangle by the spiral cord. He could hear a muffled voice on the other side.

Another nurse rushed to the screaming nurse's aide. "What's happened, Susan? What's the matter?"

The woman with the matching red nails and lips pointed past Strode, and he raised his eyebrows.

Then Susan shouted, "Charles! Charles is dead! He…" She heaved in and out as her lip quivered in panic and sorrow. "He was running in the woods. He saw the smoke."

Susan fell into the other nurse's chest and sobbed. "He's dead, Saundra! He's gone!"

Strode watched Susan's body shake and felt a tingling disturbance in his face. At first, it was sympathy. Strode's first thought was, *Maggie would've done the same thing. Maggie would've gone to see what had happened and try to help if she could. Maggie would've left the woods and followed the flames.*

Left the woods.

The fire wasn't in the woods. It was past it on the other side, where the Byers boy had come through on his bike before Teddy got him.

The other side, where Teddy was now collecting casualties.

Kills to avenge the one Strode had taken from him.

He had to get over there.

Above the crying nurses was a cubby with a folded letterman jacket and a red baseball cap. Strode grabbed the hat, stuffed some cotton balls on his wound, and went out the front door, unnoticed.

He could immediately smell the fumes from the fire. It was far more than the smell of burning wood or even a house fire. This fire reeked, causing a chill to roll through Strode— one that crept into his ear and whispered, "It's flesh."

Strode leaned against a brick column that supported the entry wing's awning. He shoved one of the pain pills in his mouth and gave himself a moment to stop his head from spinning.

He traced the lettering on his "borrowed" hat with his fingers. He felt the length of the letter L and the curve of an S.

Shit. I grabbed a fucking Cardinals hat. I don't understand Michigan.

Strode adjusted the hat on his head and scoffed. Then he pushed off the bricks and began to follow the haze.

He could feel his feet stumbling beneath him, wobbling with each step. He wondered if he had taken one too many pills, or if his head was worse than he thought.

He didn't care. He kept moving, using whatever he could to keep himself up. He made it to one nurse's car and then the next before reaching a shitty, splintering bench.

His head pounded more and more with each step he took. *Come on. Come on.*

Then a set of headlights sped to the side of the bench. It was a bright, shiny red car, and the passenger cranked the window down.

An officer with the chubbiest fingers holding a thick cigar poked his head out of the window and said, "You crazy son of a bitch." He turned to the driver. "Well, you nailed it. He busted out, alright."

Finch poked her head around Burklow. "Figured we ought to grab you before we found you facedown somewhere. Get in."

Strode opened the back door of his own Ford Pinto, smiling as he obeyed.

2

It wasn't long before the sight of the smoke ahead smothered the lightheartedness in Strode's Pinto. It filled the car the way ash fills lungs, uninvited but overpowering.

The closer they got to the backend of Warren Woods and the neighborhood where the Byers boy lived, the thicker the haze became. And the smell. Nauseating didn't do it justice. It was foul—unsettling in the grimmest of terms—and he knew they were smelling death.

Police cars and fire trucks blocked the main street of the neighborhood, which was Maple Street. Flames engulfed a house on the left side of the road. The shrubs just off the front porch and around the side of the house were on fire too.

They got out of the car as another police officer met them at the Pinto. "Stay back! Back!"

The man came closer and recognized Finch and Burklow. He tipped his hat. "Sorry, sir. I didn't recognize you in this." He motioned to the red Pinto.

Burklow nodded.

Strode and Finch stood beside Burklow, eyeing the scene. Strode pulled his shirt over his nose. The smell of burnt flesh, burnt plastic, and whatever the fuck else was on fire was worse than the bodies they'd found in the woods.

Charred bodies littered Maple Street. Some of them were burnt right to the bones while others had burns bad enough to kill but stopped before all of the skin was gone.

Finch pointed to the coils on the ground and Strode followed her finger to the melted, colored vinyl. Several of the yards and driveways had the same melted or blackened colors. Finch grabbed her flashlight from her belt and pointed it to the ends of the drives.

"Garden hoses," she said.

Her light glistened in the water, flashing across a body at the end of the road. The man lay prone with flares of black, pink, and red skin around the side of his face and down his neck.

Firefighters worked to recover the electric cords and cut off the power source. In the areas cleared of the wiring, men in thick black gloves, maybe anti-shock Strode thought, collected the bodies. Strode counted at least seven victims.

The fire in the house to the left of them climbed through the home.

Two firefighters cleared the cords from the bottom drive and hosed right into the front siding.

Burklow asked the other officer, "Is everyone out of there?"

The officer shrugged. "I'm not sure. One of the neighbors said a retired couple lives there. Their kids weren't home. They don't live there anymore."

"Is the car in the garage?" Strode asked.

"I'm not sure. My job is to keep people back. One wrong step and you're fried chicken."

Finch pointed to a man sitting on the ground on the other side of the street. He sat at the far end of a yard, one that was fortunate not to catch fire or be damaged by the fallen lines. A medic wrapped a blanket around him.

Finch looked at Strode, and he knew she was asking if they wanted to check it out. His throat still sore as hell, Strode nodded.

"Burklow, we're going to talk to a survivor."

Burklow nodded, watching the flames with helpless, solemn eyes.

Strode had been standing too long. His feet were wobbly, and his head felt as though it would do anything to detach from his body.

Finch turned and said, "You really should be resting. You know?"

He responded with a sarcastic smile, and as though he'd argued back, Finch said, "I know. I know. You couldn't miss all of this."

When they got to the other side of Maple Street, Finch snapped her fingers at the intersection and pointed to the ground. Strode began to sit across from the trembling man, and Finch sat next to him.

The smoke was thick, and Strode felt as though its hands were tightening around his throat.

Finch's eyes were red as she studied the man, who didn't even seem to notice two officers sitting in a circle with him.

"Excuse me, sir?" Finch said.

The man's irritated eyes blinked multiple times, pulling himself from a far-off gaze. He looked at Finch. "I'm sorry. Yes?"

The man looked unscathed, aside from the trauma all over his face. That, Strode was afraid, would last far longer than a burn.

Finch straightened up. "My name is Officer Finch." She motioned to Strode. "And this is Officer Strode."

The man nodded, returning his gaze beyond the circle, beyond the fire. "Jason."

Finch looked at Strode with careful eyes. "Hi, Jason. First, are you alright? I saw a medic with you, but is there anything else we can get you?"

The man shook his head and pulled the tribal-patterned blanket closer to his shoulders. Ironically, Strode thought those kinds of blankets were the ones he used in high school at bonfires.

"Okay, then," Finch continued. "My partner and I are investigating what happened here tonight. Can you tell me what you remember?"

Jason's eyes stared straight ahead as he spoke the most monotone monologue Strode had ever heard. "I heard the powerline fall. I heard it crash into the road. The loud slam took my breath away before I even opened my eyes. Then I heard a scream."

Finch nodded, "Yes. I'm sure that must've been awful hearing that as your neigh—"

"No," Jason said. He turned to Finch, and Strode could see his hair was far longer than it seemed sitting across from him. He had a dark ponytail, suspended with a dark red rubber band. Subtle traces of silver served as soft highlights throughout his hair. Maggie might've called this guy, "A silver fox." She had a thing for guys with ponytails. Plus, Jason seemed to be the artsy type. His shirt had an old forgotten painting on the front of it that Strode just barely recognized, and the sleeves had an array of pastels, blended like watercolors.

Finch waited for the man to elaborate. When he didn't, she asked, "You didn't hear your neighbors screaming?"

Jason nodded. "Of course, I did. I think I'll remember

that for the rest of my life. But a different scream came before theirs. Their screams were instant cries of pain and shock. They didn't shout words. They screamed in agony. But the first scream that came just after the powerlines fell cried for help."

Finch turned to Strode, and he knew they were thinking the same thing. He gave her a quick, impatient wave that said, *Ask already*.

"Jason, could you tell what age this person was? The one who cried for help?"

Jason finally brought his eyes to the horror of the scene. They still hadn't gathered all of the bodies. Four men stood in the front yard of the burning home, watching as the house's frame began to give out.

"All of them..." Jason stopped, swallowed, and started again, "All of them were so uneasy after what happened to the Byers boy and what happened to his sister and the others. So, when they heard a kid cry for help, they all ran to help."

Jason dropped his chin to his chest, and a wet string dangled from his nose. He used the blanket to wipe it away. "And they paid for it."

Strode's eyes were full of determination. It was as he thought.

Strode pushed on his throat with three fingers, "Di... Did anyo—"

Strode shook his head in frustration. His voice still wasn't ready, but he and Finch seemed to have their antenna pointed at the same station.

"Did anyone see the kid?" Finch asked.

"No, but it was a boy. I'm sure of it," Jason said.

So was Strode.

He rose to his feet and heard Finch thank Jason.

They huddled a few feet away as they put the pieces together. Strode pointed to the flooded street, though they had cleared the body blocking the storm drain.

"Right," Finch said. "He set up the hoses to try and flood the streets. Or even just wet them, I suppose is all it would take. But the powerlines? How does a kid do that? I've never seen anything like it."

Finch stepped closer to one fallen just inside the scene. She looked at the poles and saw split wood near one's base. The other, near its center. At the end of the road, one was still intact, with only the cords missing.

Strode couldn't explain the golden eyes he saw with Teddy. Nor could he remember if those were an illusion or reality. It could've been a fear-created manifestation—something his mind conjured as the realization of what Teddy Blackwood had become sank in.

For now, Strode only nodded, as though Finch were reviewing the facts rather than working with him to piece them together.

Finch was forgetting one other thing. The pain in Strode's throat and the ache in his head reminded him.

But just as he thought it, Finch said it, "How could he do this with a gunshot wound?"

Strode nodded, thinking again of the golden eyes. It had to be some kind of source. He had been down and out with an injury to his head and throat, but Finch had shot Teddy in the shoulder. He imagined the kid would need immediate attention, hell, emergency surgery.

Strode and Finch headed back to Burklow, who had his ass on the Pinto's front hood. When they came up behind him, he kept his eyes on the house and said, "I knew them, you know. Their daughter, Jennifer, used to babysit once a month so Sarah and I could go out. Their son was always a good kid too."

Finch put a hand on Burklow's shoulder. "We don't know that they're in there."

Finch did many things with brilliance and skill, but Strode thought she couldn't have sounded any more unsure of her own words than in that moment.

"Ten thirty-five. Ten thirty-five. Surrounding units. Surrounding units, ten thirty-five. Pricetown. Pricetown. Ten thirty-five."

Burklow pushed past his young partners and threw his top half into the open window of a squad car. Burklow's sweaty, chubby face was only inches from the cop sitting in the vehicle.

Burklow shouted into the radio, "Ten nine. Dispatcher, ten nine."

The woman on the other end repeated her message, "Ten thirty-five. Ten thirty-five. Surrounding units. Ten thirty-five. Pricetown. Pricetown. Ten thirty-five."

Burklow pulled himself from the squad car and pointed the finger at the officer inside. "Stay here. Help any way you can. And you find a way to reach me if the Mayweathers made it out. Got it?"

Still in shock from Burklow's response to the call, the officer could only nod.

Burklow hopped into the driver's seat of the Pinto and yelled, "Finch, Strode, we're going to Pricetown. Let's move."

Finch and Strode piled into the vehicle. Strode's mind was racing. Teddy had killed at least seven people that night. And now, there was an emergency in a town only a few miles past Three Oaks.

Strode wasn't sure how Teddy was doing it all, but he knew a few things for sure. Teddy was dangerous. Teddy was killing. And Teddy was moving.

Finch put a hand on the back of her seat and gave Strode a look with narrowed eyes and furrowed eyebrows that said she knew it too.

3

Ten thirty-five meant an emergency. Strode crossed his fingers and prayed to a god he didn't believe in that they would respond to anything but more murders.

They hadn't called it that yet, but Strode knew what they had just come from was calculated death. It was murder, and Teddy Blackwood was the killer.

Burklow was sweating an excessive amount, even more so than usual. The smell filled the car, and Strode wondered if it would ever leave the driver's seat.

Finch filled Burklow in on what they learned from Jason. "It wasn't just a fire. It was arson," Finch said. "It was a premeditated massacre. We asked the only survivor who responded to the screams. His name was Jason. Jason said after the powerline fell, a kid, a boy, cried for help."

Burklow nodded. "He lured them like the others."

Finch nodded, and then directed Burklow.

"There are sirens ahead." She put her head out the window. "Take a right at this light. We'll see the lights."

Strode found that Pricetown was even smaller than Three Oaks, which he hadn't thought was possible. They had a single gas station right on the edge of the town followed by a tiny trailer park, though "collection" was maybe the better word. Strode counted five trailers, and one looked like they could combust at any moment.

The streets were ill-lit with dim, dark yellow lights. Every other had burned out, and the houses were almost as run-down as the trailers. Strode looked out the rear windows and tried to determine where the hell anyone could work in a town like Pricetown.

They passed a movie theatre that seemed only to show one film at a time, and the current poster was from a Vincent Price movie that was nearly twenty years old. Is that where the town name came from? Strode assumed not. The town looked too old.

When they took a right and then a left at the next intersection, Strode saw a line of locally owned shops. The pharmacy doubled as a convenience store followed by a soda shop, a bakery, a grocery, and a bar. And, as Finch said, they saw the blue and red police lights.

An older officer, even older than Burklow, met them at the front of the Pinto. The man's deep wrinkles around his lips may have suggested he knew how to smile long ago. Just a few white hairs clung to his head and nestled on top of dark brown spots. All the hair the man had left hung from his chin in a scraggly, white beard.

The man stretched out a hand, and Burklow took it with a clear sense of discomfort. Burklow stepped aside, revealing his investigative young duo, Finch and Strode.

"I brought some help. This is, uh... Finch."

Finch reached out a hand and said, "Officer Finch, sir."

Burklow nodded. "Right. Right. And this is Officer Strode."

The man held his stern, frowny face and simply pulled the wooden "Do Not Pass" sign aside. On the other side was a red Chevy truck. In front of it was a pale, palm-up hand flat on the ground—a body.

The Three Oaks trio walked around the front of the vehicle and saw a young man in his early twenties with round glasses and dark curly hair. Another wild card, the glasses were sitting neatly beside the man's head. And over his eyes were two bright white rocks.

His throat had a deep slice straight across it, and his dark green shirt had growing black spots—blood.

Finch turned to the old officer. "Did somebody count the stab wounds?"

The frowning officer narrowed his eyes at the petite officer but didn't answer her.

"Sir?"

Burklow shouted, "For the love of God, Richard, answer her."

The man mumbled, "Six."

Finch nodded, understanding that this man did not want her help.

Strode noticed how fresh the blood seemed to be. He pressed on his throat and let out a hoarse, "Others?"

The man nodded. "That's why we called in neighboring officers. Our squad is all tied up at the farming strip. Three more just like this down there."

Finch's head snapped toward Richard. "All with the white rocks over their eyes too?"

The man didn't even look at Finch as he nodded.

Finch ignored him and said, "But why? What are we missing?"

Strode knelt to the man's face, examining the rocks. "Any witnesses?"

Richard nodded and spat into the gravel road. "Yes. The guy who called it in said he saw a kid leaning over the body. It was a man at the bar. He thought he heard shouting once, but the music was loud, so the guy said he tossed back another drink. But then the scream was louder. When he looked out the window, he saw the blood, and a kid taking off the guy's glasses. He ran for the phone to call the police, and when he came back, the kid was gone."

Burklow nodded and mumbled, "Of course he was."

Richard didn't pay Burklow any mind as he kept going. "The guy from the bar works at the pharmacy too. He said he's never seen this kid before. We got the call about a body found at the first of the farms ten minutes earlier followed by the second five minutes later. It's like we were right behind him as he was doing it. It's maddening."

It's Teddy.

Richard kicked the gravel and spat again. Then, he stuffed a thick wad of chewing tobacco on the inside of his lower lip.

"Then, this poor guy."

The man turned to Burklow. "Sarah knew him. You know?"

Burklow nodded.

"She was friends with his mother, Natalie."

Finch turned her head, and her eyebrows raised, telling Strode she knew the name too.

Burklow shrugged, seeming to fold into himself and neglect the body on the ground. "Sarah was friends with everyone."

Richard smiled, but not one that seemed sincere, and said, "But not with her good ole dad."

Finch intervened. "Richard, did the man in the bar describe the kid?"

Richard stared Finch down with a coldness that pissed Strode off to no end. He got up from the gravel and pressed on his throat, "Answer her."

Strode could taste blood. He wished he could've added, "You racist prick."

"No. The guy was wasted. All he said was that he saw the kid take the guy's glasses off. Hell, he was so far gone, he told me he saw golden cat eyes watching the kid as he did it. When I asked if he saw anyone else with the kid, he said no, just the yellow eyes."

That detail confirmed what all of them knew. Teddy Blackwood was there, he had killed, and yet again, he was lost in the wind.

4

Strode hardly slept through the night. The horror of the past twenty-four hours burned bloody and brightly each time he closed his eyes. He spent the night staring at the ceiling, avoiding the unmistakable smell of bleach and not daring to turn away. After what he had seen in his past few days in Three Oaks and Pricetown, he was confident that a run-in with Jackie Warren would send him over the edge.

Though Strode wondered if he was still on the right side of the edge. Or had Teddy already pulled him over? Was Strode so distracted by the chaos that he didn't even notice?

And once in the night, right when Strode's eyes began to close, he heard the clown. "You look like shit. Barely made it out alive, huh?"

Strode locked his eyes on the ceiling tile above him.

The clown laughed, and Strode could hear the mushy wetness of its bloodied jaw detaching from its saber teeth followed by the tapping of its feet as it laughed and hopped from one foot to the other. He imagined its paper hat popping on and off its head. Strode pulled a spare pillow from the basket beside the couch and wrapped it under his head and around his ears. He could still hear the faint chants from the clown. "Strode had a stroke. Strode had a stroke."

Strode wondered why the rocks? It was different from anything Teddy had done before, but then again, so was the Maple Street massacre. Before, Teddy had stayed hidden. And if he and the golden eyes were killing, as they had been in Michigan, which he was certain they were, they did a few here and there and then moved. But, on Maple Street, Teddy intended to kill several people and fast. It felt like more than vengeance on Strode and Finch for saving the Byers boy from his spiderweb. It felt cocky, but at the same time, urgent. Then, he went to the next town over and killed four more people. Again, with a different strategy than the last. And this time, Teddy left a calling card.

Teddy wanted the validation of being feared. It was like if they were going to see him, he wanted them to see him as something powerful.

Strode's head was pounding, and he could feel the cotton matting to the wound. He thought about showing it to Finch, but he had a feeling she would make him go back to the hospital. He grabbed the Saint Louis hat he had worn the night before and slid it over his head, wincing as the fabric rubbed on the raw skin.

When he went into the bathroom, inside Sarah's shop, he was relieved to see Burklow had taken the clown away. The smell of bleach came again, and Strode was quick to tell himself it was just from Sarah's supplies. But, when he opened the bathroom door, he kept his eyes closed and felt his way to the stairs.

When he came up the spiral staircase, Finch was already there, coffee in hand, with case reports and notes spread across the table. Some even seemed to be color-coded. *This woman is nonstop*, Strode thought. Though, he was learning, so was he.

"Is Burklow awake yet?" Strode asked.

Finch didn't lift her eyes from the gory spread before her as she said, "He is now. I told him to hurry up and get through the shower. We've got a lot of work to do."

Strode wasn't sure where that work began. So, he sat at the table and walked himself through the cases from Three Oaks. He saw at the start of Finch's timeline were two handwritten notes. *Warrens at the Starling house*, and *Blackwoods at the Starling house.*

At the center of the table was a list of names from the people identified from the Maple Street massacre. Finch worked fast.

"I got them from the coroner this morning. Nine so far."

Strode cocked his head to the side, "So far?"

"We haven't heard back on the Mayweathers yet. I'm sure they know but want to let the forensic odontologists pull dental records to confirm. That would make eleven."

Strode nodded. Finch thought they were in their home, and he was willing to bet they were too.

"How are you feeling?" Finch asked.

Strode pressed on his throat, and today he could manage short answers if he didn't put the full pressure of talking above a whisper. "Better."

Finch smiled. "Good, you little runaway."

Strode could sense a sort of awkwardness in Finch. He understood. She was freaked out. They all were. And as he had been for the past year, Finch was determined to get answers.

Burklow came down the hall and didn't say a word to anyone until he filled his coffee mug and took a few sips.

Finch spoke up first. "I think someone has to be working with Teddy. This is just a lot for a kid to do all on his own."

The men agreed.

"And to do all that walking from the woods, through the neighborhood, and then to Pricetown. It just doesn't make sense. But the guy from the bar said he saw a kid and—" Strode said.

Finch finished for him, "And Jason too, on Maple Street, heard a kid cry for help."

Burklow turned back to the coffee pot, reached for a mug in the cabinet above, and filled it. He walked the mug to Strode, who was afraid of eating or drinking anything.

Strode sipped the coffee, and the pain didn't miss the chance to remind him it was still there.

"Strode, you need to take your pain medicine. And later this afternoon, we'll take you to get your bandages changed," Finch ordered.

Strode didn't argue. He didn't even want to use his limited voice on an argument that Finch had won before it even began.

"So, now what?" Burklow asked.

"I say we go back to Maple Street. We look everywhere. Backyards, the Mayweathers', the edge of the woods, everywhere Teddy might've been. Maybe we can figure out where he was going next."

Strode whispered, "And who he might've been working with."

5

———

Strode, Finch, and Burklow piled into the red Ford Pinto. They still weren't willing to let Strode drive, which he supposed was fair. No one had ever driven that car except for him, and in just a few days, Finch and Burklow, strangers to him last week, both had.

It was weird to call them strangers now, especially Finch, who seemed to have her own secret passage to Strode's thoughts. He wished they'd talked more at the academy. In all honesty, Finch had just intimidated the hell out of him.

And she still did. But now, he expected it. He needed it to keep going.

Burklow was anxious. Strode could tell from the back seat as Burklow white-knuckled the steering wheel. A cigarette hung from between his lips, but it was more like an accessory. He hadn't inhaled a single puff of it.

Strode had a feeling that Burklow already knew in his gut that the Mayweathers were killed. Maybe they felt like a final connection he had to his daughter. Or maybe he hated the thought of their kids, though they were grown-ups now, losing their parents. Burklow had seen first-hand how hard that could be on a kid. It was something Strode realized

Teddy Blackwood was familiar with, maybe more so than any other kid who had gone through it because Teddy lost his father twice—once when they moved and again when his father died. He lost his mother on the same day. Just moments before.

Strode imagined Teddy Blackwood was the loneliest person in the world.

Burklow was humming along to The Mamas and The Papas on the radio. Finch hummed along too. Strode's throat hurt too much to try, but he swayed his head back and forth. It was one of his all-time favorite songs, "Dream a Little Dream of Me."

Despite where they were headed, Strode realized that moment was the happiest he had been in a long time. Finch grabbed the headrest, turned to Strode, and winked.

They took the road past the main entrance to Warren Woods, where he and Finch had turned the day before and where he had seen the clown. He was glad they passed it. The sky was cloudy, and Strode could see more of it once they reached the housing subdivision. However, he wondered if the dark clouds were a lingering smog from the night before.

When they turned onto Maple Street, they were all taken aback by what they saw. Not just the Mayweathers' house but the one beside it was all but gone. The Mayweathers' place looked as though the men who boarded its foundation had a strong leaning to the left. The floorwork, the dangling insulation, all sat at a slant.

The house beside it belonged to a young couple, Burklow had said. "I bet the Mayweathers were so happy to have them as neighbors."

Strode wasn't sure if the young couple were victims in the electric shock, taken by the flames that swallowed their

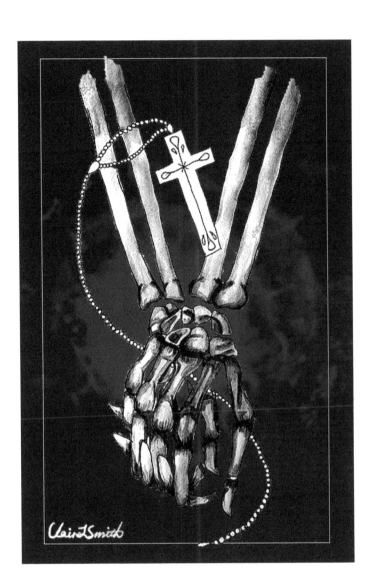

home, or if they made it out okay. Maybe Burklow was saying "they were" because the house seemed to look as sad as the chances of the Mayweathers' survival.

Burklow pulled as far up as he could and pushed the Pinto's seat back to let his gut squeeze past the steering wheel. A fireman stood on the sidewalk in front of the Mayweathers' talking to a young couple.

Finch and Strode followed along, allowing Burklow only a moment of being the leader of their ensemble. He recognized the couple, and after he said, "Hey, I'm so sorry about your place. Please let me know if there's anything we can do," they knew it was the couple who lived next door to the Mayweathers. They both seemed physically okay.

The woman sniffled while the husband nodded and managed a soft, "Thank you. We have family in Ohio we can stay with."

Burklow nodded. "Well, thank goodness for that."

The couple stepped aside, and Burklow asked the fireman, "And the Mayweathers?"

"They didn't make it out, Jack." The guy bit his lower lip and then sighed. "When we finally got it maintained enough to send someone in, it was too late. We found them in bed. We just got them out and sent them to forensics so the odontologists could confirm, but it was them, Jack."

Strode used three fingers and pressed on his throat to counteract the pressure as he asked, "They were in bed?"

The fireman stepped closer and turned his ear to Strode. Finch repeated for him, "They were found in bed?"

The fireman nodded. "Yes. Sad. At least they went together."

Strode shook his head, and Finch said, "One of our witnesses said people from all across the block ran out to help. It's possible they heard the screams later into it when people were already dead on the street, but they still would've gotten out of bed. They would've gone to the window, or out the back door, or something to see what was wrong."

Those were Strode's thoughts exactly. Something wasn't right there. And if this case had taught him anything, it was that when something didn't feel right, it probably wasn't.

With a hard, painful swallow, Strode moved a little too close to the fireman. He looked like a schoolgirl telling a secret, and asked, "What has been recovered from—"

Strode's voice cut out. He pointed to the Mayweathers' place.

They were still digging through it all. Finch, who Strode was learning would always be prepared, pulled out a baggie of latex gloves and said, "We're going in."

Burklow retrieved three masks from the fireman's equipment. He pulled one over his nose and said through the fabric, "I'm sure the ash and fumes are still pretty strong in there. And one of us," his accusing eyes pointed to Strode, "is already banged up."

Burklow returned to their equipment pile beside the truck and grabbed three helmets too. "Better safe, and, you know, all that shit."

Strode grinned. Finch hesitated, watching Strode remove his stolen Cardinals hat to reveal his blood-matted mess of a wound. He slipped the helmet over it, cringing for just a second.

"I don't know, Strode. If anything falls and hits your head... It isn't a good idea. You've been up more than you should and—"

Strode smiled with a sense of sincerity and said, "Thank you, but we both know I have to. I have to see this through, in every phase, at every turn. You didn't bring me to the World Series just to put me on the bench."

Finch ran her hands over her black hair, catching any astray. Of course, there weren't any. She put the helmet over her head. And the three of them headed inside the house.

What used to be the living room looked like the aftermath of a war. The couch sat against the back wall with no traces of what design or color it had been. Just the general curves of it here and there suggested it was once a couch.

The size of the rooms was hard to determine because the flames ate through so much of the drywall. Fallen boards and insulation blocked off space from the living room to the kitchen. So they went for the stairs. Strode didn't want to say it, but he had a brief vision of Burklow making it midway, and then the steps giving out from under him.

Under other circumstances, the thought might've made him laugh. But, the first step was soft under Strode's foot, and he thought it best to skip it altogether.

"You two wait and make sure I get up before you try them," Strode said.

Finch hopped right around Strode and skipped up the steps, taking them two at a time and not allowing her weight to settle on them. She was already turning into a bedroom before he had taken his next step.

Strode turned around to Burklow, who just shook his head laughing. Then he said, "Well, if everyone's doing it."

Strode cleared the steps and stood at the top, watching Burklow and hoping their journey didn't end with another one of them in the hospital.

Burklow felt the steps, tapping them before he took each step. He hung on to what was left of the railing and made it up in one piece.

Finch was in the first bedroom, which had a big rocket poster on the wall, and stood in front of the closet door. To the clan's surprise, that part of the house was mostly charred around the edges but not in ruins. The poster's edges were brown and orange and crinkled from the heat.

Strode stood behind her, looking into the closet. A plastic clothes hanger hung in disarray, like a shirt had been pulled off quickly. Finch grabbed the bottom of a NASA t-shirt and tugged at it, sending the hanger in a 180 spin.

"Strange," Finch said. "Burklow, didn't you say their kids were all grown up?"

Burklow came into the room, out of breath from the climb of the stairs. "Huh? Oh, uh, yeah. They're all grown up now."

Strode got it. The closet was open, and the clothes were disturbed.

"It looks like a shirt was taken in a hurry, like a kid who was late for school," Finch said.

"But they're not in school," Burklow heaved.

Finch snapped, "Exactly."

She led the group to the next bedroom and did a quick walk-through. Not much was there. That room looked untouched, despite the traces of the fire, ash, and soot that gave everything a grim coating.

The master bedroom seemed to be just as bad as the living room. It was like the fire followed a straight path and clung to the house's center. The bed was mostly ash. What they assumed were bedside tables were nothing but rubble and a few split wooden boards.

Strode broke off into the bathroom. The shower curtain was obsolete, and the nonslip rubber bath mat that every retired person seemed to have was melted against the tub. But the porcelain white sink, at least the bowl itself, still held some of its bright white color. While the fire darkened the sink's stand, the spots around the drain were a red rust color.

Finch came into the bathroom and Strode motioned for a cotton swab by balling his fists and twisting his hands around his ears, as though he were revving a motorcycle.

Finch, of course, understood. She came behind Strode and gasped. "Is that blood?"

Strode shrugged and whispered, "I believe so."

Burklow barreled in, and Strode was having a flashback of being pinned in the closet-sized bathroom in Sarah's salon. "They were old, Strode. That could've been from coughing, or..."

Finch cut him off. "Then we'll let forensics tell us that."

Burklow raised his hands in defense. "Alright. You're right."

They cleared out of the bathroom, and something in the corner of the bedroom, under a mound of ash, caught Strode's eye. He lifted the debris and threw it to the side. Underneath was a round ceramic piece. It had a deep crack down the center and a bold ring of blood at the bottom.

Strode carried it to his partners, and Burklow's whole demeanor shifted. Now they were all certain something was very wrong.

Strode swallowed hard, hoping his voice would let him get what he needed to out. He pointed to the vial Finch had tucked the bloodied cotton swab in and whispered, "Check Blackwoods. In Indiana."

Burklow blinked three times, indicating he thought Strode was malfunctioning.

"Burklow, we need to confirm the blood in this vial isn't the Mayweathers."

She took the ceramic piece from Strode, "And that this belongs to one of them."

Strode repeated in a louder but hoarse voice, "Then we go to Indiana."

Finch nodded, "To see if it matches the Blackwoods."

Strode and the others climbed back down the stairs, feeling more confident than they did going up, and returned to the barren front yard.

In addition to the three firemen were two men in navy jackets far too warm for summer. On the back were three initials, FBI.

Strode didn't feel good coming out of there and removing his helmet to reveal an unkempt wound. If these guys hadn't spoken to the police station back in Indiana, they would probably think he was crazy on sight.

The men immediately approached them and flashed their badges as Strode extended his hand to greet them.

He had seen it happen a few times but never expected them to show up with this one. It felt like *his case*, and for some reason, Strode expected others to accommodate that factor.

In a matter of minutes from collecting the stained cotton swab, the bloodied ceramic piece, and copies of the reports and notes Strode, Burklow, and Finch had on the case, it was all taken from them.

Teddy's whereabouts, his victims, his capture, was now up to the FBI.

6

It had been three days since the FBI took over the Blackwood case. Finch insisted that the Three Oaks trio kept looking for Teddy, but Strode wasn't sure where to begin. Plus, he wasn't sure what they could learn at that point that the FBI wouldn't. All Strode had that no one else did was a run-in with the golden eyes.

The morning before, the FBI had confirmed what Strode already knew to be true. The blood found in the Mayweathers' home passed the paternity test with Arthur Blackwood.

Strode was going to head back to Indiana, but Burklow and Finch insisted that he stay. Finch even threatened to take him back to the hospital if he didn't.

Strode lay on the couch until nearly ten in the morning. Finch's petite feet spiraled down the staircase, and she flipped each of the lights on. The light beat into Strode's eyes and made him more aware of the pain from his head injury.

"It's time to change the dressings," Finch said, carrying a small wastebasket.

Strode groaned and said, "You don't have to mommy me, Finch."

She sat beside him on the couch, forcing Strode to sit up, and tipped a bottle of peroxide onto a cotton ball.

"Do you know why I hate that so much? When people say I'm mommying them?"

Strode shook his head.

"Because you think it's an insult rather than a display of men needing women to point out, 'Hey, if you don't change your bandage, your wound will get infected, and you'll be back in the hospital.'"

Strode couldn't help but smile, and Finch returned it with a look that said, "Now, are you done?"

Strode helped take the old bandage off, and Finch dabbed the wound.

"You know they have everyone looking for him now?" Finch said.

Strode did. How could they not after they found his blood in the Mayweathers' house? If they couldn't prove he did any of the other things, they had evidence there.

"They had his picture on television and his description on the radio," Finch went on.

Strode winced when Finch got to the back of his head. "Have you taken your pain medicine today?"

"No. I just got up."

Finch gave him a scolding scowl.

Strode felt as though he had just proven her statement. Women had to remind men of the simplest things, like how taking your pain medicine made your injuries less painful.

"Come on. You've been moping down here long enough. We still have work to do. Let's get some food in you so you can take your medicine."

Finch went up the stairs, and Strode changed into a new t-shirt. He could hear Burklow asking how he was and Finch

shushing him. "He's fine. The best thing for all of us is to keep working."

The television in the background blared a deep, interrupting tone.

Strode hurried up the steps to find Burklow and Finch glued to the screen.

They found Teddy.

The newswoman said that officials placed him in Northern Michigan in front of a television store. The woman who called the police said he was staring at the set, in a hypnotic trance, watching the New York Yankees.

Strode's heart sank. Before, when he thought of everything Teddy had done, it was as though the boy he'd been was gone, buried under a monster. But now Strode couldn't help but wonder how much of him was still there. How much of him was still only a kid?

PART 5

CONFESSIONS OF A MAN GONE MAD

1

Teddy was led down a mustard-colored hall with peeling striped wallpaper that had heavy water stains from the shitty ceiling that leaked both repugnant-smelling water and mounds of soggy insulation. The dark green vines burst across the yellow backdrop. Their sporadic twists and turns with uneven lines of thick and thin reminded Teddy of the blood vessels in his mother's eyes as his father choked her. Only the vessels in her eyes weren't a cooling green, but a bright blood red.

Teddy had seen similar inscriptions on some of the shadow's victims. It was as if the eyes were communicating with Teddy all on their own. The burst blood vessels could say, "You've won. Well played."

The man behind Teddy was a large Black man. He had a face that would've seemed friendly had he not put handcuffs on Teddy's wrists and held them as they walked to the doctor's office. Teddy couldn't tell if the guard was from the hospital or borrowed from the prison.

The whole place had a nasty bleach smell that gave Teddy a headache. But when the doctor opened his office door and told Teddy to take a seat inside, the scent shifted to mold and must.

The doctor positioned his desk as far into the right-hand corner as possible. If he were to sit at it, his back would be to Teddy. Teddy could see it was a therapy tactic. The doctor pushed the swivel chair into the center of the room so the two chairs would face one another with nothing between them.

Teddy's seat was a vinyl chair. Its overlay was peeling, creating scratchy edges that rubbed the back of Teddy's pant legs. A bright, white light hung from the ceiling, just above their heads.

The doctor sat in his seat and pulled his jacket closer to his middle. Like the guard, Teddy thought the doctor had a nice-seeming face, but given the circumstances, niceness didn't matter.

"Hello, Teddy. My name is Dr. Lustig, and I'll be performing the psychiatric evaluation on you."

Teddy shook his head. "I don't think my head is sick."

Dr. Lustig smiled, pen and paper at the ready, and said, "Well, we can't know until we try. And the goal is just to make you better."

Dr. Lustig's demeanor caught Teddy off guard. All of the FBI officers had been calling him a twisted son of bitch or a conniving little bastard, and then this guy said he just wanted to make Teddy better. No one could make Teddy better but the shadow. It was a truth he knew they could never understand.

"So, Teddy, let's start with the house," Dr. Lustig said.

"I already talked to them about the houses. They know I was in one of them. That's how they found me. Well, my blood anyway."

The doctor took a quick, scribbled note across a yellow notepad. "No. No. I mean the house in Indiana. The one you and your mother moved to. Can you tell me about the move?"

Teddy hadn't spoken about the move with anyone aside from the shadow, whose white-hot eyes positioned themselves just above and behind Dr. Lustig.

"We moved because my parents got into a fight."

Dr. Lustig crossed his arms. "What about?"

"My dad was having my old babysitter over. I saw them together one afternoon." Teddy shook his head. "I don't want to talk about this anymore."

Dr. Lustig nodded. "I understand, Teddy. Can you tell me, did you have any friends in Oakhaven?"

Pete. Teddy still had the Polaroid picture the shadow had created for him of Pete trudging through the snow.

"Yes. One."

Dr. Lustig's hand zipped across the pad of paper again.

"And how about Indiana? It doesn't look like you ever started school there?"

Teddy had forgotten all about school. He had missed a year of it. He couldn't help but wonder, if he were still in Indiana, what he and Ali would be doing. She was going to be his summer guide. Teddy wondered if Ali knew he was alive. Then, Teddy feared she'd heard what he'd done.

"I had a friend. Her name was Ali. She lived in the house next to ours. There was a cluster of trees between our houses, and we'd swim in the pond there."

Dr. Lustig nodded and said, "Ali sounds lovely."

She was, Teddy thought.

Teddy saw the shadow's white eyes against the dingy wall and said, "I had another friend too. A best friend."

"Great, Teddy. Can you tell me about him?"

Teddy smiled. "He lived in the basement of the house in Indiana."

Dr. Lustig's smile faded. "The basement?"

Teddy nodded. "I could hear him inside my head. He would talk to me. At first, I was afraid, but then he would play games with me."

Dr. Lustig tapped the pen on his notepad. From all the games he and the shadow played, Teddy knew this meant the doctor was considering his strategy, his next move.

Dr. Lustig's eyes lit up. He had it. "What kind of games did you and this friend play?"

Teddy's lips parted into a beaming smile. "All kinds, but mostly tic-tac-toe. We didn't play it as much when we left."

"That reminds me, Teddy, what was the past year or so like for you when you left the house in Indiana? Weren't you afraid?"

Teddy looked to the shadow behind Dr. Lustig. "I was most afraid of being alone, but the shadow didn't let that happen. So, I left with it."

"And the shadow was the friend you mentioned?"

Teddy nodded.

"Teddy, help me understand something. You said you could hear the shadow in your head when you moved to Indiana. Had you heard the voice before then?"

"No. It was in the basement at the house."

Dr. Lustig nodded. "Right. Right." He took another note and seemed to underline it. Teddy could hear the fine-tip metal pen carving into the paper.

"Did you hear the shadow when you killed the man and woman on Maple Street?"

Teddy smiled, looking beyond Dr. Lustig and at his protector and friend. "Yes. The shadow is with me wherever I go."

Dr. Lustig began to turn his head, and then it seemed as though he resisted the urge. "Is the shadow with us now?"

Teddy repeated, "Wherever I go."

The shadow stepped closer to Dr. Lustig and merged with the doctor's still shape of darkness. But the eyes towered over him, growing in height. Its shoulders climbed over their resting place as its claw-like fingers arched at the head of Lustig's shadow.

The shadow gave Teddy a nod of reassurance, and its snake-like fangs broke into a subtle grin.

"Teddy, did the shadow tell you to kill those people in Three Oaks?"

Teddy didn't see the need to hide anymore. The world knew what he was and saw that he wasn't this scared little boy. Teddy straightened up in his seat.

"The shadow needs me to kill. If I can't, it has to leave me. That's the only way it would ever leave me. So, I do what my friend needs, and then it takes care of me."

"And did the shadow take care of you in the past year before you got to Michigan?"

Teddy looked onto the shadow with adoring eyes. "We took care of each other."

Dr. Lustig folded his hands together and said, "Did you hurt people during that time, Teddy? Like you did in Three Oaks?"

The shadow's eyes opened and closed, giving Teddy a shot of encouragement.

"I just took care of my friend, the shadow."

Dr. Lustig stared at Teddy, and Teddy wondered if the doctor could ever understand. Or, if like the cops, he would only see Teddy as evil.

But then, Teddy remembered, he didn't need the doctor to approve of him. He didn't need anyone to think he was good. All he needed was to find his way out so he could take care of his only friend. He needed out, so he could feed the shadow.

2

Teddy had spent five days in the psych ward. It was far more confinement than Teddy was used to, and the shadow's eyes, though still white, weren't quite as bright.

Teddy had given the shadow enough to make it the best it'd ever been. The shadow said so. With that, Teddy could bury some of the returning guilt about the people he had to hurt. Teddy had learned that people wouldn't be there for him—even the best ones, like his mother or Ali. There would always be something else. Something that mattered more or that could take them away. But with the shadow, Teddy controlled when it left, and as long as he kept it well fed, it never would.

The same broad man who had taken Teddy to his first appointment with Dr. Lustig accompanied a blonde woman with deep purple lipstick to Teddy's confinement center. That's what they called them instead of cells.

The woman couldn't look at Teddy. Every time she lifted her head, it was as if it was attached to a pull-string that tugged it back down. She handed the letter to the man and said, "Can you just give this to him? I need to get back upstairs."

The woman spun around and hurried up the steps. The man opened the envelope, keeping that part to himself, and handed Teddy the folded piece of paper. "You've got a letter."

Teddy was surprised. A letter? Who could be writing to him? Teddy opened the letter and saw scribbly yet neat letters that said:

Dear Teddy,

I have spent all this time wishing I could tell you I was sorry. When your dad came, I was so afraid. He started shouting. And I was scared. When you told me to get my dad, I ran through the house, yelling for him, screaming as loud as I could. Then I remembered Daddy left me with you while he went to the abattoir. I ran as hard as I could, Teddy, but I was too late. And for that, I'm sorry.

Daddy doesn't want me hearing any of it because he says, "It'll just break my heart," but I sneak the radio into my room at night. When they put the alert out for you, I went to your house each day until they found you, waiting to see if you'd come home.

I've heard some other things they say about you too, Teddy. It's really bad. But I want you to know that if you get out again and get to come home, please come here. Me and my daddy can help you, Teddy.

You did bad things, Teddy, but you're not bad.

Your Friend Always,

Ali

Teddy lowered the letter from his face. He had never thought of going back to Indiana. It never really did feel like home. It might've had he been there longer, but who could say for sure?

Teddy did feel a sense of relief in knowing that someone else out there, someone like Ali, still believed he was good.

He wanted to see Ali and see if she really could help him and the shadow. Teddy knew he couldn't stay at the psych ward forever. Eventually, the shadow would get too hungry, and Teddy couldn't let that happen.

The man still stood outside Teddy's bare, besides a cot, "confinement center."

Teddy looked at him, sliding a piece of hair from his forehead. It was getting long. Maybe Ali could cut it for him. Teddy could already hear her giggling as she did it.

"Sir?" Teddy asked. "Is Dr. Lustig available?"

The man's eyes narrowed. "Your appointment isn't until tomorrow."

Teddy nodded. "Yes. I know. I was just hoping to discuss this letter with him. Well, you see, it's made me feel something different than I did when we first spoke."

Another guard came from behind the big guy and said, "Oh, yeah. What's that? Insanity?"

"Guilt," Teddy said.

The guard brushed the scrawny comedian aside and looked Teddy in the eyes. His gaze was full of suspicion, but Teddy thought maybe even a touch of sympathy too. It was as he thought before. Something about this guy's face, perhaps the softness of his eyes, even when he tried to make them stern, made Teddy think he was a good guy.

"Please," Teddy said. "I need his help with this."

The guard's brown eyes looked at the letter. And then he nodded. "Alright. I'll see what I can do."

"Thank you, sir."

When the guard's boots beat into the steps as he went to retrieve Dr. Lustig, Teddy turned to the bare wall of his confinement center.

"Shadow?"

The eyes appeared, slightly more yellow than they were a few days ago but still in good shape.

"Shadow, we're getting out, but I'll need your help again."

The shadow nodded.

Well played, Teddy.

Only a few moments later, the guard appeared with Dr. Lustig. Teddy was thankful he had the hall all to himself. That made things easier and made Lustig more willing to bend the rules.

Dr. Lustig carried his notebook and pen against his chest. He smiled and greeted Teddy, "Good afternoon. What can I do for you?"

Teddy debated on whether he should let the doctor read the letter for himself.

You read it.

Teddy obeyed the shadow's instructions.

"I got a letter today, Dr. Lustig."

Dr. Lustig smiled. "I heard, Teddy. I was going to ask you about it tomorrow. Was it from anyone special?"

Teddy straightened his cream-colored shirt and matching pants that were far too big for him.

"Yes. Ali."

Dr. Lustig's eyes widened. He immediately tried to correct his response to something more conspicuous, but Teddy knew he had him.

The doctor tried to appear casual as he said, "Oh, right. Your friend from Indiana?"

Teddy nodded. He lowered his head and began to cry. "I need to write her back. Only I don't know what to say, but I have to answer her. She's just so kind, doctor. She wants to be my friend."

Dr. Lustig said, "Do you think you and I writing Ali together may help you talk about leaving Indiana and the trail to Michigan? Maybe even what the shadow asked you to do?"

Teddy nodded, wiping a tear from under his eye. "Yes."

"Very well then, Teddy."

The guard disappeared and found a chair for Dr. Lustig. He stood behind the doctor as he began writing.

"Well, where do we start? 'Dear Ali.' How about that?"

Teddy shook his head. "I need to write it. It's my guilt. I should be the one to confess it to her."

Good, Teddy.

"May we talk in your office?"

Dr. Lustig looked at the guard and nodded, giving him the okay.

"Stand back," the guard said. He opened the door to Teddy's room, and Teddy ran at him. He grabbed the pen from the doctor's hand and lodged it into the guard's eye. A clear gelatinous fluid poured from the man's eye.

Teddy held his legs around the man's torso and stabbed his other eye, ramming the fine metal tip right into the center.

Just as Dr. Lustig began to scream, the shadow opened its claws and tore out his throat before the man ever saw it coming.

The doctor lay flat on his back, and just as the others had, including Teddy's father, Dr. Lustig coughed and gagged as the blood spilled from its exposed passage.

Teddy ripped up four pieces of the white notebook paper and laid them over each of the men's eyes.

Then he tucked the letter in his pocket and hid himself within the thick doorframe on the other side of the hall as he waited for the aides to respond to the commotion.

They did.

"Dr. Lustig! Mike! Oh my god. Call nine-one-one! Call nine-one-one," one of them shouted. And while the men tended to the soon-to-be deceased, Teddy strolled right past them, smiling when he noticed some of the blood sticking to his shoes.

Teddy was fine with it. They were looking for him, but just like any other game, it required skill and strategy.

And when they saw the bloodied footsteps, they would know Teddy had won.

3

Strode and Burklow got the call around ten the next morning. The FBI reported that Teddy had escaped the psych ward in Logansport, less than an hour from the Starling house.

Burklow relayed the information from the speaker on the other side of the phone to Strode. Finch stood at the coffee pot and seemed to be solving a mental puzzle of her own.

"How?" Strode asked. "How did he get out?"

Strode's voice was a little hoarse, and he still wasn't eating solids, but his throat was doing better. Thanks to Finch, he was down to two painkillers a day too. One in the morning and one before bed.

Burklow was shaking his head. "I don't understand. How did this happen?"

The voice on the other end explained, and Burklow said, "That little fucking bastard." Then after a pause, he continued, "Oh, no. You've got the wrong guy. That would be Officer Strode."

Burklow handed the phone to Strode, and given that he hadn't spoken much in the past two weeks, he was reluctant. Strode took the phone and said, "Hello?"

The voice on the other side was quite higher than any other man Strode had ever heard before, which sort of sounded like one of Santa's elves was reading him a murder novel.

"Officer Strode. This is Special Agent Borr. We met at the Mayweather place the morning after the fire."

Strode was tempted to say it wasn't much of a meeting but thought better of it. This was the first time the FBI was calling him directly about the Blackwood case.

"I was just telling your partner that Teddy's means of escaping were quite horrific and tragic. We have agents set up across Michigan waiting for him if he comes back. Sometimes killers like to revisit their scenes. I have my money on Maple Street. He'd probably consider it his most grand achievement."

Special Agent Borr made a "tuh" sound, mocking Teddy.

"How did he escape?" Strode asked.

Special Agent Borr sighed. "It was awful. Honestly, I don't know what's sadder, the deaths of these people, or the fact that it's a kid doing them."

Strode had never said it aloud, but he knew what Borr meant. Of course, the innocent lives lost were sadder, or they were supposed to be. Strode hated it all. But what he hated most was that a kid like Teddy, one he thought he and Maggie would've loved to have, had gotten so lost.

"He stabbed the guard with a fine-tip, metal pen."

Strode cringed a little but then nodded.

"In the eyes," Borr clarified.

Strode quivered and then mouthed, "In the eyes," to Finch. Her bottom lip curled in disgust.

"Jesus. Were there any others?" Strode asked.

"Yeah. The psychiatrist who was evaluating him was there. They were sitting outside his cell, or I guess they call it a confinement center, though it is just a room with a toilet and a cot."

Strode had a feeling, but he asked anyway. "The doctor, how did Teddy kill him?"

"We've seen it a few times in this case. Or I suppose you have. He somehow ripped the throat clean out. It was just like those kids we found in the woods the other day. They were only in high school."

Strode knew what he was referring to, and he'd read the reports on those boys. The bodies were rotten and turned to goo by the time they found them. No torturing for those guys either. That thing that tried to do it to Strode had torn out their throats too. And one of them had a stick shoved into the center of his neck.

"The kid left a literal trail of blood. He stepped into some on his way out. Police said they followed the trail, but then it faded right before a wooded area. There's not much else out there. No sign of him."

Teddy had to be moving. He was always moving.

"How many miles is the wooded area from the hospital?"

Strode could hear Borr flipping through some papers on his desk.

"Only about two and a half miles northeast."

Strode mouthed the distance and direction to Finch. Strode watched as she set her coffee mug down on the counter, almost missing it, and hurried to the dining room table. She had tried to recreate all of her notes that the FBI had taken. Strode was sure she did more than a fair job of it.

She ripped a large multi-colored sheet of paper from the table, turned Burklow around, and held it up to his back for Strode to see. With a black marker, Strode circled Logansport and then Interstate 25, going northeast.

Strode said into the phone, "Well, thank you for the report. I'll let you know if I think of anything else that might help."

"Whoa, wait a minute, Strode. Do you know where he might be going?"

Strode held the bottom of the phone, shaking his head from side to side, the way the clown hopped from foot to foot when it shouted, "Strode had a stroke. Strode had a stroke."

Strode looked at Burklow—spun around and confused as always—and then at Finch's confident face. The three of them had to be the ones to go. They knew more about the case than anyone else. And Strode knew the most about Teddy. He needed to be the one to find him.

Strode tried to ease the sense of urgency in his voice and said, "I'm sorry, Borr. I don't. I'll talk to my colleagues, and if we think of anything, we'll be sure to let you know."

Borr thanked him and Strode hung the phone on the wall. He stood only a few inches away from Burklow and forgot the map was pressed against his back. He traced the black line Finch drew with his pointer finger. It went northeast, just as Borr had instructed.

Burklow shivered and let out a little, "Woo."

Strode was too shocked to care about anything else.

He was going to find the missing kid-turned-killer, because Teddy Blackwood was going home.

4

Strode and Finch climbed into the Ford Pinto with Burklow close behind in his Three Oaks squad car. Burklow flipped his lights on once they got out of town and the whole time on the interstate. The instructions were clear. If another district's officer or state trooper radioed in, Burklow would respond immediately with a ten thirty-five code. Strode and Finch were not to stop for anything.

Strode gripped the steering wheel with anger and nerves as Finch stared straight ahead, focused. Then, she said, "Strode, have you given any more thought to who could be helping Teddy?"

Strode hadn't because he had a good idea of who it was. He had seen them in the woods. It had tried to kill him the same way Teddy had killed the psychiatrist and the boy in the woods. Right after Strode thought it, he said, "Teddy didn't try to rip my throat out. The eyes did."

Strode turned to Finch, waiting for her to at long-last give him a look that said, "Okay, everyone was right. This guy is out of his fucking mind."

But instead, she said, "Yes. The golden eyes."

Strode turned his head, leveling one eye with the road as best as he could. "What did you say?"

"The golden eyes," Finch repeated. "I saw them too. It made a hissing sound too, right after I shot Teddy. When I saw them, I froze. It wasn't like anything I had ever seen before. I thought I was in shock, but then, the more we talked about someone helping Teddy, and the more unusual the circumstances, like taking down powerlines, the more I thought what I saw was real. And whatever it is, it's helping Teddy."

Strode had an uneasy feeling growing in his gut. It didn't quite fit together. Why would this thing help Teddy?

Strode's voice was drying out from talking, but he said what he had been thinking for weeks now. "That thing isn't helping Teddy. Teddy is helping it."

Finch sat back in her seat. She smoothed the top of her head to catch any loose-hanging hairs. There weren't any.

Strode turned the radio dial and landed on a Beatles tune he had forgotten about. It was called, "Devil in Her Heart."

Strode listened to the lyrics, and each line made him hurt more for Teddy. The poor kid lost his family and then was all alone and outwitted by the devil.

Either way, Teddy killed people, and it was up to Strode to bring him in.

They drove on Interstate 25 for about thirty more minutes before reaching the little township he had left just a couple of weeks ago. In just that short time, the place had grown to feel less like home. Instead, it was something Strode wanted to avoid, like whiskey, the first alcoholic drink he had ever gotten drunk on.

Just the thought of it made his stomach turn.

The car rolled down a gravel road, and bits of rock chewed into the cracks of the tires. Strode took inventory of the familiarities, like the rusty train cars and rows of trees, and thanks to Abraham's Abattoir, the smell of fresh blood. The copper smell followed them past the Abrahams' house and to the driveway of the Starling house.

Finch leaned forward, looking up at the house as the legend it was. Her eyes were wide, and maybe even a little afraid.

She turned to Strode, "One step at a time."

Strode nodded. He could do this. He had to do this.

Burklow decided to stay in his car in case Teddy came out running.

Finch and Strode walked up the drive. Strode could feel the house watching him. It had sat alone, empty for over a year, and Strode thought it seemed to say, "I've been waiting for you."

Finch nearly lost her foot to one of the front porch's gaping holes. Strode steadied her, and she was quick to smooth her hair back.

Strode reached for the door handle, feeling as ready as he'd ever been. The doorknob barely turned.

"It's locked," Finch said. "How can we get inside?"

Finch began looking around the porch for a hiding spot for a spare key.

Strode wasted no time, and with three hard kicks, the rickety front door fell to the living room floor. The mouth of the Starling house opened wide.

"Jesus, Strode. What the hell are you doing? We can't just break in."

Strode stepped inside and waved Finch aside. "*We* didn't. I did. They'll expect nothing less from the nut case cop."

Strode laughed while Finch looked at him with unease.

Finch pulled her gun from her belt as Strode did the same. Finch pointed for Strode to take the kitchen and the back porch while she took the stairs.

"Together," Strode said.

Finch nodded and followed Strode's lead. He crept through the living room and saw that the record player's needle was still sitting atop a vinyl record. The needle hung at the inside of the disc. When Strode came through after the Blackwoods' deaths, it played "Being for the Benefit of Mr. Kite."

Only the Sgt. Pepper's album was not the record loaded. It was Elton John.

Strode fell to his knees and flipped through the music collection.

"It's not here. Why isn't it here?"

Finch crouched beside Strode. "What?"

Strode tossed records aside. "The Beatles album. Sgt. Peppers. That album was on the last time I was here. Someone changed it. And the Sgt. Pepper's album is gone."

"Teddy?" Finch asked.

Strode nodded. "It had to have been. We might have already missed him."

Finch and Strode walked together, guns ready, and went up the stairs. Sneaking around was pointless. Strode had kicked the front door down and made a loud fuss over the records. Now, they had to stay together to have each other's backs.

The stairs creaked the whole way up. Strode stared into the office and imagined Mr. Warren giving his warning message right before he slit his own throat.

Strode believed now that whatever had a hold on Teddy had a tight grip on Mr. Warren too. The room was empty.

Next, Strode went for the room he knew was Teddy's. Tally marks and a wall-splitting message that read "Hello" made the room feel even more harrowing this time around.

"Was he talking to it all this time?" Finch asked.

Strode nodded. "I think so."

They checked the other rooms, and they were clear.

"I don't understand," Strode said. "Why isn't he here?"

Finch looked at the peeling, the cracks in the walls, and said, "I don't think Teddy liked it here. Or even if he was starting to, I don't think he did in the end. So, if he came back here, it was for something specific. It has to be more than the record."

Strode remembered the neighbor asking to keep him posted on Teddy because his daughter was his friend.

The Abrahams.

"We have to go to the Abrahams' house."

Strode hurried past Finch and out the front door.

Burklow cranked his window down and poked his head out. "Anything?"

"Nothing," Strode said. "We need to go to the Abrahams' house."

Burklow nodded. "Okay. Where's that?"

Strode pointed through the trees. "It's the house just before this one."

"There wasn't a car in the drive," Finch said.

Strode tried to think fast. Where could Teddy be going?

"There's one more place we can look—the abattoir at the end of the road. The Abrahams own it."

Strode stared down the Starling house as he backed out of the drive and said, "I hope you sit here all alone and rot away to hell."

5

———

Abraham's Abattoir sat amongst the grim, grey clouds with the tall rows of corn behind it. Some of the leaves were bright and alive, while the others seemed just a step away from death's icy grasp.

Strode felt somewhere in between the two.

The copper smell of blood was unmistakable, and the sound of squealing pigs sent a chill down Strode's spine. He could see the dread on Finch's and Burklow's faces. Finch was anxious but focused. Burklow was outright sweaty and pale like he was going to be sick.

Deciding he was the leader on this mission, Strode straightened up, shook off his own angst, and said, "One step at a time, guys."

Giving advice felt foreign to Strode, but he tried to look and sound as confident as possible. But as he stared up at the big aluminum center of animalistic gore, Strode realized he hadn't been to Abraham's since the night of the Warrens' deaths. Strode remembered how afraid he was to be alone at the abattoir that night. Like a child, he envisioned the cornstalks curving into hands, ready to catch whoever came running by. Everything was evil at night. Strode thought he'd spend that entire night praying some dipshit teens didn't make him go running into the cornfield.

The bloodied massacre that called him away turned out to be far worse. That was a haunting that had followed him ever since, a haunting he knew would always plague him.

Strode studied the metal can of a building and tried to remember where the door was. An officer ahead of him made him walk the grounds before he staked it out that fateful evening over a year ago.

Off to the left there was a matching metal door that had a small window cut out. Strode cupped his hands around the glass and peeked inside.

"Okay," Strode said. "This is it."

Just as Strode reached for the door handle, it eased itself open. It didn't screech like the old doors in the Starling house. It was more like a hollow whine. The metal, he supposed, was the cause of that. Everything was old and weak in the Starling house, but things were sturdy and already bloodied in the abattoir. An image that seemed to say, "Others have dared and failed, and you will too."

Uncertain of where Mr. Abraham was, Strode decided to stay quiet in case they could get the jump on Teddy. Strode put a finger to his lips, instructing the others to do the same. Both officers nodded and pulled their guns from their belts.

The three of them crept through the abattoir, with the potent smell of blood intensifying with each step. The cement floor hummed below as the grinder churned through thick muscles and fat. In the distance, there was a ripping noise. It was the same kind of sound that came when he bit into Maggie's glazed chicken wings. It was meat tearing from the bones.

The walls were a dull grey but had a yellow tint to them. It was like something dark had splattered them, and the cleaner could only lift so much. That's how Strode's mind worked; even on his good days, the stains of trauma entombed him.

The three officers passed what looked like Mr. Abraham's office. It was an ill-lit closet space with a single chair and square desk. There were papers scattered across the desk and the floor, and he had left several filing cabinets ajar. Above the desk was a picture of a woman with long white-blonde hair that framed her face in loose waves. In her arms, she held a baby wrapped tightly in a polka-dotted blanket.

Burklow came behind Strode and said, "That's a sweet picture."

Strode nodded, "I think her name was Lynn."

Strode stopped himself, with the help of a fierce look from Finch, from saying she had died.

Either way, Burklow seemed to have caught the *was* in Strode's sentence, and he turned out of the office without the others.

Guilt didn't linger. It sank its teeth right into Strode.

Before Strode had a chance to try to reason with it, he heard the switch-click of a cocked gun.

"Fuck," Burklow said.

Strode's eyes met Finch's, and he took a hand and lowered it, telling her to hide. For the first time in the hundreds of hours they had worked together, Finch followed Strode's order, which meant she too thought it was the right call.

Strode stepped out, his gun still pointed. The dark hall only allowed a spotlight of light, and into that light stepped a man holding a gun with Burklow just at the other end of it.

Burklow was calm. Strode thought Burklow appeared more rattled by his mentioning the dead wife than the firing end of a loaded gun in his face.

Strode knew the man. He was John Abraham.

Strode held his gun in one hand, and with the other he tried to steady Mr. Abraham.

"Take it easy, John."

Mr. Abraham held his eyes on Burklow. The end of the dark steel barrel was only centimeters from the Three Oaks officer's sweaty, wrinkled forehead.

"John, it's me, Officer Strode."

The man didn't budge. Strode could see the sweat around his eyes, and worse, the desperation in them. Whatever he was doing, Strode knew he had good reasons, to him at least, to see it through.

"Drop your gun," Mr. Abraham ordered.

Strode only hesitated for a moment, and then he let his gun fall to the floor.

"Okay, here's what we're going to do," Mr. Abraham said. "We're going to the next room over."

Mr. Abraham sighed but held his focus. "If we do this the easy way, only one of you has to die slowly. The other, we can make it quick."

"We?" Strode asked.

The man turned the gun on Strode.

"Come stand beside him. I'll get behind the two of you and tell you where to go. If either of you steps out of line, I'll shoot."

Strode wasn't sure Mr. Abraham had it in him. He never knew him well, but everyone else in town did. He was the town's handyman, and he befriended each family that came to the Starling house.

In Strode's hesitation, Mr. Abraham pressed the gun to Burklow's head. "I *will* shoot him. I *will* do it."

Mr. Abraham's voice was frantic. Even when he was trying to be authoritative, Strode could hear his fear. He did as the man said.

"Good," Mr. Abraham said. "Now, we're going to go back to the main room where you came in. On the far right, there's another hall."

The men trudged through the abattoir, and Strode's stomach turned at the smell of the blood. It worsened the longer they were there. The most disturbing part was that he couldn't tell exactly where the smell was coming from, because it was everywhere in the abattoir.

The sounds of rotating gears worked against Strode and worsened the hammering in his heart. *Focus. Focus.* Strode looked for a way out, but he was in the dark.

Just as Mr. Abraham said, on the far right was another hall. Down it was a series of grisly stalls with butchered carcasses. The bright colors of the flesh and the wetness of the blood told Strode that someone had caught Mr. Abraham in the middle of his work.

Strode knew Teddy was there. Where else would a killer take comfort than in a place of slaughter?

Toward the end of the hall was an empty stall. Mr. Abraham put the gun to Burklow's back and shoved him in.

Across from Strode was another. "You, in that one," Mr. Abraham said to Strode.

Strode obeyed, eyeing the drain at the center of his enclosure with a dark rim circling it.

Mr. Abraham stood between Burklow and Strode, waiting. After a moment, Mr. Abraham closed his eyes, and with sheer terror and a heavy tremble in his voice, said, "Which one do you want?"

Strode stood in the pin and could see over the ledge and to the way they came.

Already blood-soaked from god knows what was Teddy Blackwood. Beside him was a dark figure, far taller than Teddy.

Its eyes gleamed in hunger, and Strode noticed the bright whiteness of them had shifted to a slightly yellowish hue.

"I've done my part. Everything you need is here, the drain, the saws," Mr. Abraham said.

Strode noted the long, jagged-edged teeth of a saw on the other side of Burklow's stall.

"Now, please. Don't make me watch."

Teddy smiled. "You know, sometimes, when we have an audience, the meal is even more fulfilling. It's like the victim's fear soaks up all the fear around them, and it cooks with their own."

Teddy wasn't even armed. Strode looked to Mr. Abraham, holding the rifle, the only thing keeping him and Burklow in their confinement.

"John, what are you doing? You have a daughter. She needs you," Strode pleaded.

The figure standing beside Teddy hissed.

"She needs you, John. Lynn is gone. She needs you."

Mr. Abraham shook his head. "It's too late, Strode. They'll take her from me anyway."

"It's not too late, John. You don't have to do this. You don't have to become a killer. Let us go, and you can still see your daughter. Don't go away, making your daughter think you're a murderer."

Burklow nodded. "Listen to the man."

Teddy laughed. "Mr. Abraham is in far too deep. He has been for some time."

Strode ignored them all and held his eyes on Mr. Abraham. "I can help you. I can make sure she is taken care of. Fuck, I will take her myself. This doesn't have to end badly for her."

Mr. Abraham kicked his rubber boots in the ground and quivered. "You don't get it, Strode. I've been in it for so long. I helped him. I helped him hide the bodies and clean the blood from his clothes. Then he killed them all, and then himself. I thought the shadow was gone that night, but it was only waiting for someone like Teddy."

The shadow's hissing grew louder, but Teddy only laughed.

Strode inched closer to Mr. Abraham, with his hands raised in surrender. "John, who did you help?"

Mr. Abraham's eyes glistened with tears.

Strode played back one part of Mr. Abraham's confession. *He killed them all and then himself.*

Now Strode sounded desperate, "Mr. Warren? You helped Mr. Warren hide bodies?"

Strode's eyes zipped back and forth as he started putting it all together.

"Jackie! John, what happened to Jackie?"

Mr. Abraham lowered his gun and said, "The shadow made him kill her. All of them." Mr. Abraham fell to his knees. "And I helped him. I thought he was sick. And now, they're going to take me away."

"Hold them there," Teddy ordered Mr. Abraham.

"Don't do this," Strode said.

Steady tears fell down Mr. Abraham's cheek. "You'll make sure she's taken care of? That she's safe?"

"Yes, John. I swear. Just don't make this worse."

Mr. Abraham turned the barrel of the rifle to the underside of his stubbly chin.

"No!" Strode yelled.

The gun fired.

Strode hurried to his feet and retrieved the rifle. When he rose, Teddy stood on the other side of the cold barrel and gripped his hand around it.

Strode looked into his silver eyes, and Teddy smiled.

"Where is the Abraham girl? Where is Ali?" Strode asked.

Teddy's smile widened, and at that moment Strode knew nothing was left of the sweet boy he had searched for. Teddy had become just like the being he served. He feasted on suffering and blood.

"Are you going to shoot me, Strode?" Teddy asked. The stone color of his eyes warmed to a soft brown. His voice lost its edge and reinstated its innocence.

Strode shook his head. "You're not Teddy Blackwood. You're just a shell of him. A cruel killer, who had everything taken from him, so now he takes from everyone else."

Strode could see Burklow moving in his peripherals, which he knew meant Teddy could too. Strode pressed the gun to Teddy's face, "Don't move."

The shadow hissed and slithered from behind Teddy to Burklow's stall.

"I'm warning you. If that thing hurts him, I'll shoot you square in the face," Strode said.

Strode was pleased to see some alarm in Teddy's face.

Good, Strode thought. *He's not invincible.*

"The hunger is heat for us, Strode. If we don't eat, we burn."

Strode could see shiny, pink flares of skin on Teddy's forearms.

Teddy nodded. "And that's a mild one. Without the bodies, the death, the blood, it's constant heat."

"You let it make you into that, Teddy," Strode said.

"You could never understand. You're always alone. Friends help friends. I help the shadow eat, and it heals me and gives me strength."

Burklow charged at Teddy, wielding a carcass saw. From the shadow figure emerged a three-dimensional skeletal hand. It pressed on Burklow's shoulder and into his skin. Steam arose from the heat and Burklow screamed a blood-curdling cry.

Strode didn't hesitate. As soon as Teddy ran at him amid the chaos, he pulled the trigger.

Teddy fell to his knees and grunted in anger, like a bull ready to trample its prey. Strode had only grazed Teddy's neck.

Strode pulled Burklow to his feet and, with everything he had, tried to guide his hefty body back through the front of the abattoir.

Strode struggled with the rifle and Burklow, and when he made it to the office, he heard a quick mumble, "In here. In here."

There was a door just past the office where Burklow and Strode had left Finch.

When the door closed, Strode and Burklow saw a small blonde girl with bright blue eyes. Strode recognized her. Ali Abraham.

"Okay, Officer Finch says we have to get them to turn into the office."

"Where is she?" Strode asked.

Ali shook her head. "She made me swear that I wouldn't say anything other than her directions."

Burklow held a hand to his sizzled shoulder.

Strode was panicking. They would find them, and they would kill them all.

"Ali, you need to go. Get out of here and get help."

Ali shook her head. "No. No. This is the way. Finch says so. I watched for her as she followed behind Teddy and the shadow. When she came back, she had a plan."

Strode didn't like it, but that woman had yet to fail him.

"Alright. I can do that."

"Good," Ali said. "Finch said as soon as they get in there, shut the door and count to thirty."

"And then what?" Strode asked.

Ali untied one of her black high-top Converse sneakers and handed it Strode.

"And then, be ready."

* * *

Teddy and the shadow came around the corner while Strode held his position in front of the office door. The plan was simple. There was an assortment of desk supplies—staplers, cups of pens, pads of paper—piled on Mr. Abraham's desk. When Strode heard Teddy and the shadow coming, he would throw Ali's shoe at it. He could hit any of the targets, and he knew it would be enough noise that they would respond.

Strode still had no idea where Finch was hiding. He just hoped that whatever the hell she was doing, she would be safe.

A moment later, Strode heard the hissing of the shadow.

"You have to heal me more. It's still bleeding."

The shadow didn't answer, but Teddy responded as if it did.

"Fine, but we can't drain them. It has to be fast again. We can get a few more on the way out, to get your strength up."

Strode waited one more second, and when he saw Teddy's shadow, his real inanimate shadow, he threw the little sneaker at the tower of office supplies.

"Found them," Teddy said. Strode could imagine the sadistic smile on Teddy's face.

Strode tucked himself into the nook of the opened door just a foot away from the office. Teddy and the shadow stepped into the office and Strode ran behind them, closing the door. He pulled outward on the doorknob as hard as he could, preventing Teddy from turning it on the other side.

Through the glass, Strode could see a white fog transcending. Teddy immediately began to scream, and the shadow's hiss became a deafening screech.

Strode had seen that fog only one other time, in training.

It was tear gas. Only one officer passed Strode's first tear gas test. Her name was Officer Finch. The rest of the men knew the effects, and as Strode had done, they recited them in their heads until their skin crawled with unbearable heat and their eyes melted.

Of course, a timed test's purpose was psychological.

But the gas ate at Teddy's skin far quicker. His skin welted and blistered, as though he was sitting in flames.

It was the heat.

Teddy had said he and the shadow felt constant heat and that if they didn't eat, they burned.

Well, Finch had found a way to add fuel to the fire.

Remembering the thirty seconds rule, Strode pulled his weight from the door, and petite Officer Finch fell out.

Strode saw Teddy convulsing on the floor like a worm under a heat lamp in the background. And Teddy's weakening vessel left the shadow figure shriveled into a dark splotch on the carpet. There was nothing almighty about it. In that moment, it looked like nothing more than a stain that had gone unattended.

Strode hurried Finch to the room with Burklow and Ali. She coughed, and her eyes were red with irritation, but she waved Strode to stop minding her.

In the office, Strode watched the burns eat Teddy's skin, far worse than the shadow had Burklow's arm. It crept up his neck and ate chunks from his face.

When the gas subsided, Strode put one arm under his nose. The gas didn't spare his eyes, but Strode knew they would heal. That was something he could walk away from, unlike letting that murderous kid back into the world.

Strode lowered himself to Teddy and saw the red that filled his eyes encapsulated a warm, chocolate brown. But the burns on his face, the dried cracks in his flesh, said it all. They were unlike any burns he had ever seen on a person. Running between the singed flesh were scraggly strands of black, of death. It looked just like the ashen trees in Warren Woods.

The black navigated into the crevices of Teddy's face. It burned away his rosy pink cheeks, or any sign or dimples, if he ever were to smile again. All it showed was the wickedness within.

Strode cuffed Teddy's nearly charred wrists.

"And now, when the world looks at you, they'll see what you've truly become. A monster."

6

Strode and Finch saw to it themselves that Ali Abraham collected her things from her home and was all set for Florida. Mr. Abraham's wife, Lynn, had a sister there. Lynn's wishes were for her sister to take Ali if anything happened to her or her husband.

Strode stood in the foyer of the well-kept farmhouse waiting for Ali. Finch was upstairs, helping her pack. Burklow sat in the car. He was Ali's ride to the Indianapolis airport.

When they finally came down the stairs, Ali was holding a book to her chest. It was leather-bound and worn.

Ali handed it to Strode. "I think you should see this. Daddy thought he kept it hidden, but he wasn't good at keeping things from me. That's why I was never allowed to talk about the Warrens." Ali tucked a piece of her blonde hair behind her ears. "Because I knew about this. I think he always knew I'd find it at some point."

Strode opened the book and saw it was a journal.

Strode skimmed through the passages, all confessions of a man gone mad, a man he knew as Mr. Warren.

Tonight, I killed a man coming home from work. I stood in the corn, and when I heard him coming by, I waved him down.

Before he knew it, I stabbed him in the eye with a screwdriver. Blood and gelatin merged into a thick, dark goo. In the moment, I felt powerful. I had done what the shadow wanted. Now, I'm afraid there isn't a shadow at all, just my mind split in two, like Jekyll and Hyde. And that, I think, is far scarier than the golden eyes I see and the murderous voice in my head.

Strode flipped through the pages to find more than fifteen detailed descriptions of Mr. Warren's murders with plenty of clean-up help from Mr. Abraham.

In one passage, Mr. Warren wrote,

I fear that, as we do with most things in life, Mr. Abraham sees me as he wants rather than as I am. He wants to believe the world is safe for his wife, for his daughter. He told me that men like me aren't killers. Instead, we're unmade. We haven't known much of support or kindness in our lives, so we take longer to detach from our inherent primitive ways.

It's a sweet notion, truly genuine. Although, I believe he has it wrong. I have known love in each of my daughters, Laurie and Jackie, and in my adoring wife. And no matter where I go next, or whether the monster within swallows me whole, I want them to know that I knew love, and I knew it because of them.

I think the shadow wants me to forget.

Ali sat on the steps as Finch read over Strode's shoulder. "Officer Strode?"

Strode raised his eyes from the journal, forgetting where he was. "Yes, Ali?"

"If you skip toward the last few pages, I think you'll find what you were looking for."

It was written two days before the Starling nightmare.

"I don't even remember doing it." That's what I said again and again when Mr. Abraham found me in the cornfield, leaning over my daughter's body. The shadow had already

collected a kill that night through my own hands. I had bleach, ready to douse the body, and sweet Jackie, curious as ever, came running into the field. "Daddy, Daddy. I could see you from my window. I didn't want you to play all by yourself."

Then, her sweet little eyes fell from me to the body at my feet. Jackie took a step away from me. I could see in my own daughter's eyes that she knew I was a monster. I unwound the thick hanger wire from my pocket and placed it over her head, the way I might've her grandmother's ruby necklace on Jackie's wedding day. Of course, I knew then, that was a day neither of us would ever get to see. She coughed, and I could see empty gums from where I had pulled teeth from her the day before, just to feed the shadow her pain.

When she stopped kicking, I hurried to the shed, grabbed the shovel, and buried her in the cornfield. Not more than fifteen feet into the field. I lay beside my wife that night, knowing our daughter was dead. Dead because of me.

But the shadow was pleased.

Strode's eyes were full of over a year's frustration and angst. Part of him had always known Jackie was dead, but seeing it on paper, the finality of it, sank his heart into the pit of his chest.

Finch rubbed the center of his back, just as she had when he panicked outside Warren Woods.

"We'll stay another day, Strode. We'll get her out and put her with her family. Okay?"

Strode fell into Finch's chest and cried. "I wanted her to be okay."

Finch hushed him. "And now, she is free to rest."

Strode nodded. He pulled from Finch and looked at the poor little blonde girl on the step. He got on a knee beside her and said, "Thank you, Ali Abraham. You are one of the bravest little girls I've met. Now, I promise you, everything is going to be just fine. Okay?"

Ali wiped a tear from her eye and hugged Strode.

* * *

The next day, Strode, Finch, and Burklow stood in a circle around Jackie Warren. They didn't tell the town yet. Strode wanted her to have a day of being remembered as the sweet, innocent little girl she was, and not a victim of the state's hottest murder mystery.

Strode looked down at the small coffin Finch had found for Jackie and said, "Thank you, Jackie. For everything. You were with me through it all and you showed me that sometimes our lowest moments, our worst tragedies, are simply stepping off points to something better." Strode turned to his two partners beside him and smiled. "You helped me find the truth, but more than anything, you helped me find my family."

Burklow and Finch put an arm around Strode. Burklow went first and said, "Thank you, Jackie. For bringing me this crazy son of a bitch, who has reminded me what it means to be a good cop."

Then Finch said, "Thank you, Jackie, for showing this man that in all the bad, there's always good. We just have to be willing to find it."

They each set a red rose on the coffin and stepped away.

As Strode walked alongside his new partners, he couldn't help but feel weightless. He supposed people never really know how much they were carrying until they let it go.

EPILOGUE

They transferred Teddy to a facility in Oakhaven to await trial. They kept Teddy in isolation, and each day, the heat of hunger worsened. The shadow was starving.

The shadow didn't need to touch Teddy any longer. They'd shared heat for so long Teddy could feel it, even when the shadow wasn't strong enough to inflict it upon him.

Teddy screamed and cried for help, hoping to lure a guard into his cell. He managed to get three in the first week, but each time Teddy tried to jab his fingers into a guard's eyes or strangle another with his sheets, they overpowered him. He was too weak. They then revoked another "privilege," like showering unshackled and alone, or covers at night. Though Teddy only missed the familiarity of his sheets. In reality, he spent the night waking to the shadow's whisper or the endless sweating.

For the first time since Teddy had met the shadow, he felt as helpless as the little boy watching his father beat his mother. He felt the same fear he imagined Mrs. Mayweather did when she saw Teddy raise the bedside lamp. Or maybe the same kind of fear of the boys in the woods before the shadow ripped out their throats. Only Teddy imagined death would be better than a life alone.

Teddy knew if he couldn't get out, he would suffer.

I need to eat.

"I know. I can't get anyone."

I need to eat.

The heat would rise each time the shadow spoke to him.

When he thought the heat had subsided, the shadow would whisper again.

I need to eat.

"I know. I will try to think of something."

After a few days, there was nothing.

Teddy stared at the cement wall before him. There were no tally marks or cracks with spelled messages. He tried to clear his head.

There was nothing.

Teddy tried running through thoughts, hoping one of them would be interrupted, hoping he would hear his friend.

But there was nothing.

"Please, Shadow. Where are you?"

There was nothing.

After three days of total silence, Teddy felt a chill like he never had before. He sat in the damp corner of his cell and shivered.

"Help me, Shadow. I'm so cold."

The hall lights flicked on. Teddy could hear footsteps of what sounded like two people, a guard, and a new prisoner.

"Alright, Dae. This is you. It's a great place. Recently remodeled with an ocean view. Nothing but the best for creeps like you."

The man grunted as the guard shoved him into the cell, just as he had to Teddy.

The guard poked his head past the other prisoner's cell and looked in on Teddy.

"You've finally got a friend, Blackwood."

The guard laughed and tapped his knuckles against the metal bars.

"Dae, maybe you can get him to introduce you to his imaginary friend."

The guard laughed again, and darkness consumed the hall.

Teddy could hear the man on the other side spit and spread the saliva with the bottom of his shoe.

Teddy's lip curled in disgust.

Teddy whispered, "Shadow, we have someone. We can get him somehow. I know it. Please, Shadow. Talk to me."

"Is it true?"

Teddy jumped at the sound of a voice but was disappointed with the rugged tone on the other side of the wall as it repeated, "Is it true what you did? To all those people, I mean?"

"Yes," Teddy said.

Teddy wanted the man to fear him. He hoped it would serve as a seasoning, like garlic butter on steak, before he and the shadow could make their move.

But the man laughed. "Shit, kid. I've never seen anything like it. What was it like?"

Teddy wiped a tear from his face as his expression went cold. "It was like I was God. I held their life and then took it away."

Teddy thought that ought to get him, but the man laughed and said, "Wow. You really are a twisted little bastard. Huh?"

Teddy pulled his knees to his chest and buried his head.

"Shadow, I can get him. Please, talk to me."

"Well, kid. I imagine you're going to be here for a very long time. I'm lucky. Took a plea deal. I'll be out in a few months. I have parole for two years, but that's nothing. Not like I murdered kids or anything."

The man laughed, and Teddy wished so badly that the shadow would rip out his throat already. But Teddy knew the shadow was far too weak. Maybe even too weak to talk to him, and it wasn't like it had doors to slam to remind him it was still there.

* * *

Two weeks became three, and there was no sign of the shadow. Teddy felt more and more alone.

He screamed in frustration, and the man beside him mocked him by screaming louder.

"Blackwood, Dae, shut the fuck up," the guard yelled.

"Kid, you're way past the insanity card. They're not going to make that mistake again. Was it the doctor or guard you killed that day?"

"Both," Teddy said.

A tear fell down his cheek, and Teddy swatted it away like a gnat.

Teddy sat in the corner of his cell, alone with his thoughts. Teddy thought of his mother, the way she hummed "Puff the Magic Dragon" that afternoon his father found them. How peaceful she looked. It made Teddy wonder if his dad never came, would his life have turned out differently?

It was such an aged thought for a person his age.

Teddy didn't know how to sift through the ideas and images in his head. The shadow had guided him for over a year. Without it, Teddy wasn't sure he even knew who he was. With or without it, Teddy knew that to everyone else, he would always be a monster. And the only thing worse than being a monster was being a caged one.

＊ ＊ ＊

"Can anyone else hear you?"

Teddy sat up in his cot and heard the man on the other side of the wall whispering.

"How have I helped you? What do you mean warmer?"

Teddy scrambled from the creaky cot and pressed his ear between the bars. His legs felt wobbly and weak beneath him.

"What does that mean?"

Teddy closed his eyes and listened for the shadow. It was faint, but he could hear it say, *You noticed me.*

"I'm sorry, but you're better off with the kid next door. I won't be here long."

The man spat onto the cement and dragged his shoe across it.

"Well, how do I take you with me?"

Teddy beat into the wall, "Shadow! Shadow! I'm over here. You have the wrong cell!"

Both the shadow and the man on the other side were quiet.

"Shadow, please! We'll get out. I promise we'll get out."

Teddy pounded his fists into the cement, watching his own blood smeared across them.

Teddy wiped the blood off with his palm and held it out as an offering. "Here, Shadow! Take mine! Take mine! Please, Shadow. I'm so scared."

The next morning, the guard whispered to Dae. "I have a daughter and a son. My daughter is the same age as Marlene Byers. Do it, but do it fast. Just as we talked about."

The metal cell door echoed through the hall as it opened.

"Okay, is there anything else you need me to do? Just this, right, and then we're set?"

Then, in front of Teddy's cell stood a man. He didn't have anger or even determination on his face. Instead, he wore hesitation and regret, and that scared Teddy even more. He knew that feeling. He had carried it several times when he helped the shadow. And Teddy knew that kind of killer was easier to sway than the one who came to crave the blood themself.

The man put a key in the door and slid Teddy's cell open. The man held a ball of white cloth. It was his bedsheets.

Teddy stood and ran at the man. Teddy curved his hands around the man's throat. The man dodged Teddy, bent him over, and kneed him in the gut.

When Teddy fell to the floor, a cotton noose formed around his neck, and the man tugged it back. Teddy gasped and clawed at the man's hands, but that only made him tug harder.

Teddy saw yellow eyes before him. He reached out for it, and then his hand went limp.

Teddy's body fell to the floor.

ACKNOWLEDGMENTS

———

This one is for my readers, whether this is your first time with me or if you've been here since my first novel, *Not Another Sarah Halls.*

Readers have asked, "Was it easier writing this book, now that you've already written one?"

Long answer short, no. *Take Your Turn, Teddy* felt like my Everest. I related to both Strode and Teddy, as I'm sure you did too. I empathized with Strode's pain, Teddy's sense of isolation, and both of their day-to-day struggles of feeling worthy.

In their struggles, I wanted to highlight control, the shadow's control over Teddy, his fear of his father and being alone; and with Strode, the power he relinquished to his trauma.

Control is difficult to hold onto, but it is not an allusion. Rather, the loss of it is.

Thank you to my readers for delving into this dark tale with me. It was one of the greatest challenges of my life, and I wouldn't be here without you.

Secondly, thank you to my incredible editor Clayton, who gave me a push when the shadows in my head called me away from this story. Also, for helping me "kill my darlings" and produce the polished piece this book became. I never could've done it without your editorial touch.

Thank you to my family for celebrating my love of the macabre and keeping me sane while I embark on the maddening journey of writing a book. I love you all.

Lastly, a special thanks to everyone who supported me early on by pre-ordering the book, e-book, or donating to my pre-sale campaign.

Jeremy Griggs
Hanna Newlin
Lisa Newlin
Mike Eiler
Paige Manning
Grant Gernhardt
Dennis Gernhardt
Susan Griggs
Mary Jane Wireman
Ariel Turenne
Matt East
Tyson Hurst
Ashley Cavuto
Keegan Luna
Charles Williams
Eric Gray
Jill Arman
Tommy Skinner
Natalie Pilla
Sue Beam
Jessica Rucker
Victoria Cervantes
Shelby Pritchard

Larry Griggs
Michelle Haynes
Priyanka Surio
Britney Mitchell
John DeWeese
Anne A Brickler
Kayla Dispennett
Sarah Dykes
DJ Davis
Traci Terrell
Kathryn Tague
Mike Overby
Nicola Thompson
J. Rougeau
Heather Rodrigues
Linda Addison
Chantelle Rodrigues
Maryn Hamilton
Elizabeth Ivanecky
Justin Hall
Haley Sopko-Berg
Michael Goodwin
Eleni Madiar

Rachel Lutack
Audrey Bowers
Peyton Hurst
Jeff Robertson
Nick Simpson
Ilia Epifanov
Scott Graves
Todd Young
David Hoernig
Carissa Svoboda
Kay Smeal
Jada Henry
Clayton Bohle
Gabrielle Roessler
Bailey Brouillette
Rebecah Gray
Halley Skidmore
Grace Hasson
Tristan Crutchfield
Noelle Schultz
Christian Gualajara
Katie Herget
Kelsey Cook
Kyra Dawkins
Martin Fernandez

Howard Crouch
Nicole Spindler
Lacey Maffett
Peyton Stovall
Jeremy Streich
Keelan Berry
Miguel Robles
Tamar Haddad
Rosie Anderson
Shawna Lashley
Frankie Reynolds
Brady Bove
Joselyn Garduno
Eric Koester
Kaylee Simms
Gloria Kitchens
Tess Farmer
Sidney Whitten
Tamara & JD Newlin
Robin Reynolds
Traci Barnhart
Ashley Bylund
Victoria Lipscomb
Lindsay Bonty

CPSIA information can be obtained
at www.ICGtesting.com
Printed in the USA
LVHW080500140222
711067LV00013B/396/J